ACCLAIM FOR COLLEEN COBLE

"Colleen is a master storyteller."

—KAREN KINGSBURY, BEST-SELLING AUTHOR OF
UNLOCKED AND *LEARNING*

"Suspense, action, mystery, spiritual victory—Colleen Coble has woven them all into a compelling novel that will keep you flipping pages until the very end. I highly recommend *Without a Trace*."

—JAMES SCOTT BELL, AUTHOR OF *DEADLOCK* AND *A HIGHER JUSTICE*

"Coble's books have it all, romance, sass, suspense, action. I'm content to read a book that has any one of those but to find an author like Coble who does all four so well is my definition of bliss."

—MARY CONNEALY, AUTHOR OF *DOCTOR IN PETTICOATS*

"Coble captivates readers with her compelling characters. Action-packed . . . highly recommended!"

—DIANNE BURNETT, CHRISTIANBOOK.COM

"[*The Lightkeeper's Ball*] has romance, mystery, secrets and a bad guy. Coble wows the reader with a fresh storyline. Readers will enjoy peeling back the layers and discovering this is more than your average romance book. The characters are strong not only in themselves but also in their faith."

—ROMANTIC TIMES, 4 STARS

"Coble's historical series (*The Lightkeeper's Daughter*; *The Lightkeeper's Bride*) just keeps getting better with each entry. Coble has a strong feel for the time period (in this case, 1910) and has scripted believable characters in suspenseful situations."

—LIBRARY JOURNAL, STARRED REVIEW

ALSO BY COLLEEN COBLE

A novella included in *Smitten*

THE LONESTAR NOVELS
Lonestar Sanctuary
Lonestar Secrets
Lonestar Homecoming
Lonestar Angel

THE MERCY FALLS SERIES
The Lightkeeper's Daughter
The Lightkeeper's Bride
The Lightkeeper's Ball

THE ROCK HARBOR SERIES
Without a Trace
Beyond a Doubt
Into the Deep
Cry in the Night

THE ALOHA REEF SERIES
Distant Echoes
Black Sands
Dangerous Depths

Alaska Twilight
Fire Dancer
Midnight Sea
Abomination
Anathema

BLUE MOON PROMISE

UNDER TEXAS STARS

COLLEEN COBLE

THOMAS NELSON
Since 1798

NASHVILLE   DALLAS   MEXICO CITY   RIO DE JANEIRO

Published in Nashville, Tennessee, by Thomas Nelson. Thomas Nelson is a registered trademark of Thomas Nelson, Inc.

Thomas Nelson, Inc., titles may be purchased in bulk for educational, business, fund-raising, or sales promotional use. For information, please e-mail SpecialMarkets@ThomasNelson.com.

Publisher's Note: This novel is a work of fiction. Names, characters, places, and incidents are either products of the author's imagination or used fictitiously. All characters are fictional, and any similarity to people living or dead is purely coincidental.

Unless otherwise noted, Scripture quotations are taken from the King James Version.

Library of Congress Cataloging-in-Publication Data

Coble, Colleen.
  Blue moon promise / by Colleen Coble.
    p. cm. — (Under Texas stars ; 1)
  Previous title: The cattle baron's bride
  ISBN 978-1-59554-915-0 (trade paper)
  I. Title.
  PS3553.O2285C38 2012
  813'.54—dc23   2011044565

Printed in the United States of America

12 13 14 15 16 17 QG 6 5 4 3

DEAR READER,

I'm excited to share *Blue Moon Promise* with you. It is a very personal book to me, and I hope you love Lucy because you're seeing a bit of me in her. All those control issues she has? Yep, that's me. I'm a fixer and I mother my loved ones within an inch of their lives. ☺

I came face-to-face with my serious defect this year. My dear Dave was diagnosed with an aggressive prostate cancer. I found myself vacillating between putting it in God's hands and then jerking it back and wanting to fix it myself. So poor Lucy had to suffer through her own issues with lack of control until she came to the same place I did—where she realized how futile all that effort was. God is in control.

I recently came across Proverbs 16:9 again and saw it with new eyes. "A man's heart deviseth his way: but the Lord directeth his steps." I realized that no matter how much I might think I know the path I should take, only God knows the best journey for me. All I have to do is let go and trust him.

I think many of us are like Lucy. We say we trust God and are content to rest with what he has for us, but when the hard times come, we try to rely on our own strength way too often. God wants to carry our burdens for us. He wants us to trust him with our future. I've resolved to try to do a better job with that. How about you?

As always, I love to hear from you! E-mail me anytime at colleen@colleencoble.com. Let me know how you liked *Blue Moon Promise*. I pray you can take away a little insight into learning to trust God more.

Your friend,
Colleen

P.S. Dave is doing well following his surgery. And although the cancer had moved into the seminal vesicles, his first PSA was 0. So we're rejoicing!

For my husband, Dave.
Your faith and courage under fire have been an
inspiration to all of us.
Love you!

ONE

~~❧❧~~

Lucy Marsh pulled her threadbare coat around her neck and hurried down the snow-clogged street. Glancing behind her, she saw only the snow drifting onto run-down houses. The rapid thump of her pulse began to calm, and she managed to breathe through her tight lungs.

Maybe it was her imagination. For the past week she'd caught a glimpse of the same man every evening after work, and until today, she told herself he must live in the same general area. But she'd left early today and he had still been there. This time he seemed to watch her. A black coat covered him and he wore a hat pulled low over his face, so only the twitch of his smooth-shaven chin appeared. When she stopped and stared at him, he darted around the corner of the building.

She took the opportunity and dashed across the street, skirting the horse and carriage blocking her path to the house. The roof leaked and wind blew through the boards and under the windowsills, but it had been home for ten years. Glancing behind her again, she saw no sign of the man so she hurried up the steps.

Pressing her hand to her stomach, she paused and wished she

didn't have to go inside. What was she going to do now? Mrs. Hanson had been apologetic about letting her go. It was hard times and not her work that necessitated firing her. But the hard facts didn't feed them. While 1877 had been a bad year so far, Indiana had been particularly hard hit.

But she would find a way. She always managed.

The steps to the porch took careful navigation. They tilted to the front, and it was easy to lose her balance. She paused outside the door. The children would worry, so she tried on a smile. When it stayed in place, she turned the doorknob. Before she could open the door, Amos Cramer's gruff voice stopped her.

"One moment, Miss Marsh," he panted, hurrying up the steps toward her. He was a large, red-faced man with sparse gray hair and a handlebar mustache. He parked himself in front of her door and wheezed, struggling to catch his breath.

She had tried to be kind to their landlord until Mr. Cramer mistook her kindness for romantic interest. Now she just tried to stay out of his way when he came to collect the rent. Her back against the door, Lucy pressed away as far as she could to escape the strong odor of stale perspiration that drifted toward her.

He crowded closer. "I'm afraid I have some bad news for you." His muddy gaze slid avidly over her face and hair.

Lucy pressed tighter against the wall, though it gained her no space between the odious man and herself. What now? She didn't think she could endure more bad news.

"I've decided to sell out and go back to New York. I've had an offer I can't refuse for this place. The new owner plans to tear it down and build a store here." He hesitated and rubbed his lips with a dirty handkerchief. "I'm afraid I must ask you to leave within the next seven days."

Lucy gasped. "A week? How can I find something else in a week?"

Amos shrugged. "I'm sorry, my dear. You might try that boardinghouse over on Canal Street. They might have an opening." He pursed his lips and raked her figure with his gaze before turning and waddling away.

Lucy's throat grew thick. She couldn't cry, not now. Tears would frighten the children. Fingering her locket, she straightened her shoulders and pushed open the door.

Her three-year-old sister launched herself against Lucy's legs. "Lucy, you was late." Eileen stuck out her lower lip. "We has company."

Lucy looked toward the single chair in the tiny parlor. A man with gray hair and penetrating charcoal eyes sat regarding her calmly before he stood. There was something forbidding in his face, and she inhaled. *Please, God, have mercy.* Her gaze sought and found her brother, Jed. Twelve years old, he'd been a handful all year. His hangdog expression did nothing to calm her fears.

"Jed?"

His gaze remained on his worn shoes. "Uh, Lucy, this is—"

"I'll introduce myself," the gentleman interrupted. He stepped toward her and stared into her eyes. "Henry Stanton of Larson, Texas." He shifted his gray Stetson in his hands. "Your father was my boyhood friend. I came as soon as I heard of his death."

Henry Stanton. Lucy struggled to remember if her father had ever mentioned him. She knew her parents had grown up in Texas. Her Uncle Drew was still there. "I'm delighted to meet you, Mr. Stanton. How did you hear of our father's death?"

"His wife wrote me asking for help, so I decided to make a stop here on my way back from Chicago. Is she here?"

Lucy shook her head. "Catherine left right after Father died."

The man frowned. "Left? I don't understand."

She didn't like to speak ill of anyone, but he had to know why Catherine wasn't here. "Her, uh, friend showed up and she left with him."

"She abandoned her children?" His voice rose.

Lucy looked to where Eileen was playing with her doll. The child didn't seem to be paying attention. "I cared for them anyway," she whispered. "Catherine wasn't good with children."

"I see." He pointed his hat at Jed. "Your brother is in a heap of trouble, miss. He lifted my wallet when I talked with him on the porch."

Stealing? She stared at her brother and the guilt washed over his face. "Jed, how could you?" It was too much. She sank onto the edge of the bed and buried her burning eyes in her hands. Her shoulders heaved as she tried to get her emotions under control. The events of the past few weeks had drained her. When she raised her head, she found Henry with a speculative look on his face.

"Please don't distress yourself, Miss Lucy. Young Jed's behavior will be corrected on the ranch."

"On the ranch?"

"Tell me, Miss Marsh, are you a Christian woman?"

Standing again, she straightened her shoulders and exhaled. "Why, yes, sir, I am."

"I thought as much. God has led me here for a purpose." He smiled. "I have a proposition for you."

Her pulse quickened. Perhaps there would be a way out of these dreadful circumstances yet. "What would that be, Mr. Stanton?"

"Have you read in the Bible how Abraham sent a servant out to find a wife for Isaac?"

"Of course." Lucy's heart sank before beginning a rapid beat against her chest. Surely he wasn't offering for her hand. He was *old*. Older than her father.

"That was my main purpose for this trip, though my son has no idea of my mission. Now that I've met you, I believe you will do nicely. Nate needs a wife like you."

His son. Lucy's limbs went weak. The room spun, and she sat back on the edge of the bed.

"I can see I've shocked you."

Lucy eyed the man. "Is—is your son a Christian?"

Mr. Stanton smiled. "That just confirms the Lord's leading me here. As soon as I clapped eyes on you, something reared up inside me and I knew you were the right one for my Nate. Yes, my boy is a Christian." He put a hand on her shoulder. "I have my son's signature to act as his agent in all business matters for this trip, so if you agree, I will arrange a proxy marriage. Right after the ceremony we'll leave for Texas. A train leaves at one o'clock tomorrow afternoon."

"Why would we not return to your ranch and see if your son and I would suit?"

"You don't know my boy. He is apt to send you packing rather than listen to reason." He shook his head. "No, this is the only way."

It felt wrong to surprise this unknown Nate. Lucy held up her hand. "I'd rather know we suit before I pledge my life to a man. And give him a chance to get to know me as well."

He thrust out his chin. "This is my offer, Miss Lucy. It's the only one I'm making." He nodded at her siblings. "Think of your brother and sister. They will have warm beds and plenty of food to eat. Fresh Texas air and plenty of room to grow up."

Her main consideration was the children. While the thought of marrying someone she didn't know was most unappealing, Lucy had to consider the offer. They were about to be evicted, and she'd lost her job. How could she possibly support the children? "I'd like time to pray about it."

"I would expect nothing less from a good Christian woman. I'll return tomorrow at nine for your answer. If you're accepting my offer, have all your things packed. There will be no time to spare." His walking stick thumped on the floor as he walked to the entry.

When the door closed behind him, Lucy clenched her hands in her lap and turned to her brother. Too angry to speak, she just looked at him.

Jed swallowed hard and took a step back. "It was a dare, Lucy. I didn't mean to do anything wrong. I was just funnin'. I gave it back to him."

"A dare? You risked jail for a dare?" She buried her head in her hands. "Lord, help me," she whispered.

She lifted her head, opened the locket, and stared at the face of the unsmiling young woman. What would her mother have her do? Lucy squared her shoulders. This wasn't beyond her capabilities.

"On your knees, children." She sank to the floor. "We must pray."

LUCY PREPARED THE last of the beef in a thin stew for her brother and sister. She picked at a piece of dry bread and watched them eat. She'd always risen to the challenge, but tonight all she wanted to do was climb onto her cot and pull the covers over her head. The task appeared overwhelming and she was tired, so tired.

There was a rap on the front door, and she rose from the table to answer it. A glimpse through the window to the porch made her stomach plunge. Albert, Catherine's *friend*, was standing at the door. She wanted to throw the bolt and ignore the summons, but she forced herself to open the door.

His gaze skewered her. "Miss Lucy. You look lovely today."

His smile made her feel unclean. "What do you want?" She peered past his shoulder to the vehicle in the wash of gaslight, but no one was in the buggy that waited in the street.

He tipped his hat up with a finger. "Your mother sent me by for Eileen. If you'll just get her things together, we'll be off."

She blocked his entrance with her body. "I have no way of knowing if what you're saying is true." She couldn't turn her little sister over to this man. "I find it odd that you don't ask for Jed as well."

"I'm sure Catherine will want him eventually too, but right now, she wants Eileen."

Lucy tensed, her fingers on the door. "Then why is she not here herself to claim her daughter?"

His smile twisted to a snarl and he stepped toward the doorway, but Lucy slammed the door before he could block it. She threw the lock. "Go away!"

His shoulder hit the door, and it shuddered. "Open up," he growled.

The wood vibrated against her, and she held her breath. *Please let it hold.* Eileen had left the table and was hiding her face in Lucy's skirt. Lucy touched the top of her sister's soft hair. Staring at the lock, she prayed again for it to hold. After a moment, the battering against the door stopped. She wanted to peek out the window, but she was afraid the sight of her face would inflame the man even more.

Eileen whimpered. "It's okay," Lucy said in a soft voice. "I won't let him near you."

"He scares me." Eileen trembled against Lucy's skirt.

Lucy didn't dare admit the man terrified her as well. She had to be strong for Eileen and Jed. She glanced across the room and saw Jed with a rolling pin in his hand. "Check the back door," she mouthed.

He hurried to the kitchen. When he returned a few moments later, he gave her a nod. Lucy dared a glimpse through the curtain. Albert paced along the porch. He glanced at the door, then to his buggy before heading down the steps.

"You haven't seen the last of me," Albert shouted over his shoulder.

He lurched into his buggy. The whip came down on the horse's back, and the animal reared, then took off down the street. Albert glared back at the house as the buggy pulled away.

Lucy sagged against the window frame. He'd be back. She had only delayed the fellow. Next time Catherine might come too, and then what could be done? If Lucy refused to let Eileen go, Catherine would likely call the police.

Lucy's arms were leaden as she gathered the sobbing child in her arms and walked back to the table with her. "It's okay, he's gone, darling." All they had was one another.

While Eileen finished her stew, Lucy thought about her options. She made a list of possible places to apply for work, but the likelihood of finding a position was slim. Many were unemployed in Wabash. Even if the town had a poorhouse, that wasn't an option now that a new law forbade children from residing there. Without a job, she would have to turn the children over to their mother or they would all end up on the street. So what was she to do?

Hiding her fear from the children, she took the dirty dishes to the dry sink. Putting water to boil, she stared out the window at the yard. A tire swing hung from the lone tree. This place was the only home Jed and Eileen had ever known, but they were bound to have to leave no matter what happened. If she accepted Mr. Stanton's offer, at least the children would have food to eat and a place to sleep.

The thought of marriage to a man she didn't know was fearful, but she would do anything to keep them all together. It seemed she had no choice.

TWO

～～⟋⟍～～

Nate should have felt a sense of contentment and peace, but something was off tonight, and he couldn't quite figure out what it was.

Standing in the corral, he went through the list of chores. The shapes of the cattle shifted on the darkening hillsides as they milled about. He'd checked the windmills and they were all pumping water, so the stock was hydrated. The chicken coop was locked up for the night. The horses were stabled and curried. Yet he struggled to relax the tense muscles of his shoulders.

He walked back to the barn and shoved the door along its tracks. The good scent of hay and horse rushed to his face as he stepped inside. He heard a sound behind him and turned, then saw Percy.

"Boss, supper is getting cold," the cook said. "I called you twice."

"I'm coming."

"What's eatin' you? You look like a new calf spooked by a goat."

There. "Did you hear that?"

Percy tipped his head to the side. "Hear what?"

The noise came again. A sliding, shuffling sound. "Someone's in the back stall," Nate whispered.

He pulled his gun and approached the stall. A figure burst from the shadows. The man leaped past Nate and darted out the open barn door. Nate ran after him. He caught a glimpse of the man's shirt as he vaulted around the corner of the barn. As he raced after him, Nate heard a jingle of horse tack. He rounded the barn in time to see the fellow mount his horse and ride off.

"Bring me a horse!" Nate ran toward the barn.

Percy was standing in the doorway, but at Nate's command, he ducked back inside. When Nate reached the barn, Percy was leading Whisper from his stall. Nate quickly saddled his horse and mounted, but by the time he got to where he'd last seen the intruder, there was no sign of the man.

His gut told him the man would head toward the road. Setting off in that direction, he chafed at the slow pace he had to take with the uneven ground. He didn't want to risk Whisper breaking a leg.

An hour later darkness had descended. He sat back in the saddle and looked down the hillside toward the road where the dim light of a lantern glowed by the darker shape of a buggy. The lantern swung in a man's hand as he stepped out to greet the rider who reined in at the sight of him. The light allowed Nate to recognize the man. Drew Larson.

He watched Larson talk to the intruder, and though Nate couldn't make out any words, there was no mistaking Larson's angry tone. Larson climbed into the buggy and took off. The other man followed on horseback. Had Larson hired the guy to poke around in the barn? It seemed likely. Deep in thought, Nate rode back to the Stars Above.

When he arrived at the ranch, he lit a lantern, then went to the stall where the fellow had been hiding. Holding the light aloft, he studied the space. One corner held a small pile of wood. Nate knelt and picked up one of the logs. The odor of kerosene was strong, and it wasn't from the lantern. The wood had been soaked in the stuff. Nate's gut clenched.

Did Larson hate them so much?

NATE RODE TO town and reported what he'd seen to the sheriff, who wrote it down with a bored expression and promised to look into it. Nate didn't believe a word of it. The man was lazy through and through. And a good friend of Larson's to boot.

Still disgruntled, Nate stalked down to the café, skirting the puddles in the stockyard. He paused to scrape the noisome muck from his boots before stepping into Emma's Café at the end of the street. Nate went to the only empty table on the opposite side of the dining room.

He'd no more than stretched his legs under the red-and-white tablecloth when Emma Croft appeared through the door to the kitchen. She was one of those ageless women who could have been forty. Her smooth olive skin held no wrinkles, but Nate knew for a fact that she'd come to the Red River area back when his dad was a young man. She had to be at least sixty. She didn't take any guff from the men, and most of the trail riders knew better than to say a smart-mouthed word to her.

She plucked the pencil from her hair bun as she came toward him. "Thought I'd see you today, young Stanton. Where's your daddy? I thought he and Paddy would be in today."

"Due back from Chicago later this week." Nate had always suspected Paddy O'Brien held a special place in Emma's affections, but he'd never had the nerve to ask. "Arranging a sale of our spring herd."

The light in her eyes dimmed. "That so? Well, tell him when he gets back that I'll have a chocolate cake ready for him and Paddy."

"They surely love those cakes of yours. I'll tell him." He hid a grin. "And Paddy, too, when I see him."

She put the pencil to her pad of paper. "What will you have?"

He ordered a roast beef dinner and a piece of that famous cake. "Emma, have you seen any strangers around town?" He described the man he'd found in his barn.

Emma frowned. "A fellow like that had lunch with Larson yesterday. Didn't catch his name."

Nate pressed his lips together. More evidence, not that it would do any good to report it to the sheriff.

Emma sauntered back to the kitchen. The front door opened and Margaret O'Brien stepped inside. He lifted his hand and motioned to her.

A smile lifted her full lips when she saw him. "Nate, I didn't expect to see you here!" Dressed in a plain, heavy skirt and her battered cowboy hat, she hurried toward him.

He stood and pulled a chair out for her. "Where's your pa?" He thought about mentioning that Emma would be sorry he wasn't here, but he wasn't sure how she felt about her pa seeing a woman, so he said nothing.

"Home."

"You came to town alone?"

She settled into the chair and took off her cowboy hat, revealing gleaming red hair. "I'm not some hysterical female who jumps at every shadow, Nate."

He knew that well. His pa and hers had pressed them both to consider joining the two spreads. Maybe it was time to think about that. Margaret was a handsome woman, though he would have found it hard being married to her. She was a little intimidating. Not the kind of woman who would be wooed with flowery words and sweet talk. Discussions with her usually went to stock and horses.

He corralled his thoughts. "What brings you to town so late?"

She held his gaze. "I saw you come in. Pa's been on me to commence with pursuing marriage between our families."

He choked on the swallow of coffee he'd just taken.

Her green eyes softened but her chin stayed up in a defiant gesture. "Pretty forward of me, isn't it? But we've been friends long enough for there to be no pretense between us. So I'm here to ask your intentions, Nate."

His lungs constricted. "I—I haven't given it much thought, Margaret."

She leaned back and folded her arms across her chest. "I reckon we're going to have to make a decision soon. Otherwise, my pa is going to be thrashing the bushes to find another landed suitor. Not that he'd have much luck. Most men seem to want tiny, helpless wives who can hang on their every word. That's not me."

At least Margaret was up front about what she wanted. He couldn't say the same about most women he'd come in contact with. "If we're going to think about marriage, don't you think we should have some feelings for each other?"

She shrugged. "I like you fine, Nate. I'm sure you're no worse in the morning than Pa."

He grinned. "I reckon we're going to have to think about it some."

LUCY TOSSED AND turned on the narrow cot in the tiny parlor. A thin blade of moonlight slashed the floor and spread to the foot of the cot. If she could just climb that moonbeam and disappear . . . This burden was more than she could bear. God must have thought she could handle it or he wouldn't have allowed it. She was a strong woman and this would just make her stronger.

Maybe hot milk would help her sleep. She rose and went to the icebox. Her hands closed around the glass jug and she held it up to the faint light. Nearly empty. She bit her lip and put it away. The children would need it more than her.

Turning back toward the cot, she heard a faint click. Almost like the door latch. Surely Jed wouldn't be sneaking out. The wood floor was rough and cool against her bare feet as she tiptoed back toward the entry. She didn't call out for fear of awakening Eileen. As she neared the door, a figure loomed out of the shadows, and she smelled a man's hair tonic. The fellow was much too big to be Jed. It wasn't Albert either. The figure was too burly.

Her memory flashed back to the man who'd been following her, and she recognized the shape of the hat. In her haste to back away, she stumbled over the hem of her nightgown and fell, banging her back against the leg of the cot. She bit back a cry at the pain that gripped her and struggled to scoot away from the intruder.

A man's voice growled out of the blackness. "Where is it?"

She scrambled to her feet and felt for her footstool. It had to be here somewhere. Her fingers closed around it and she whirled to brandish it over her head. "Get out of here!" She swung the stool and it collided with the thug's head.

He swore at her, and his calloused hand seized her arm. He tore her weapon from her hand.

"Help!" She darted away from the man and raced for the door that showed a crack of light from the way it hung slightly ajar. A middle-aged couple lived next door, and the husband was a burly ironworker. "Mr. Thomas!" She had no idea what time it was or if her choked cry was loud enough to summon help, but she was too small to deter the brute.

She threw open the door and screamed again before the man shoved her. She stumbled to her knees, then regained her feet and lurched to the porch, screaming for Mr. Thomas again.

A faint shout came from the house next door. "Coming."

She whirled to face her attacker. He wore tan pants with suspenders over a dingy plaid shirt. He was tall and thick with a shock of pale hair that fell over angry eyes peering from under his floppy hat. His gaze flickered to the street. His scowl darkened, then he plunged into the wash of light from the streetlight before the shadows beyond swallowed him up.

Lucy gasped as Mr. Thomas, still belting his pants under his nightshirt, rushed up the steps to the porch. His wife was behind him. "A man broke into our house." Lucy pointed down the street. "He ran that way."

"I'll summon the police." Mr. Thomas rushed down the steps.

"Are you all right, my dear?" his wife asked, leading Lucy into the house. "Did he . . . ?"

Lucy shook her head. "He didn't harm me, Mrs. Thomas, thanks to you and your husband." She lit a gaslight, and its comforting glow filled the room. "I must check on the children. If they heard me scream, they'll be frightened."

Still clucking, the older woman followed her. "I'll prepare some tea. You've had a shock to your nerves."

Lucy nodded and rushed to the tiny bedroom at the back of the house where her siblings slept. Eileen lay curled up on her pallet, but Jed's cot only contained rumpled covers. "Jed?" she whispered. She touched the cot in case her eyes deceived her, but her hand grasped only cool sheets.

Maybe her brother was in the privy. Retracing her steps, she crossed the parlor to the kitchen where she lit a lamp and carried it to the back door. She stepped onto the back stoop. "Jed, are you out here?"

Jed's form appeared in front of the outhouse. "What's wrong?" He rushed up the steps.

She hugged him. "There was a man in our apartment." She released him long enough to draw him inside.

"Maybe he was looking for money," he said. "He broke into the wrong apartment if he was."

"He's been following me."

Jed went still in her arms, then pulled out of her embrace. "I'm scared to stay here. Scared for Eileen too. What's going to happen to us now that Pa is gone?"

Lucy's gaze jerked to her sister, who was rubbing her eyes in the bedroom doorway, before veering back to Jed. "I could marry Mr. Stanton's son and get us out of here."

His eyes were moist. "I think you have to, Lucy. Where will we go if you don't?"

A knock came at the door, and a man's voice called out, "Police, Miss Marsh."

JED LISTENED TO the policeman question his sister. His heart rebounded against his ribs. He'd nearly told her. Dad would have been disappointed after he'd specifically said not to tell anyone, not even Lucy.

Eileen tugged on his arm. "I have to go potty, Jed."

"Use the chamber pot."

Eileen wrinkled her nose. "It smells."

Sighing, Jed took her hand and led her to the back door. The outhouse loomed in the backyard. He took her to the building that listed to the left.

She snatched her hand from his. "I can go by myself."

"I'll wait outside." He leaned against the door she closed and tried to make sense of what had happened.

His head ached every time he tried to remember the night of the accident. Flashes of the horse screaming, the rain pounding on his head, and the sound of the carriage screeching along the cobblestone swarmed in his head. Every time he tried to remember, those thoughts filled him with panic. He swallowed hard. There was something on the edge of his remembrance, but it always played hide-and-seek with him.

He straightened when Eileen came out the door, tugging down her nightgown. "Ready?"

She nodded and took his hand. As they walked back to the house, he thought he heard something rustling in the bushes. "Who's there?" When there was no answer, he rushed Eileen to the back door and pushed her inside.

It might be one of his friends who dared him to lift Mr. Stanton's wallet. He sidled to the shrubs. "Joe?" he whispered.

But a hand much larger than Joe's grabbed his arm. "Where are the dollars?" a harsh voice growled.

"I don't have any dollars." In trying to tug his arm away, Jed fell against the fellow, and the tight grip loosened enough that he was able to tug free and run for the house. He stumbled inside, then jumped up and threw the dead bolt.

The acrid taste of fear clung to his tongue. If only Dad were still alive. He'd know what to do with the danger that drew closer every minute. Jed wanted to go to his cot and cover his head, but he wasn't a little kid anymore. Lucy and Eileen needed him to figure out what to do.

He turned back toward the window. Something moved at the edge of the outhouse, but he couldn't see in the gloom. And it didn't matter. Nothing on earth would make him go out there again.

THREE

The policeman took out his notebook. "Did you recognize the man?" he asked.

Details came back that Lucy hadn't consciously noted. "No. He was maybe five-eleven and burly. No beard. Big nose. Blond hair."

"Sounds like the same fellow," the policeman muttered, jotting it down in his book.

"What fellow?"

Consternation crossed the man's face. "Uh, we've been watching your place, miss, ever since your father died."

"I don't understand."

"We're not sure his death was accidental. We suspect whoever robbed the pawn shop that night had something to do with it. We think your father saw something or had something they wanted."

Lucy couldn't think about it. Not yet. "What could he possibly have had that was worth killing him for?"

The man shrugged. "Maybe stolen goods that had been pawned and would have led us to the thief. We're not sure yet. We'd hoped no one would bother you and your brother and sister, but now that they've found you, you'll need to be careful." The policeman glanced around. "I hate to worry you, but this is a bad part of town. You need to be somewhere safer. Is there anyone you can stay with?"

She shook her head. "We have no one. My mother's brother lives in Texas, but I have no way to get there."

"I'd suggest you find a way." He put his notebook away. "We'll have a man watching, but that's no guarantee, as you saw tonight."

"This place is being sold anyway. We are all being evicted this week."

His eyes were sympathetic. "I see. Well, good luck to you, Miss Marsh. I wish I could be of more help."

Lucy shut the door behind him and leaned her forehead against the cool wood. What was she going to do? She had a way to get to Texas, but it meant selling herself. Was it worth it? Her gaze went to Eileen sleeping in Lucy's cot. She'd been frightened by the commotion and had insisted on crawling into Lucy's bed. She and Jed were everything to Lucy. If she could get to Texas, maybe she could find her uncle. Maybe he would take pity on Jed and Eileen and see to their future.

And Catherine could show up anytime. Lucy knelt beside the bed and pleaded with God for a way out of the mess she was in. She sensed no permission from the Lord to turn down this offer. If she said no to this man, what would become of her and her siblings? God had promised that he would provide. What if this *was* his provision? God was in the business of bringing blessings out of unexpected circumstances, but Lucy didn't *want* this twist to her life. The very thought of marrying a man she didn't know seemed ridiculous, but didn't God ask the seemingly impossible at times? And if it assured the future for Jed and Eileen . . .

She finally sat up and put her head in her hands. "Okay, Lord. Whatever you tell me." She lit a candle and took her Bible in hand. If she remembered correctly, the story of Abraham was in Genesis 12.

> Now the LORD had said unto Abram, Get thee out of thy country, and from thy kindred, and from thy father's house, unto a land that I will shew thee: and I will make of thee a great nation, and I will bless thee, and make thy name great; and thou shalt be a blessing.

The words imprinted on her heart as though God had spoken them to her. *A blessing.* She could be a blessing. Warmth that had nothing to do with the pitiful bit of coal in the fireplace enveloped her. God was behind this. It had to be so. Marriage was an honorable thing. And this had come at a time when she saw no way to support the children and herself. Marriage was something God had ordained, and Mr. Stanton said his son was a Christian. She closed her Bible.

Holding the lantern aloft, she went down the rickety basement stairs. They creaked under her bare feet. The leather-strapped trunk was shoved under the stairwell. She set the lantern on the floor and tugged the trunk out. Jed would have to help her carry it up. Picking up the lantern again, she glanced around the space to see if there was anything down here she needed to bring with her. A rough wooden shelf held empty canning jars and the canner. She picked one up, then realized a rancher would own such equipment.

She turned back to the trunk and opened it. All it contained was a blue dress. According to her father, her mother had been married in this dress. Lucy ran her fingers across the silky material. It was much fancier and more lavish than anything Lucy owned. She wished her mother were here to instruct her on what to do. How was she to be a wife when she had no role model? She'd been an infant when her mother died. She clasped the locket again. What would her mother have advised?

She lifted the dress into the light and examined it. It had a high collar and voluminous skirt. The sleeves were ruffled. It was heavy too. Draping it over her arm, she took up the lantern and mounted the steps. She would wear the dress when she met Nate. It would give her courage to face whatever the future brought.

NATE LEANED BACK in the saddle and surveyed the ramshackle house that stood on a barren hillside swept by the north Texas wind. He heard a horse whinny from inside the barn, so he knew someone was here. Larson only had one horse, an old paint he'd ridden into town two years before. Nate dismounted and tied the reins to the hitching post before stepping onto the rickety porch. The wind drowned out the sound of his boots on the old boards.

Before his fist could fall on the door, it opened and Larson's form filled the doorway. Nate dropped his hand to his side. "I need to talk to you."

"I got nothing to say." The man started to shut the door.

Nate put his boot against the doorjamb and glanced at Larson's belt. No gun. "Well, I do." Past Larson's shoulders he could see the one-room cabin. It appeared to be empty. "Where's your henchman?"

Larson's eyes narrowed. "What henchman?"

"The man you hired to burn down my barn."

Larson smirked. "You have a mishap, son?"

"I'm not your son. I tracked the guy, you know. I saw you meet him."

Larson brushed past Nate to stand on the porch. "I don't know what you're talking about."

Nate turned to face him. "I saw you, Larson." He jabbed his forefinger against the man's red-checked shirt. "I'm here to warn you to let it go. My pa didn't do anything wrong."

Red rose up Larson's neck and lodged in his face. "He took advantage of my father. He's got no right to my land."

Nate was tired of the old argument. "Where'd you get the money to hire that guy?"

Larson took a step back. "You can't prove I hired him."

"The sheriff will be keeping his eye on him. You might as well send him packing."

"It's your word against mine."

Nate managed to keep his rising temper in check. "I *saw* you with that guy, Larson."

Larson shrugged and turned to his still-open door. "It's not against the law to talk to a fellow. Sounds to me like you got an enemy, Stanton."

"I'm going to see that those men are run out of town. The money you paid them is going to be lost."

Larson faced Nate. "You think you own this town, but you don't. Larson blood built this county. My ma was killed by a Comanche arrow."

Something inside responded to the pain in the man's words. "I'm sorry about your ma, Larson. But this argument is going nowhere."

Larson flashed him a glare, then turned and stomped through the door. It slammed behind him, and Nate made no move to go after him. Maybe the sheriff would listen. He mounted his horse and rode to town.

DELICIOUS AROMAS FILLED the air as Lucy sat in the dining car. The train vibrated along the track, but the experience of seeing the train station fade in the distance exhilarated her. The white linen tablecloth was finer than anything she'd ever seen. She took a spoonful of consommé and the flavor brightened her spirits. The children had already eaten and were tucked into their cots in the luxurious accommodations Mr. Stanton had purchased for all of them.

She smiled at the woman across from her, Mr. Stanton's cousin, whom he had brought along as a chaperone. Mrs. Walker was in her fifties yet still trim. Her blond hair held a few strands of gray but was lustrous and thick.

Lucy took another spoonful. "It's quite delicious, Mrs. Walker. Thank you for choosing for me."

"You're quite welcome, my dear. Are you feeling better?"

The woman had discovered Lucy weeping in her berth and had been quick to comfort her. Lucy managed a smile. "Much better, thank you. At least until I meet Nate." She stared down at the simple gold band on her left hand. Standing in front of a justice of the peace with her husband's father hadn't been the way she'd dreamed of marrying. "What if he's cruel or physically repulsive?"

Mrs. Walker smiled. "Oh, my dear, you have no need to worry.

Nate is quite handsome. All the young ladies in town would give anything for him to pay attention to them."

"Why was he unable to find a woman on his own, then?"

"Nate only has one goal in mind—to make the Stars Above Ranch known in all of Texas. He works much too hard and is too exhausted to spark any young lady. He seldom attends church socials or town dances." The woman's eyes were gray but not as shrewd and determined as her brother's.

"Stars Above Ranch? I like that."

"Nate's mother, God rest her soul, named it when Henry brought her to the original cabin. They arrived at night and she said she'd never seen so many stars."

It sounded so romantic. The name alone eased Lucy's fears. "Did your cousin tell you h-how we met?"

Mrs. Walker inclined her head. "He did."

Lucy put down her spoon. "I'm encumbered with the responsibility of raising my brother and sister. That's quite a challenge for a new husband when Mr. Stanton could have found a carefree young woman."

"Henry prides himself on being a good judge of people. He believed he'd found his Rebekah for Nate."

Lucy liked the sound of that. "I desire to belong somewhere."

"What happened to your parents, dear girl?"

"My mother died when I was an infant. Father was killed in an accident three months ago."

"What did your father do?"

"He owned a pawn shop."

The woman's eyes were kind. "And there was nothing of value left for you to use to raise your siblings?"

Lucy hesitated, then shook her head. "Father's shop was broken into just before he died, and his most valuable merchandise was stolen. We were fine, though, because I had a good position as a seamstress. Then my employer was forced to let me go yesterday."

"So Henry said. He has sung your praises since he met you." Mrs. Walker reached across the pristine tablecloth to pat Lucy's hand. "And I quite concur. You'll make our Nate a superb wife." Her gray eyes studied Lucy's face. "I haven't known you long, but I can see you are the sort of person who quickly takes charge of things. While I heartily endorse such courage, you can fall into the trap of thinking you are in control. Do not forget that God does with us as he wills."

"Of course I know that," Lucy said quickly.

The woman smiled. "You're a God-fearing young woman. But in Texas you will need more than courage—you'll need wisdom. Listen to God, Lucy."

"Yes, ma'am. I always do." But her conscience stirred. Did she really? Or did she tend to rush into things and then ask God to bless her decisions?

She ate her dinner and said good night, then made her way through the car to her sleeping quarters. She first peeked in on her brother and sister. Jed's red hair fell across his forehead, and his freckles stood out on his pale skin. A wave of love for him choked her. He'd had a rough year. He and Papa had been so close. The trauma of seeing their father die in a runaway buggy had scarred him. He'd been in the buggy as well but had been thrown clear before the horses plunged with their father into a swollen river. In one crushing blow, they'd been orphaned. Papa's body hadn't been recovered for three days. Jed hadn't been the same since.

She dropped the curtain back into place and entered her own compartment. A lingering scent of hair tonic hung in the air. Lucy had smelled it before. It was the same scent she'd noticed on the intruder last night. She froze and stared at the berth. Hadn't the covers been straight and taut when she was last in here? Now the blanket had been pulled back.

She pulled her valise from under the berth. She was sure it had been rifled through. Who would search her belongings? She sniffed the cologne again and wished she could talk to the kind policeman again. It was surely a common hair tonic and she was jumping to conclusions.

She exited the compartment and peered in on Jed and Eileen. They still slept. She couldn't tell if anything had been disturbed and she didn't smell the cologne. She rubbed her head and tried to puzzle it out. She went back to her compartment and gathered her pillow and a blanket, then settled on the floor by Jed and Eileen. If anyone came, she intended to stop him from harming her siblings.

FOUR

❧❧❧

Nate pushed his broad-rimmed Stetson away from his forehead and leaned back in his saddle. He'd lost ten head of cattle from the frigid cold in the past twenty-four hours. He couldn't remember ever enduring cold like this, not even in February. And snow. The most they usually got was an inch or two that quickly melted away, not six inches like that covering the ground now.

He squinted toward town. Pa should have been home two days ago. A dart of worry kept Nate on edge. He hoped this sudden and unusual snowstorm hadn't trapped Pa somewhere. Turning Whisper's head, he plodded toward the house. Smoke curled from the chimney, and his mouth watered at the aroma of steak that blew in with the smoke. It had been a long time since breakfast. He would be glad when Pa got home. Their cook, Percy, didn't talk much. Nate rode into the barn and curried his horse before heading to the house.

Not for the first time, he wondered what it would be like to come home to a wife and family. Someone strong and knowledge-able who would discuss cattle and ranching with him. Maybe someone like Margaret O'Brien. She was almost as tall as Nate was himself and could rope a calf nearly as well too. She was attractive enough, but she was more like a sister than a lover.

He bounded up the steps and had his hand on the door when he heard the rattle and clank of a wagon coming across the snow-covered meadow. He turned and shaded his eyes with one hand while he studied the approaching convoy. Three wagons. It had to be Pa with provisions. His spirits lifted.

As the wagons neared, he recognized his father's gray head. Nate lifted a hand in greeting and went to meet him. Then he saw the young woman clinging desperately to the wagon seat beside his father. Her youth and beauty seemed to bring sudden color to a blank landscape. She peeked at him from under her bonnet, then stared down at her hands.

He stared harder. What had Pa done? Nate remembered his father's ramblings about the place needing a woman's touch. *"One of us needs to get married."* That was one of the things Pa had gone on and on about. He wouldn't have. Would he? But this woman was young enough to be his daughter.

Nate eyed her. Could he have hired a housekeeper? Studying the tiny woman, Nate couldn't see it. Pa wouldn't have hired someone so puny. Nate gritted his teeth. The little wench probably took one look at Pa and saw him for a rich sucker. And if that fancy blue dress was any indication, she'd expect him to lavish pretty dresses and fripperies on her. Well, if she thought she was getting any money out of this ranch, she was sadly mistaken.

Nate waited for his father to step down from the wagon and explain. Maybe he hadn't married her yet. Maybe there would be a chance to talk him out of such a fool notion. His thoughts were interrupted when his father enveloped him in a bear hug. Nate tried to return the embrace, but his agitation kept his shoulders stiff.

His pa released him. "Boy, you did good while I was gone. We passed the south pasture and saw the herd there. They look fat and sassy." He jabbed a thumb back toward the wagon. "Help Lucy down while I get her luggage."

He didn't wait for an answer, but then, he never did. Nate suppressed a sigh and offered his hand to the young woman. Lucy, his father called her. She was a cute little thing. Tiny, barely five feet if he had to hazard a guess, with huge blue eyes. A wisp of fine blond hair had escaped her bonnet and lay across the delicate pink of her cheek.

She took his arm and nearly fell when she tried to step down. He caught her in his arms, and the contact sent a shock of awareness through him. He hastily set her on her feet and backed away. "Miss Lucy." He tipped his hat.

She stared at him with those enormous blue eyes. He'd never seen eyes so big and blue. A man could get lost in those eyes. No wonder she'd snared his pa.

He heard an excited shout and turned to look at the last wagon. A boy of about twelve, his cheeks red from the cold, came bounding through the snow. His amazingly red hair stood up on end, and he carried a little girl who looked like a tiny version of Lucy.

"Did you see how big everything looks out here, Lucy?" He turned his gaze on Nate. "How far's the nearest neighbors, Mr. Stanton?"

Nate softened a bit at the lad's exuberance. "Nearest would be the O'Briens, about ten miles away."

Lucy gave a timid smile. "Uh, Mr. Stanton, this is my brother, Jed, and my sister, Eileen."

Nate shook the boy's hand brusquely and nodded to the little girl, then turned to lead the way to the house. That boy might be her brother, but he'd bet the little girl was her own daughter. Percy and Rusty, the foreman, had come to help with the provisions and the luggage, and he followed them into the house. Lucy had a bit of difficulty walking through the heavy snowdrifts. What had Pa been thinking? If he wanted a wife, why hadn't he picked one who had some gumption? This pale lily wouldn't last long out here.

He took her elbow and helped her along near the house where the drift went clear up on the porch. She shot him a grateful look from those amazing eyes again, but he was much too cautious to be caught in her little web of deceit.

In the parlor, Lucy sighed and sank into the rocker near the fire. She held out her arms for Eileen and took off the little girl's coat, then spread it out in front of the fireplace. Lucy set Eileen on her feet, then stood to take off her own cloak, bonnet, and mittens. When she pulled her small, white hands from the mittens, his heart sank when he saw the plain gold band on her left hand.

She'd gotten Pa to marry her.

Nate's eyes met hers, and he saw the fear in them again. He stared her down with a contemptuous curl to his lips. She paled and looked away.

His father came into the room, rubbing his hands. "I'm famished. We haven't eaten anything since breakfast. Let's eat while it's hot."

"Aren't you going to introduce me properly?" Nate asked. "Is Miss Lucy your new housekeeper?"

"There's time for all that after lunch." His father avoided Nate's gaze. "After we eat, we'll have some coffee here in the parlor by the fire, and I'll explain everything."

Lunch was a stilted affair. Nate saw the glances Jed kept tossing his way. Lucy grew more strained and silent. Her knuckles were white from gripping her fork, and she kept her eyes trained on her plate throughout the entire meal. His father tried to draw her into the discussion several times, but she wouldn't look at him and answered in the briefest of words.

Finally, his father pushed back his chair and gave a satisfied sigh. "I missed that good grub of yours, Percy. Now how about some of your famous coffee? They just don't know how to make the stuff in the city. Bring it to the parlor when it's ready." He stood and led the way down the hall.

Lucy pleated her dress nervously. "Could I put Eileen to bed? She's exhausted."

"Of course, dear girl." His father turned to Nate. "Show her to the little guest room, son. The coffee should be ready by the time you get back."

Nate had been watching for an opportunity to talk to her alone all evening. The candle in his hand cast a flickering light ahead of them as he led her up the stairs and down the hall. He pushed open the door to the smallest guest room. Lucy slipped past him into the room. A blue quilt his mother had made covered the bed, and a small cot was pushed up against the wall.

"I'll be outside the door. Let me know when you're ready to go back to the parlor." He closed the door and leaned against the wall. The soothing murmur of her voice to the little girl sounded motherly. He heard her singing in a low, sweet voice for several minutes, then the door opened and Lucy stepped into the hall.

She eased the door shut. "She's asleep."

He took a step closer and lowered his voice. "I want to know what's going on."

Lucy lifted her chin toward him. "I don't think you do, Mr. Stanton. You're not going to be happy about it."

The certainty in her voice alarmed him. "I've seen your kind blow through here before. You're just out for all the money you can bleed out of Pa, but you'll have to go through me first," he said, gritting his teeth. "So why don't you just pack your things and get out before you get hurt?"

Lucy smiled wearily. "It's a bit late for that."

"You can't mean you actually care for Pa. He's an old man."

"It's not what you think."

"Oh, I think it is." He spun around and stormed out of the room. He hadn't handled that well. She'd stayed too calm, as if she knew something he didn't. Had Pa already given her money?

Moments later Lucy joined them in the parlor. Nate stood, staring morosely out the window at the driving snow. He turned when she entered the room and glared at her. He thought he saw tears shimmering on the tips of her lashes, but he had to be imagining it. She was much too calculating to cry.

His father rubbed his hands together. "Ah, Nate, I've got some explaining to do."

Nate gave him an ironic smile. "I reckon so, Pa."

Pa stared at him with a steady gaze and a hint of compassion in his eyes. "This is Lucy, your wife."

NATE'S FACE WAVERED through the tears that rimmed Lucy's eyes. He hadn't spoken since his father told him that he had a wife. She had felt a thrill of joy at the first sight of her handsome husband, so strong, so manly, his feet planted apart like the king of his realm here in Texas. But with his rejection of her, all those hopeful wonderings had vanished like yesterday's sunshine.

"You mean *your* wife," Nate corrected.

But his lips went white, and shocked comprehension settled over his face. She wished she could take her trunk and run off. Find her family and not face this man's wrath. She twisted her hands together.

Mr. Stanton shook his head. "No, son, I mean *your* wife. It's time you settled down and saw to raising a family. I won't be around to help you forever. You need a passel of strong sons to build our cattle empire."

Nate sank onto the sofa, and the lines deepened in his tanned face. "Pa, what have you done?" he whispered.

Mr. Stanton hunched his shoulders and raised his voice. "If I waited for you to find a wife, I'd be too old to enjoy my grand-children. Lucy here, she's a good Christian girl. She'll make you a fine wife."

Lucy saw the shudder that passed through Nate's frame. A lump grew in her throat. Did he find her so unattractive? She had no claim to great beauty, but he had barely glanced her way to even know what she looked like.

Nate waved a hand in her direction. "Look at her, Pa! What were you thinking? The work here is hard. The vision we've talked about will take a woman who can carry her own weight."

Lucy's tears dried up with the bolt of rage that shot through her. She drew herself up to her full height of just under five feet and glared at her new husband. "I'm stronger than I look, Mr. Stanton. I've worked long hours at the dressmaker's shop, and I'm not afraid of hard work. I can tackle any chores you care to throw my way."

She was wasting her breath. He was determined not to give her a chance. She could see it in the hard line of his jaw and the fierce glare in his eyes. But something inside her screamed to be allowed to prove her worth. To take control of this situation. She would prove to him her value. He would see just how capable she was.

"I can learn to do anything. And I'm a good homemaker and organizer. You'll see."

The muscles in his jaw hardened. "You aren't staying long enough to find out, Miss Marsh. I aim to put you on the first stage back north."

"We are married," she reminded him. "I don't believe in divorce." He would not send her away. She had a brother and sister to care for. Her appearance might disgust him, but marriage was more than physical appearance.

He took a deep breath. "Neither do I. But this is no real marriage. I never agreed to any such arrangement." He turned and frowned at his father. "You should have known better, Pa."

Henry was pale but resolute. "For once in your life, listen to me, Nate. This ranch needs a woman's touch. You need a woman to soften you before you turn to granite."

"If you want a woman around the house so bad, *you* marry her," Nate shot back.

"That advice is a little late," Lucy said. "I'm married to *you*."

Mr. Stanton opened his mouth to speak, then gasped and clutched his left shoulder. His face turned red and darkened to nearly purple before the color drained from his face, and a gargle escaped his open mouth.

"Pa?" Nate's voice rose, and he jumped to his feet and rushed toward his father. Henry Stanton reeled away, crashing to the floor like a great tree felled by a logger's ax.

Lucy bit back a shriek and ran toward her new father-in-law. Nate rolled Henry over onto his back and peered into his face. The older man was still breathing, but his pallor was pronounced and he was unconscious.

"Let me." Lucy pushed her way closer to Henry. "I know something of nursing. Is there a doctor in the area?"

Nate nodded. "Doc Cooper in Larson."

"Send Percy to fetch him, and you help me get him into bed." She checked Henry's breathing and was relieved to see a bit of color coming back to his face. She snatched a quilted throw from the chair and tucked it around him.

Bellowing for Percy, Nate ran to do what she said. Lucy pressed her fingertips against her father-in-law's chest and frowned at Henry's irregular heartbeat. He'd had some kind of a heart spasm.

"Please, God, please keep him alive," she whispered.

If this man died, she would be at the mercy of her new husband.

Nate returned and lifted his father's shoulders. "Grab his feet."

Lucy complied and Jed jumped in to assist as well. They carried him up the stairs. Lucy's muscles protested, but she held on to his inert body and managed to do her part.

"His room is the first on the left," Nate said.

Lucy pushed open the door with her foot, and they laid Henry on the bed. Her muscles still burned even though they'd been relieved of the burden. Nate jerked his father's boots off.

Lucy pulled the quilts up around him. "We need to keep him warm."

Nate nodded, then ran his hand through his sandy blond hair. His gray eyes held a deep fear that tore at Lucy's heart. She laid a hand on his arm. "We should pray for him."

He nodded again and moved so her hand fell away. She couldn't help the stab of disappointment at his rejection of her comfort. Bowing her head, she prayed aloud for this man she'd already come to admire and care about.

When she lifted her head, she became aware that Jed and Eileen hovered at the doorway. She straightened her shoulders and moved away from Nate. She had to be strong for the children's sakes. "I'll fix us all some tea."

Nate grimaced. "I can't abide that sissy drink, and I'm not about to start drinking it now."

Hot words bubbled to her lips, but she choked them back. No wonder Henry had to find a wife for his son. No woman in her right mind would choose to put up with him.

Henry stirred and his eyes fluttered open. "Quit your wrangling," he said in a weak voice. "I can't endure petty quarreling." He struggled to sit up. "Besides, the sight of Nate sipping tea like a woman would finish me off for sure. Fetch me some coffee. That's all I need."

"I'll just be a moment." Away from her new husband's stern presence, she felt reprieved. She hurried down the stairs to the kitchen, with Jed and Eileen on her heels.

FIVE

〜❦〜

When they reached the kitchen, Eileen tugged on Lucy's skirt. "I don't like it here, Lucy." Tears rolled down her cheeks.

Lucy scooped Eileen up into her arms. "Hush, darling, it will be all right. There's flour for biscuits and beefsteak for dinner. That's more than we had in Wabash. I know it's going to be an adjustment, but let's wait and see how things are tomorrow. We're all at sixes and sevens with Mr. Stanton's illness and the long trip. I'll make sure things work out for you both."

Jed crossed his arms and glowered at her. "Mr. Nate acts like this was all your fault. Is he going to send us back?"

Lucy had been wondering the same thing, but she managed to smile. "Nate is just shocked at what his father has done. It will be fine once he gets used to the idea."

She hoped that was true. She was willing to give Nate the benefit of the doubt, but her charity was growing thin. The thought of their tiny home, rude though it might be, filled her with a sense of nostalgia and longing.

But no. Danger lurked in Indiana. She had cut ties and no one knew where they were. It was better that way. This was a new start away from whatever danger had come calling.

Lucy put Eileen down and surveyed the kitchen. Dingy cotton covered the open shelves. A teakettle and coffeepot sat atop the wood cookstove, blackened by years of abuse. The wooden table was battered and smooth with use. She peered into the coffeepot and the dark liquid inside smelled horrible. But then, the entire kitchen reeked of stale food.

Wrinkling her nose at the strong smell, she poured the black coffee into a cup. She eyed it. Maybe she should see if it was any good. She took a cautious sip and shuddered at the bitterness. From the strong, acrid taste, it must have been made this morning. There was no time to make fresh though. A sugar container was on the table, so she took it, then stirred some sugar into the cup.

Sugar. What a luxury. There seemed to be plenty too. She dipped her finger into the coffee and tasted it. Shivering at the still-bitter taste, she added more sugar, then poured another cup for Nate and added sugar to that cup also. At least it might be drinkable now.

"Watch your sister," she told Jed.

She carried the coffee back to Henry's bedroom. He was sitting up against the pillows. Though Henry looked wan and weak, his eyes were not so dull. He took the coffee eagerly, and she handed the other cup to Nate. Both men took a big gulp. Nate's eyes widened and he choked but managed to keep it down. His father was not so charitable. Sputtering, Henry spewed the coffee from his mouth. The dark liquid pooled on the quilt in front of him.

The eyes he turned to Lucy were full of reproach. "Sugar! You put sugar in my coffee?"

"I'm sorry." Lucy took a step back toward the door. "It was bitter. I think it was old."

Nate wiped his mouth. "It's supposed to be bitter." He took the cup from his father and brushed by Lucy on his way to the door. "She doesn't know coffee from syrup. You should send her back to where she came from."

Henry scowled. "Lucy is your wife, and the sooner you adjust to that fact, the better."

Nate put a hand on his hip. "She's not my wife, Pa. I never gave you permission to bring me back a bride."

"You signed a proxy statement, Nate. It's all legal, and you'd best make the most of it."

"The proxy was to sell cattle! Not marry me off."

The two men glared at one another, and Lucy thought they looked like two roosters squaring off for a fight. If she had the nerve, she'd douse them both with cold water. They deserved it. Henry for bringing her here without telling her his son hated women, and Nate for not giving her a chance to prove herself. Well, she would show them. She wasn't afraid of hard work, and when Nate realized it, his apology would be sweet.

Still lost in a pleasant daydream of Nate groveling at her feet, she didn't notice Henry's gray color until he choked. Sinking weakly back against the pillows, he clutched his left arm again. Lucy started to his side, but Nate beat her to it.

Drops of perspiration beaded Henry's face. "Quit fussing," he muttered. He rallied a bit and clenched his son's hand. "Promise me you'll try to care for your new wife, Nate," he whispered. "If I thought I'd done anything to harm her and those children, I would turn over in my grave."

Nate patted his father's shoulder. "You're not going to die, Pa."

Henry tried to rise in the bed. "Promise me."

Nate stilled, and his shoulders slumped. "I promise." He shot a dark glance toward Lucy as if it were her fault his father was so insistent.

"I want her and the children to move in with you. I'm not sure the noise would be good for the old ticker." Henry's voice was weak, but the odd gleam in his eye made Lucy wonder if he was using the situation to his own advantage. "Once I'm well, we'll see about getting you a decent house for a family."

Nate's brows drew together, but he nodded. "Whatever you want, Pa." The look from his gray eyes as he turned toward Lucy was anything but meek.

The time ticked by slowly. When Lucy had finally begun to wonder what had become of the doctor, he came bustling in. A stringy man with grizzled hair, Doc Cooper reminded Lucy of a miner rather than a doctor.

"What's this nonsense, Henry? You're too ornery to die on us. Let's take a look at you." Dr. Cooper jerked his head at Nate, Lucy, and the children, and they obeyed the silent admonition to leave him alone with Henry.

EILEEN RUBBED HER eyes and leaned back against her brother in the rocker. "I don't like our new brother. I want to go home."

Holding her, Jed gave the rocker a push with his foot and somehow managed to give her a reassuring smile when he wanted to tell her they'd just pack up and leave. "We have to make the best of it. We don't have anywhere else to go right now."

Lucy had told him they had an uncle in the area. Maybe they

could find him and he'd help Lucy get a job. Jed too. He could stock shelves or something at the general store. Maybe take care of horses. He liked horses.

"Is our new grandpa going to die?" Eileen asked.

"I hope not." Jed looked around the ranch. As far as he could see, there were cattle grazing on a thousand hills. Several white-washed barns were in the back lot and fences penned in a remuda of horses. A few chickens pecked in the dirt in the side lot by the barn. He'd never been in a place where he felt so alone. No city, no people. Just the big, blue sky overhead and the sense that he could see forever.

Eileen tugged on his shirtsleeve. "Look, Jed, kittens."

Half a dozen kittens played in the dirt by the barn door. "I see them." He slid off the rocker and set her on her feet, then took her hand. "Let's go look around."

Even the dirt was different here. Dry and dusty. It left a fine red layer on his shoes as he led his sister across the scrubby yard. While his sister knelt and cooed at the kittens, he studied the landscape back here and imagined himself riding the low-lying hills. His friends back in Wabash would be envious if they could see him now. They had read of the exploits of Jesse James and Cole Younger and dreamed they would be the hero to bring them down. He pretended to draw a gun from a holster and shoot at the chicken pecking near the water trough. If that had been Jesse James, he would have nailed him.

A horse's nicker from inside the barn caught his attention. He walked into the cool, dim building. A beautiful gray horse stared at him from a stall. He'd never seen a horse so fine.

He touched the horse's nose and found it soft. Its lips nuzzled his chin. "I don't have any sugar for you." A bag of oats hung on the far wall. He took a handful from the sack and held his cupped palm to the horse. A thrill shot through him when the horse ate it. If only he could have this horse. It was love at first sight.

When a sound came behind him, he assumed it was Eileen until he smelled an unfamiliar hair tonic. When he turned, he saw no one.

"Hello?"

No one answered him, and if it weren't for the spicy scent still in the air, he would have thought he had imagined it. That smell . . . Terror enveloped him and he couldn't move. Why was he so afraid? It was only hair tonic.

He swallowed hard and shuffled his feet. With the paralysis broken, he listened. The hair on the back of his neck prickled at the ominous silence. He wanted to run, but he was part of this family now. If the man wasn't answering, then he was up to no good. Jed took a pitchfork in his shaking hands and sidled toward the darker areas of the barn. He pushed each stall open with the tool.

When he was in the last stall, he heard Eileen call his name. He whipped around to make sure she was okay, but when a rustle came behind him, he knew he was in trouble. He half turned, but a blow came out of nowhere and knocked him to his knees.

His ears rang and he nearly blacked out. He shook his head and staggered to his feet in time to catch a glimpse of a man's jeans and boots disappearing out of the stall.

"Eileen, run!" He stumbled to the front barn door. When he exited into the sunshine, he blinked to clear his vision. Eileen was picking up the kittens as though she were trying to save them too. At least that man hadn't hurt her.

He heard hoofbeats and ran to the side of the barn where he

saw a rider galloping away on the back of a black horse. He'd never be able to identify the intruder. All he'd seen was the man's clothing and hat. Not his face.

He needed to tell Mr. Stanton, but what if the news made him sicker? Maybe he should wait and tell the younger Stanton when no one else was around.

"Something wrong, kid?" a voice said behind him.

He turned to see a young cowboy atop a huge roan. The man's cowboy hat was pushed to the back of his head, and his blue eyes were smiling though his lips were in a straight line.

"There was a guy in the barn. He hit me and ran." Jed turned to point to the rider, but he was already out of sight. "He's gone."

The cowboy frowned. "He hit you?" He dismounted and came to stand by Jed. "You've got a knot on your head."

"It's where he hit me." Jed became aware that he was still clutching the pitchfork. He loosened his grip and put the tines in the dirt. Suddenly dizzy, he leaned on it. "Don't tell my sister. I don't want to worry her."

"Who's your sister?"

"Mr. Nate's wife. I'm Jed. Who are you?" Jed eyed him. What if this guy was in cahoots with the other one?

The man's eyes registered shock. "Nate's married?"

"Mr. Stanton arranged for the marriage by proxy." The man still hadn't said who he was. "Who are you?" Jed asked again.

"Roger Stanton. I think I'd better see what Pa has done to my brother. I'll be in as soon as I take care of my horse. Pa has some explaining to do."

Jed started to tell him that his father was sick, then decided to hold his tongue so he could get inside and tell Lucy there was another Stanton to deal with.

SIX

Lucy strained to hear past the closed door but heard only the murmur of the doctor's voice and couldn't make out any words.

Her brother came into the kitchen with Eileen by the hand. "Lucy, I—"

Nate interrupted her brother. He crossed his arms and leaned against the wall. "You may have killed my father."

She wetted her lips and tried to think of a suitable response, but before she could respond, Jed stepped between her and Nate.

His fists clenched, he thrust his face into Nate's. "My sister is worth two of you, mister. Eileen and me would be in the orphanage if Lucy hadn't found a job at the dress shop and kept us all together. She's come home with her fingers bleeding from the pins. And she's small 'cause when there's not enough food, she makes sure me and Eileen eat first. Lucy may not be big, but she's all heart. You don't deserve her."

The man's eyes widened and he glanced at her, then at Eileen, with an expression of puzzlement on his face. He studied her as if seeing her for the first time. Lucy refused to look away before he did.

When his attention finally returned to Jed, Lucy put a hand on her brother's arm. "Hush, Jed. This is God's will."

Nate gave a bark of laughter. "I find it hard to believe the Almighty told you to agree to such a plan. I don't need a wife."

She could take offense at his tone or she could do the right thing. The Bible said a soft answer turneth away wrath. If she'd been hit with something this huge and no warning, she'd be angry too.

She chose to forgive his manner and forced a smile. "No, you don't *want* a wife, and that's a completely different situation. We must make the best of this situation. You should respect your father enough to do that much. I haven't known Henry long, but he seems a wise man. Maybe he knows more about what you need than you do."

Nate ran a hand through his hair, and Lucy's heart softened even more at the vulnerability on his face. This had taken him by complete surprise. She'd had time to get used to it, but Henry's actions had left Nate reeling. She glanced at her brother and saw a trickle of blood on his forehead.

"Jed, what's happened to you?" She rushed to the sink for a rag and pumped cold water onto it, then hurried back to tend to him. "Sit down." She pushed Jed into a chair.

He winced. "There was a guy in the barn. He hit me."

"He *hit* you?" Nate half turned toward the door.

Jed stared at him then at Lucy. "There's another Stanton out there too," he said in a rush. "A younger brother, Roger."

Nate whipped back toward them. "Roger is home?" A light lit his eyes. "He's been gone a year."

Lucy tried to hold on to her composure. One more Stanton to deal with didn't appeal. "Where has he been?"

"Wandering out west. Last I heard he was fighting Indians with Custer."

Lucy put her hand to her mouth. "Custer?"

"He left the cavalry before the Little Bighorn. I'm not sure what he's doing now. I didn't think he'd ever come home. Where is he?" he asked Jed.

"Taking care of his horse. He said he'd be in after that."

"What about this fellow who hit you?" Nate asked.

Lucy's stomach clenched as she listened to her brother's story. "Bandits?"

Nate shrugged. "Hard to say. Could be a drifter looking for anything he could steal."

The tightness in his shoulders made Lucy think he wasn't saying what he really thought. "You don't think you should check it out?"

"You heard your brother. The man rode off. He's long gone."

She decided to let it go too. Jed was going to be fine. "We'd better get that coffee for your pa, or he'll take a switch to you."

Surprise flickered across Nate's face, and he lifted one eyebrow. "Figured him out already, huh?" He stared into her eyes, then his shoulders slumped. "I guess we'd best declare a truce for now. But don't think this situation will stand, Miss Lucy. I can't quite see you happy here."

Lucy bit her lip and held out her hand. "Truce, Mr. Stanton. I see I shall have to prove myself to you."

Her small hand was enveloped by his large, calloused one. The contact sent a thrill of awareness through her, and she nearly jerked it away. She searched the gray depths of his eyes. Did he feel the same attraction she did? If he did, he hid it well.

Nate released her hand and turned toward the cookstove. "I

reckon your first lesson better be coffee. A cattleman can't live without it. It warms him up on those cold nights on the cattle drive and wakes him up after a night spent tossing on the hard ground."

Lucy followed him to the stove. Nate grabbed the handle of the battered coffeepot and poured the dark liquid into a tin cup. "Sugar ruins the taste." He handed her a cup. "Take a swig."

Repressing a shudder, Lucy took the cup of coffee and raised it to her lips. She mustn't let him think she was too weak to even stand up to the taste of coffee. If learning to like the vile liquid was a necessity, then she would do it. She took a gulp of the coffee, and the bitter taste nearly made her gag. Managing a smile, she lowered the cup.

"That wasn't so bad, was it?"

"Do you want the truth?" A smile tugged the corners of her lips.

"Yeah."

"It's not as bad as cutting my finger off with a dull knife, but that's about all I can say for it."

Nate stared at her for a moment, then a laugh rumbled in his throat. A shiver skittered through her at the sound. With his face lit with amusement, he was entirely too appealing. A dimple in one cheek and the white flash of his teeth softened the tanned planes of his face, and even his towering height and broad shoulders seemed less intimidating.

Nate poured a cup for Jed. "Here, boy. If you aim to be a cattleman, you'd best learn too."

Jed took it cautiously, then sniffed it. His nose wrinkled, but he took a big swallow. His eyes widened and he coughed. "Good," he choked out.

Lucy and Nate both burst into laughter. The moment of

camaraderie warmed Lucy's aching heart. Maybe things would turn out right yet. She hadn't come this far to fail now.

NATE PUSHED OPEN the door to his father's room with Lucy and her siblings on his heels. What would he do if something happened to Pa? It had been just the two of them so long. Cholera had carried off his mother when he was two, and he had only vague memories of a gentle voice singing to him and a soft lap that smelled of something sweet. And Roger had been roaming the country for years. Maybe Pa was right. It might be time for him to take a wife. But he wasn't some greenhorn who needed his father to pick out a wife for him.

His pa was sitting up in the bed, some color in his face. He smiled when he saw the cup in Nate's hand. "Coffee, just what the doctor ordered. And Lucy's pretty face will help as well." He winked at her, and Nate heard her soft laugh.

"I don't remember ordering any such thing, Henry." Doc Cooper put his stethoscope into his black bag and closed it with a snap. "I reckon one cup won't hurt, but don't go drinking too much of it. You need to rest. I'll be back in the morning."

He jerked his head, and Nate followed him into the hallway. "How is he, Doc?"

The doctor slipped an arm into his coat. "I won't lie to you, Nate. He's getting old, and his ticker is just wearing out. See that he starts to take it easy, even if it means hiring more help. And try not to get him excited or upset. I know that's not easy to do with a man as active and vital as Henry has been."

Pain squeezed Nate's chest. "I can't lose him, Doc."

The doctor finished buttoning his coat. "Death comes to all of us eventually. Lord willing, your pa will be around a few more years, but he's got to step back and learn to enjoy life. That new wife of yours will help. Henry thinks a lot of her, and she'll make him slow down, you mark my words." Doc Cooper opened the door. "I think he'll be fine if you follow my instructions."

Nate walked the doctor out onto the porch and stood staring as he rode off down the dirt lane. His mind was numb. He couldn't make himself believe that his pa was getting old. Pa had always been there. He was too strong to ever die, wasn't he? Nate willed it to be so.

A soft hand touched his, and he jumped. Turning, he stared into Lucy's anxious face. "Is Pa okay?"

She nodded. "What did the doctor say?"

"His heart is weak. He needs to cut back and take it easy." Nate blurted out the words, but it didn't ease the pain. "He'll never do it. He loves the ranch. I'd have to hog-tie him to get him to stay in the house."

Lucy's eyes looked luminous, like sapphire gems. "I'll take care of him."

"He's my pa. I don't need any help." He regretted his words when he saw her bite her lip. "Sorry," he muttered.

He didn't know how to act around women, which was probably the reason he was still unmarried at thirty. He'd had no lack of partners at the few county dances he'd attended, but he invariably said the wrong thing and ended up riding home with Pa. He swallowed hard. He was no longer unmarried. This young woman with the dazzling blond hair and sparkling blue eyes was his wife. *His wife.* He couldn't get his mind around it.

Lucy straightened her shoulders. "Well, you're going to get my help whether you want it or not, Nate Stanton. I'm your wife and your father is now my father. The kids and I have already learned to love him. This isn't about you. It's about your father. Our problems can wait."

She was right. Lucy was entrancing with her golden curls and pink cheeks. Her full lips looked soft and inviting. Nate jerked his thoughts away from that direction. His priority was to see Pa better, then he could worry about getting rid of Miss Lucy and her siblings.

The door banged and they both turned. Nate's heart thumped at the sight of his brother striding toward him. "Rog!" He embraced his younger brother, then stepped back to study him. Roger looked older, wiser. "Just seeing you is going to make Pa feel better."

Roger's smile vanished. "Pa is sick?"

Nate nodded. "His heart. He's going to have to take it easy. You're home in time to pick up some of the slack."

Roger's blue eyes clouded. "I'm not staying. This is just a visit for a day or two before I head for Oklahoma."

He would not react. That always made things worse. "What's in Oklahoma?"

Roger shrugged. "That's what I aim to find out."

"Can't you at least stay until Pa is on his feet? I'm going to need some help."

His face expressionless, Roger stared at Nate. "I know how it will be, Nate. Little by little, you'll want more and more from me. Things I can't give. I don't want to be stuck here all my life. I want the city, people. It's like being buried alive here."

Roger had never been happy on the ranch. He had to choose his own path, but Nate wanted to grab his brother by the throat and pound some sense into him. What more could anyone want than the ranch? And Roger was a Stanton. Shouldn't he want to be part of building the Stanton cattle empire?

"Don't look at me like that," Roger said. "I know you love this place, but we're all different. I want more than running cattle for my life."

"Like what? You still don't know, do you?"

Roger shrugged again. "Give me time. I'm only twenty-nine. I'll figure it out. But I'll do it my way, not yours."

And that was always the way it was. Nate took his brother's arm. "Let's go see Pa."

SEVEN

~ের্জ্য

Carrying the tray of coffee cups, Lucy hung back as the two men entered the master bedroom. Henry was propped up on pillows with a Lone Star quilt over his legs. His eyes were closed and his mouth hung open slightly, the expression accentuating his pallor. With his hat off, his hair looked thinner and grayer. Pity welled in her chest as she saw him like that, his strength gone and his age showing.

"Maybe we should come back later," she whispered, herding the children back toward the door.

At the sound of her voice, Henry's eyes opened. He blinked, then looked past Nate to where his younger son stood. He reared up in the bed. "Roger?" His voice was weak and disbelieving.

Roger crossed the few feet to the bed and took his father's hand. "It's me, Pa."

Henry kicked the quilt off his feet. "Did someone telegraph you that I was dying or something?"

"No, I was traveling through Dallas and decided to come home for a visit. I won't be here long." Roger shot a warning glance at Nate. "Just a few days."

Henry's lips pressed together, and the animation faded from his face. "I reckon we'll take what we can get, then, son. If you can just pitch in for a day or two, I'll be on my feet in a few days."

Roger smiled, but it seemed forced. "I can do that, I reckon, Pa."

Lucy edged toward the bed, eager to know more about the family dynamics. Roger was most handsome and dashing. What had brought about the rift she sensed?

Henry leaned back against the pillows. "What have you been up to?"

Roger pulled a chair closer to the bed. "I did a stint as a stevedore on a steamboat until the thing blew up near St. Louis. Then I worked for the railroad as a conductor for a few months. I quit when the train reached San Francisco and worked at the shipyards for a few months. I was with Custer for a while, but luckily, I lit out before the Little Bighorn. After that I worked at a bank awhile. I decided to come back this way and see what it's like in Atlanta."

"I thought you were going to Oklahoma." Nate's frown was ferocious.

"There's a girl I want to say hello to in Oklahoma first," Roger said.

"Be careful if you're traveling by yourself. There are still some renegade Comanche bands around. Neighbors got burned out two months ago."

Roger returned Nate's frown. "I'm always careful."

Lucy wanted to find a way to end the tension rippling in the room. "I made you some fresh coffee." She brushed past the men with the tray and let Henry take a cup. "Nate showed me how to make it. No sugar this time."

Henry grinned. "You'll make a rancher's wife yet, Lucy."

Roger cleared his throat and glanced at Lucy. "About that wife thing. Young Jed tells me you arranged the marriage, Pa. I just want to make it clear to you that I won't stand for anything like that."

"Roger," Nate hissed. "Now's not the time to upset him."

Henry waved his hand. "I'm not an invalid, Nate. It was just a little spell. Your brother can speak his mind."

Roger pushed his cowboy hat to the back of his head and sat back in his chair. "You can't run our lives for us, Pa. You've lived your life. Let us live ours."

Lucy's cheeks scorched. She didn't want to hear this. Had Roger seen her small size and found her wanting too? Nothing she could say would change their minds. Only action would do. The thought of facing the cows in the barn made her shiver, but she was going to learn how to milk them and chop wood. And anything else it took to show these men she could be the best rancher's wife they'd ever seen.

Henry caught her eye. "You're being rude to Lucy. I won't have it."

Roger glanced up at her. "I mean no disrespect to Lucy. I'm sure she's a fine lady."

Henry sat up. "This is ridiculous. It's not your business, Roger."

"It's not yours either," Roger shot back. "You had no business arranging a marriage for Nate without his knowledge."

"I think your brother can speak for himself," Henry said.

Lucy glanced at Nate, expecting him to put in his displeasure as well, but he merely sat in the chair with his arms folded across his chest.

Lucy's fingers curled into her palms. "I would prefer you not discuss me as though I'm the bedside table."

Roger lifted a brow, then rose from the chair. "I seem to have left my manners in San Francisco. I'm sorry, Miss Lucy. I don't know you, but I'm sure you're a suitable wife for Nate." He went toward the door. "I'm going to have a bath. See you at supper."

Lucy's legs felt wobbly, and she sank onto the chair he'd vacated. It was bad enough to have one Stanton opposed to her presence. How was she going to convince them all that she could do this? Especially now that she was beginning to have doubts herself.

A FIRE BLAZED in Lucy's fireplace, and the warmth enveloped her. The wind rattled the window but failed to flutter the curtains. The house must be tighter than the old house in Wabash. Her room held a large bed covered with a feather top and several quilts. It appeared to be a woman's room with rose wallpaper and pink curtains.

Her siblings were across the hall. Eileen had wanted to sleep with her until she'd seen the lavender room that held a white single bed and some toys. In the closet she found a toy train and several carved toy soldiers as well as a stuffed bear with a missing eye. Lucy suspected the toys were Nate's.

Her trunk was by the closet, and she crouched beside it. When she opened it, her hand hovered over the top dress. Hadn't it been on the bottom? It was her work dress, and she'd been careful to put her only good dress on top.

She lifted her meager clothing from the trunk and shook out the two dresses. Her arms were tired, and her good dress felt heavy in her hands. When a knock came at the door, she laid the garment on the bed and went to open it.

Nate stood in the hall. When he saw her, he tugged at his collar and shifted his feet. "I would like to speak with you."

"Is your father all right?"

"He's sleeping. I checked on him."

She stood aside to let him pass, but he shook his head. "It would be better to talk in the parlor."

A perverse impulse to add to his discomfort kept her standing in her room. "We *are* married," she reminded him. "I'm unpacking. You can talk to me while I put my things away. If you wish, you can leave the door open."

He frowned, then hesitantly stepped into her room. "I haven't been in here for years."

"It appears to be a woman's room. Whose was it?"

"I believe my mother used it as her sewing room."

Lucy lifted her good dress and shook it again, then hung it on a hook in the closet. "What did you need to speak to me about?"

He was staring at the closet. "Are those all the dresses you have?"

Heat rose to her cheeks. "I'm sorry if my attire fails to impress you."

"It's not that—it's just that I thought women loved pretty dresses. I expected you to have others like the one you're wearing. Expensive and lavish. The gray one on the bed is worn. Even the one in your hand has seen better days."

She looked at the brown dress in her hand. "I wore my mother's best dress to give me courage. I didn't want you to be introduced to a frumpish wife."

When he didn't answer, she peeked up through her lashes and saw his expression soften.

He walked to the window and gazed out. "How did you hear

of my father and his desire to marry me off? Did he run an ad? I want to understand how all this transpired."

Her hands stilled. "You should ask your father such questions. Suffice it to say that he persuaded me. I was not looking for a husband, if that's what you are asking."

He turned from the window and stared at her. "Most men would be reluctant to take on the responsibility of your siblings."

She drew herself as tall as she could. "Mr. Stanton, I have no interest in fleecing you or your father. I came here in good faith, intending to pull my weight and be a helpmeet to a kind, Christian man. So far, I've seen little evidence that you possess either of those traits."

His gray eyes darkened, and his lips tightened into a firm line. "It's hardly unchristian to question the motives of a woman who would marry a man sight unseen. There is more here than you're willing to tell me."

The fact that he was right took the wind out of her sails. She was hardly representing Jesus well herself with her evasiveness. She slumped onto the bed. "Very well, Mr. Stanton. I would not want you to question my integrity, so I shall tell you the unbridled truth. Your father came to see how we were getting along. He'd heard of my father's death and had received a letter from my stepmother asking for assistance. He came to see what he could do."

Nate frowned. "Pa came to *you*?"

"He did. He was friends with my father in their younger days. When he heard of our circumstances, he put forth the proposal of marriage. I was quite unsure about agreeing to something so extreme."

"So why did you?"

She forced herself to hold his gaze. "Several reasons. I lost my job at the dressmaker's shop, and we were being evicted from our home. Then someone broke in and threatened us. The policeman said a man had been watching us since my father died. He thought it a good idea to get out of town." Lucy was tired, so tired, but she lifted her chin.

"You told Pa all of this?"

She nodded. "Most of it. I didn't mention the intruder, only our circumstances. He was so kind . . ." And shrewd. Henry knew exactly what he wanted.

He lifted a brow. "Pa is a sucker for a hard-luck story, especially when the person caught in the circumstances has a bit of pluck. So he offered you a way out and you snatched it up."

"That's not what happened at all. Your father basically talked me into accepting his proposition."

"Come now, Miss Marsh, you can't expect me to swallow that."

"It's *Mrs. Stanton*. Or just call me Lucy and be done with it. And if you don't believe me, ask your father. I—I thought perhaps God was opening a door so the three of us could stay together. Without a job or a home, I would have had to take the children to an orphanage."

He absorbed her statement in silence. "I can see where you might believe God had done this," he said finally. "It was a very queer thing for my father to suggest."

"I was shocked. But he assured me you were a fine man and would welcome a helpmeet." She'd better tell him all of it. "One of Jed's friends dared him to pickpocket someone. While your father was waiting for me, Jed decided to take the bet. He tried to lift your father's wallet."

Nate's eyes widened. "Pa thrashed him?"

She shook her head. "He used it to persuade me. He promised

you and he would take Jed in hand. I came for my brother and sister. So they would have a better life. So Jed would become a man I was proud of."

She rose and stood as tall as she was able. "I'm a hard worker. I will not let you down in any way. Just give me a chance." She held her breath as she studied his conflicted face. "I'm a good house-keeper. I will take charge of the chaos here at the ranch, and you'll be surprised how smoothly things will run."

"I like dealing with things as they come up. Our chaos is con-trolled. We don't need our routine changed."

She'd already seen ways she could make their lives easier, but she held her peace. "Does this have anything to do with your brother? About him saying you were letting your father run your life?"

His lips tightened. "I am my own man. My father knows better than to try to control what I do." He stepped to the door and into the dark hall, closing the door behind him. "Good night, Miss Marsh."

"That's Mrs. Stanton!" Exhausted, she fell back onto the bed. If he cast her off, what would they do? How could she keep them all together?

EIGHT

❧⟡❧

The next morning Nate went to his pa's room and found it empty. Panic made his mouth go dry. He rushed down the hall and found him in the kitchen with Jed and Lucy. They were laughing around the table like they'd done it every morning for years. He felt like an intruder as he stood in the doorway and watched them.

"There you are, my boy." Pa pointed to a seat across from him. "Breakfast is ready. Lucy fixed the best flapjacks I've ever feasted upon."

Nate eased into the seat and looked at the platter of flapjacks. They did look good. His stomach rumbled. "How'd you get Percy to give up his kitchen?"

"He didn't give it up. He shared it." Lucy's smile seemed to brighten the sunshine flooding through the window. "He fixed the coffee and eggs and let me do the flapjacks."

Truly, Lucy was a miracle worker. Percy guarded his kitchen like a mama bear guarded her cubs. The kitchen was cleaner too. Or else it was the presence of women and children that made it seem sunnier and more welcoming.

Nate transferred a heap of flapjacks to his plate and spread jam on them. The flapjacks were light as thistledown, and Nate dug in with gusto. "I'll say one thing," he mumbled past his mouthful of food. "You sure can cook."

He wished he dared ask his father about the circumstances that brought Lucy here. Could her wild tale possibly be true? He aimed a glance at his pa. "You're looking better."

His father leaned back in his chair with his coffee cup in hand. "I feel fine. Dr. Cooper is an old woman. I aim to rest up another day, then get out to the barn and shoe the horses."

Lucy opened her mouth, but Nate shot her a look of warning and she quickly closed it. Arguing with Pa would do no good. "Good idea," he said with a shrug. "But don't you reckon it would be bad manners to leave Lucy alone all day?"

"You're probably right. You get your chores done, then get back in here to entertain her," his father said.

He gave a sly grin, and Nate had to grit his teeth to keep from spewing out his thoughts. He still hadn't changed his mind over Pa's fool-headed scheme to marry him off to this tiny girl. When she saw the cabin where he spent most of his week, she'd soon be hightailing it back to Indiana.

Pa pointed his fork at Lucy. "She tells me you asked how she came to be chosen as your wife. What she told you is true. It was all my idea. I even used young Jed here to persuade her."

"Why would you do that?"

His father shrugged. "It was a test, boy. I wanted to see if I'd judged her faithful heart right. And I did. You need a wife who will stick with you when the droughts come. One who won't let the tarantulas scare her off."

Lucy's eyes went wide. "Tarantulas?"

"They won't hurt you," his father said. "And Lucy has that big heart we need here. I'm a good judge of people, and you know it."

Nate didn't want to admit it, but his pa had rarely been wrong. "I'll take her to the cabin when I finish up with chores."

"I was going to suggest that," Pa said. "Lucy here is eager to see her new home."

"She may change her mind when she sees it."

Lucy lifted a brow. "I'm not staying here? I already unpacked."

"Well, pack up again. Nate doesn't live here. He just eats here." His pa poured more coffee into his cup from the battered tin coffeepot. "And don't you go scaring her, Nate. That place just needs a woman's touch. It's what your ma and I had when we were first married. You'll build her something better soon."

"It's fine like it is. She'll have to get used to it."

"You needn't discuss me as though I'm not here," Lucy said. "You did enough of that last night."

Nate felt a shaft of grudging respect. She knew how to hold her own. Footsteps clacked behind him, and he turned to see Roger coming through the door. His hair was still damp and his sideburns curled from the moisture. "You just now getting up?"

Roger shrugged. "I was up late."

Roger had been playing poker with the ranch hands in the barn when Nate went to bed, well after midnight. "I need help mending the corral. Trip knocked out some boards."

"I'll be along in a bit."

At least Roger wasn't planning to shirk work while he was here. "Appreciate it," Nate said. "We're heading to the cabin to get Lucy and the children settled in."

Jed shot to his feet and practically pranced around his chair. "Can we ride a horse there?"

Nate aimed a glance at Lucy. "Can you ride?"

She swallowed and looked away. "A little."

A tenderfoot, just as he suspected. He shrugged and got to his feet. "Wanda is real gentle so you'll be okay on her. And Jed can ride Buck. I'll put Eileen in front of me."

Lucy stood and began to clear the dishes. "By the time you get the chores done, I'll have these dishes cleared away and Eileen fed and dressed."

"Let Percy see to those dishes. You young'uns run along." Pa waved a hand. "You need to start settling into your new life."

His new life. Maybe he wouldn't have been kicking so hard if he hadn't been dragged to it like a roped calf. "I need to check the stock," he said, heading for the door.

Walking the back paddocks, Nate kept his coat around his neck. He broke the ice on the water troughs, then went to the barn to check on the injured cow he'd corralled yesterday. Inside the barn he smelled an unfamiliar odor. Some kind of hair tonic maybe, but none of his hands sissified themselves that way. Frowning, he walked through the barn and checked the stalls. In the back right corner one he found a heap of hay covered with a man's shirt. A makeshift bed? And if so, whose? The man who had tried to burn the barn?

AT ABOUT TEN o'clock Nate came in from the barn lot, bringing a rush of cold air with him. Lucy watched the play of emotions across her new husband's face. It was clear he didn't think she was up to ranch work, but it couldn't be any harder than dressmaking, just different. She'd repacked her few belongings, and Percy had brought the trunk down by the door.

"Ready?" Nate stood in the kitchen with his feet apart and his coat still buttoned. "Let's get your coat." He jerked a thumb toward the entry.

"I really should help Percy," she told Nate as she followed him from the kitchen.

"I don't need no help. I packed you sandwiches for lunch." Percy handed Nate a sack.

Nate took her arm in his free hand. "Pa won't rest until he knows we're on our way. So we'd best get it over with, then check back and see how he's doing."

Lucy nodded and went with him. Her bag was on the table by the door, and she picked it up. Jed carried his belongings, and Nate hoisted her trunk to his shoulder. The sunlight nearly blinded her when she stepped outside, and the cold air stole her breath. There was white on the ground.

"I hadn't been expecting snow," she told him.

"Don't get it often," Nate said. "A skiff of snow is about all we ever see. I can't remember ever having this much." He put the luggage on the back of a mule, then led Lucy toward a black-and-white horse whose markings reminded her of a cow. Its forlorn stance with its shaggy back to the wind softened her heart.

"This is Wanda. Riding her is like sitting in your mama's rocking chair."

"Why can't we take a buckboard?"

"Mine is at the cabin. Pa will need his for supplies later. Besides, we need to get these horses to the cabin for our future use. Don't be afraid of Wanda. She won't let you fall." The horse nuzzled Nate's hand and he laughed, then dug his hand into his pocket and pulled out a lump of sugar for the mare. She lifted it with soft lips from his hand.

Lucy's trepidation eased. Wanda glanced at her with gentle brown eyes, then dropped her head again. Lucy let Nate help her into the saddle. He'd had the foresight to provide her with a side-saddle. It was old but well oiled and in good condition. This high up, she could see out across the land. Stanton land. And she was as much a possession of Nate's as these boundless acres. In that moment the thought terrified her.

Jed bounded onto his horse, a small buckskin that shied nervously at his exuberance. Nate lifted Eileen in his arms and showed her how to pet his horse. "This is Whisper, Eileen. Would you like to give him a lump of sugar?"

Eileen's face was white with fright but she nodded, and Nate gave her a lump of sugar. The gelding's lips closed gently around the sugar, and Eileen gave a squeal of delight. "I feeded the horse, Lucy!"

Lucy gave her an encouraging smile, full of pride. "You're a brave girl, Eileen." Something in the way he spoke to Eileen—gently and respectfully—eased her unsettled feeling.

Nate set Eileen at the front of his saddle, then swung up behind her. "Follow me," he told Lucy and Jed.

Clutching the reins, Lucy managed to get her horse to follow Nate's lead, but she had a sneaking suspicion it had more to do with her mare's determination not to be left behind. As the horses labored through the snowdrifts, Lucy kept stealing glances at Nate's firm jaw. She had so many questions she wanted to ask him, but her tongue seemed stuck to the roof of her mouth.

They traveled over a hill, and a frozen creek appeared in the valley below. A building crouched beside it, the siding gray and worn. A small, leafless tree, shaking in the wind, seemed to cower under the cabin for cover.

Lucy smiled. The way he'd talked, she was imagining a soddy or something even worse. He didn't know how rude their former lodgings were. This little place was simply waiting for her. Its forlorn appearance warmed her with the desire to make a difference. This would be home, and she would make Nate glad his father had found her. She would earn his admiration and respect yet.

Nate pulled his horse to a halt and jumped down, then pulled Eileen down against his chest. His gaze scanned Lucy's face, and puzzlement clouded his face when she gave him a serene smile.

"It's not much," he said. There seemed to be regret in his voice. Was he ashamed of the little cabin?

Her smile warmed. "It's charming."

His eyes widened, and he gave her a sharp look, then turned to go inside.

Jed dismounted and thrust his hands into his pockets. Surveying the shanty, he turned to Nate with a grin. "This doesn't look so bad, Mr. Stanton. Lucy's real good at fixing stuff up. You should see the house we used to live in."

Lucy felt the heat of a blush on her cheeks. Such faith was humbling. Her gaze was drawn to the cabin again. It seemed to call her like a long-lost child. In her mind's eye she could see a small garden patch out front and wild roses climbing on a trellis under the kitchen window where she could enjoy the fragrance.

Eileen sidled closer to Lucy and thrust her small hand into her sister's larger one. "I have to go potty, Lucy," she whispered.

Nate's expression softened. "Outhouse is out back. I'll show you, Eileen."

The little girl shrank back and put her thumb in her mouth. Her blue eyes sought her sister's face. "I want Lucy."

Nate nodded. "Let's get inside, and then you can go out the back door instead of traipsing through the snow."

His voice was gentle when he spoke to Eileen. Studying him, Lucy thought he might make a good father once he lost that gruff exterior. He wasn't nearly as hard as he tried to convince everyone he was. She followed him into the cabin and looked around.

Her first impression was of dark, dingy wood and dust. The floor was unpainted plank. It needed a good cleaning more than anything else. A hastily constructed table and a single chair were shoved against the wall by the woodstove. A wood box beside the stove was heaped with kindling that had spilled onto the floor.

She walked to the kitchen. The stove needed scrubbing and several dirty plates and cups sat in a dishpan on the dry sink. She shivered, not so much from the temperature as from the coldness of the room's atmosphere. But she would fix that.

"I know there aren't enough chairs, but I wasn't expecting company." Nate pulled the single chair out from the table and nodded toward it. "Have a seat."

"I need to take Eileen out back." Without waiting for a reply, she took Eileen's hand and quickly stepped to the back door. The privy was sturdy and well made. While she waited for Eileen, Lucy glanced at the back of the cabin. It was well constructed too. Nate seemed competent in whatever he decided to put his hand to.

She could only pray he'd decide to put his hand to being a good husband.

NINE

After lunch, Nate handed Jed an ax. "Just break the ice up in any troughs you see." He pointed at the open range where the cattle stood forlornly in the blowing snow. "I'm going to haul some bales of hay out for them."

Jed nodded and tucked his coat around his neck. His bare hands gripped the ax with determination, and he started off toward the first trough. "Hold up," Nate called. When the lad turned, he tossed him some gloves.

"Thanks!" Jed tugged them on and tromped off in the snow again.

Nate headed for the barn, then stopped and stared back at the cattle. He counted heads. He only saw fifty in this section. There should have been two hundred. And what about his bull? He yanked open the barn door and stepped inside. The silence was his first clue that something was very wrong. His bull usually snorted at first sight of him. Sure enough, the bull's paddock was empty. He wanted to throttle someone. Was this Larson's handiwork?

He checked on the calf but waited to feed it until he had Eileen with him. He hauled some bales of hay to the field, then turned to look for Jed. The lad had his head down against the wind and was walking toward him. The boy would have to learn anyway, so when Jed reached him, Nate told him about the missing cattle.

"What can we do?"

"Maybe nothing. Sometimes the rustlers ship them out of town right away, and I haven't counted heads in a couple of days. The cattle had water and food and there was no need." But he intended to check out Drew Larson's property.

Jed clenched his fists. "Someone *took* them?"

"They didn't just wander off by themselves." Nate stared at the boy hard. "Now you know what it feels like to have someone steal something."

Jed's face went scarlet. "I know it was wrong." He paused. "I think there's more trouble coming our way."

Nate's senses went on high alert. "What kind of trouble? You've done something else?"

Jed shook his head. "It was something my dad asked me to do. He said some bad men might come looking, but that I was supposed to keep it safe. A man showed up before we left Indiana."

"Keep *what* safe?"

Jed's eyes squinted to narrow slits. "Dad made me promise not to say. I can't even tell Lucy."

Nate didn't want to press the boy to break a promise, but if danger was coming, he needed to be prepared. "How am I supposed to protect Lucy and Eileen if I don't know what's going on?"

Jed hesitated. "Just watch for any strangers. And if they ask who we are, don't tell them."

"That's not good enough, boy. You can't leave me in the dark. If I know the whole story, I can help you figure this out."

"Don't ask me because I can't tell you." Jed smacked his

forehead. "I can't remember, all right! Something bad happened the night Dad died, and I just can't remember." The boy's voice broke and he ran out of the barn.

What kind of trouble could Jed be in? And why would a father embroil his son in something dangerous? Nate needed to find out more about Lucy's parents to see if he could figure this out. But first he needed to find his bull.

He walked across the sparse vegetation in the field to the hill on the west side of the ranch. A few cattle grazed in the valley below, but no bull. And not enough cattle. Rustlers had definitely been busy. Getting the cattle back would be close to impossible when he didn't know where to look. He was most upset about the bull.

Could it be at Larson's? He'd hired someone to try to burn down the barn, so Nate wouldn't put anything past him. He changed course and jogged back to the barn where he saddled a horse and rode toward Larson's small plot of land. The place appeared deserted when he leaned back in the saddle half an hour later and surveyed the small cabin and barn.

He whistled to see if his bull would respond. When the sound faded, there was only an answering trill from the quail dashing to a bush. Nate wanted to search the barn, but he couldn't bring himself to trespass with only suspicion on his side. If his bull had answered his whistle, he would have shoved open that barn door in a heartbeat.

All he would be able to do was report the theft. But it didn't feel like enough.

LUCY PUT HER hands on her hips and surveyed the room. They could put some beds against the west wall and there was space for some extra chairs by the fire. The loft overhead was empty. It would serve as the main bedroom.

Heat scorched her cheeks at the thought of sharing a room with Nate. *Not yet, Lord,* she prayed. She wasn't ready yet. It was a blessing from God that Nate was so uncertain about the marriage. Time would help them both adjust to the thought that they were tied for life.

She had finished taking inventory of the house by the time Nate and Jed came back inside. She'd never succeeded in getting the fireplace to do more than smoke. Both fellows seemed pensive and distant, but she didn't question them as she went to try fixing the fire again.

"Let me do that." Nate stepped outside, then returned with smaller kindling. The fire began to flare, then heat began to ease the chill of the room.

"Thank you," Lucy said. "I'll need hot water for my work."

"Work? There won't be anything to do today. The cattle have been fed, and Jed broke the ice for them to water. You can stay inside and keep warm."

Lucy waved a hand. "Look at this place. We can't sleep in this filth."

Nate's brows drew together. "Filth?" His voice went up at the end of the word. "There's nothing wrong with my cabin. It's not the fanciest home in the Red River Valley, but it would suit any other woman who was used to homesteading. I knew a city girl like you would turn your nose up at it."

Lucy refused to let him rile her. "The accommodations are fine, Nate. It's the lack of cleanliness I object to. We're going to need some beds too. See what you can do. When you get back, you'll see how much better it looks."

Nate's mouth hung open and he stared at her.

"I wouldn't argue with her, Mr. Stanton."

Lucy didn't wait to see if Nate would take Jed's advice. She took Eileen by the hand, grabbed a bucket, and headed for the door. "I'll need some water for scrubbing."

"I'll get it." Nate roused from his stupor and snatched the pail from her. "The pump is out back, but it might be hard to start. I haven't used it for a few days. Just stay put and don't touch anything."

Lucy nearly smiled at the alarm in his voice. Jed followed him out the door.

She found an apron in her bag and tied it on. "Eileen, would you like to help me?"

The little girl nodded. "I can do the dishes."

"All right. As soon as Mr. Stanton gets back with the water, I'll heat some and you can wash up." Lucy looked around again. There wasn't even a broom.

The front door opened, and Nate and Jed stumbled inside with the scent of moisture and a blast of cold air. Nate stomped the snow from his feet, then carried a bucket of water to her. "Where do you want it?"

"There by the stove. Do you have a pan to heat it in? And I need a broom."

"A broom?" Nate said the words as if he'd never heard of a broom before. He looked around the room as if a broom might materialize from the mere thought.

"I need to sweep."

"It's just a rough plank floor. Sweeping won't do any good."

"Even a plank floor can be kept clean, Mr. Stanton."

His bewildered expression deepened. "But why? You just walk on it."

The corner of Lucy's mouth turned up, and she bit her tongue to keep from laughing. "Just find me a broom, and you'll see what I mean."

Nate scowled. "Let's go, Jed. There's no pleasing a woman."

"I'll be very pleased with a broom," she called after them. Smiling, she went to heat the water. By the time the water was hot, Nate was back with a makeshift broom of straw.

When he gave it to her, she handed him the bucket again. "I need more water."

He rolled his eyes but didn't protest. Jed giggled. "I think you're getting domesticated, Mr. Stanton."

Nate widened his eyes. "I'm just doing what needs done for my own protection, Jed. Your sister may be small, but she's determined." He dropped the bucket and swung Eileen into his arms. "Hey, honey, there's a new calf in the barn. You want to see it after we're done with the cattle?"

Eileen squealed with delight. "Can I pet it?"

"He might suck your fingers."

Eileen looked doubtfully at her hand, then turned her sunny smile back to Nate. "I don't mind."

"Can I come too?" Lucy asked. The thought of a new calf was suddenly much more appealing than cleaning.

"Sure you can spare the time from your sweeping?" Nate's grin clutched at her heart.

"I'll take the time."

"Just don't blame me if you have to sleep with the spiders."

Spiders? Lucy eyed the room. There were a great many cobwebs. "Maybe tomorrow."

"The cleaning or the calf?"

"The calf," she said reluctantly.

His grin widened, and he went to the door with Jed following behind. "You don't know what you're missing. Come on, Eileen. We'll go see that calf."

This was a side to Nate she hadn't seen before. But sometimes duty was more important than fun. Broom in hand like a sword, Lucy swept through the cabin like an avenging angel. Spiders scuttled from her attack. Stomping and shouting, she killed all she could find and swept the room clean of dirt and cobwebs. At least she saw none big enough to be a tarantula. When the water was hot, she washed the dishes, then used the still-warm water to scrub the floors, swirling the water around with her broom before mopping it up on her hands and knees.

All that was left was the loft. She was almost afraid to check up there where she suspected she'd find even more spiders. With shaking knees, she climbed the ladder. Poking her head over the top, she looked around. It was as she feared. The entire loft was crisscrossed with spiderwebs laden with fat bodies, alive and dead. Shuddering, she backed down the ladder. There was no way she could do that herself. She would get Jed to make the first pass. Or maybe even Nate.

The thought of Nate's derision was almost enough to make her go back up, but she couldn't quite make herself mount that ladder again. She should have cleaned upstairs first. Now some of those spiders would probably come down here.

Her earlier euphoria vanished. Maybe she really wasn't cut out to be a cattleman's wife. If she couldn't face up to something as small as a spider, what would she do with a bull? But the thought of a bull wasn't nearly as daunting as those plump bodies upstairs.

She looked around her new kitchen. She could at least start the midday meal. She went to the small pantry and opened it. She backed away, a scream lodged in her throat. She shrieked with all the breath in her lungs and bolted for the door.

TEN

❧

N ate's mind whirled with all he'd have to do to accom-
modate a family. What was his father thinking?

He spotted a collie drinking from the trough. "Where'd
you come from?" He paused to scratch the dog's ears and noticed
how thin it was. Probably some traveler decided not to bother with
it any longer. That was how he got his last dog. "We'll have to get
you some grub."

He stepped into the barn with Eileen by the hand and led
her to the stall where the cow and calf lay. "He likes his nose
scratched." Nate guided Eileen's small hand to the calf's nose.

"What's his name?" Eileen rubbed the calf's nose, then giggled when its mouth opened and it began to suck on her finger.

The little girl was so cute with her blond curls and big blue
eyes. She'd be a beauty like her sister. "He doesn't have one. This
is a working ranch. We can't get attached to our livestock."

"Why not? She's pretty." Eileen patted the calf with her small
hand. "Can I call her Louise?"

Before Nate could explain why it wasn't a good idea to get

attached to the calf, a shriek echoed from the house. He jerked and knocked over a pitchfork. The scream was full of panic and terror. Renegade Comanches?

"Stay here and hide," he ordered the children. Jed instinctively grabbed his little sister and pulled her behind a feed barrel. "Jed, take care of your sister."

Nate grabbed a shotgun by the door and raced toward the house. The blood thundered in his ears. Lucy screamed again, and the sound made his blood curdle. He reached the front of the house and stood for a moment, collecting his wits. Maybe he should try getting in the back door. Indians likely were watching this one. But before he could move toward the back, the front door flew open and Lucy came stumbling out.

Her face was white, and her blue eyes mindless with terror. Those eyes widened when she saw him, then the next thing he knew, she was burrowing into his arms. She barely came to his chest, and still holding his rifle, he held her close. Her shoulders shook, and she made frantic little mews of panic. Holding her close, he tried to peer into the cabin as he steered her back to the barn.

"Indians? The kids are hiding in the barn."

She shook her head so hard pins flew from her hair, and golden strands fell to her shoulders. "Spider," she gasped. She shuddered, and his arms tightened around her.

"A spider?" he asked, pushing her away.

Lucy returned to his grasp. "It was as big as my hand. And—and hairy." She burrowed deeper into his jacket.

"Probably Zeke, my tarantula." The corner of his mouth lifted, and he felt almost giddy with relief. His chest rumbled with the effort to hide his mirth.

Lucy lifted her head. "Your tarantula?"

A chuckle escaped. "He was in the pantry, right?"

Her eyes wide with horror, Lucy took a step back. "This spider *lives* there? And you named him?"

Nate was surprised to find he regretted letting go of her. "Sure, he eats the bugs."

Lucy shuddered again. "You have to kill it."

"Nope. Zeke stays."

She crossed her arms. "Then I go. I'm not sharing my home with a hairy spider."

Nate narrowed his eyes. "Fine. I didn't want you here anyway."

"I'll stay with your father until you get that, that *monster* out of there."

If she went back to the big house, it might upset Pa. He would think Nate wasn't being a proper husband. And maybe he wasn't. It was clear that Zeke had terrified her. Didn't he at least owe her the same courtesy he'd give any guest? "I'll take Zeke to the barn."

"Then I won't go in the barn!"

Nate let out a sigh and shook his head. Women. There was no pleasing them. "I thought you wanted to learn to be a proper rancher's wife. That includes making peace with beneficial insects like tarantulas."

"Spiders aren't insects—they're arachnid. And they're hideous."

Tears shimmered on her lashes, and Nate realized that this was not some power ploy. She was petrified. Backing away from him, a sob rose from her chest and she hiccupped.

He put a hand on her shoulder. "I'm sorry, Lucy. Zeke won't hurt you."

Lucy burst into tears and covered her face with her hands.

"I've been trying so hard," she sobbed. "You must think you've been saddled with some weak woman who needs pampering. Truly, I can carry my side of the bargain, but I can't abide spiders. Especially ones that need a close shave. Preferably with a very sharp blade."

Nate suppressed his grin when she shuddered. He pulled her back into his arms. She seemed to fit there. He rested his chin on her head and breathed in the fragrance of her hair. It smelled clean with a hint of something sweet, maybe lavender. Something stirred in his heart. Whether he'd planned it or not, this woman was his wife. He might not love her, but he had to make accommodations for her in his life, even if it meant ridding the house of creepy crawlies.

God would expect no less. They were both Christians. Surely they could find a way to create a comfortable home even without love. He hugged her. "I'll get rid of Zeke."

She turned her wet face up to him. "You will? It won't even be in the barn?"

"I'll take him out somewhere and let him loose."

She smiled, and it was like the sun burst through the storm clouds. "Thank you, Mr. Stanton," she whispered. A shadow darkened her eyes.

"What's wrong?"

"Um, there're other spiders in the loft. Could you get rid of them too?"

He grinned. "Those I can kill." He released her and went inside.

"I'll just stay out here until the spiders are gone."

Nate stepped inside the room and stopped short. Was this the same place? It was spotless. He whistled softly through his teeth.

He hadn't even noticed all the dust and cobwebs until they were gone.

He strode through the house until he found Zeke crouched in a corner of the pantry. "Sorry, old friend, you have to go out into the cold." He held out his hand, and the tarantula crawled onto his sleeve. He carried the spider out the back door and walked out into the field until he couldn't see the cabin anymore, then shook Zeke off into the melting snow. The spider seemed to look at him reproachfully, then scurried off toward a stand of cottonwood trees by the river.

Now for the rest of the spiders. Nate went back to the cabin. He grabbed the broom and climbed the ladder to the loft. He swatted and squashed spiders until all that was left were dead remains, then swept them all up onto a piece of tin he found. He carried them out the back door so Lucy wouldn't see them and tossed them into the field.

He was still smiling when he went looking for Lucy. She was in the barn with the children, and she jumped when he stepped through the door. Her face was still pale, but she met his gaze bravely.

"It's gone. So are the ones in the loft."

Relief flooded her face, and she gave him a tremulous smile. "Thank you, Mr. Stanton. Are you hungry? I'll start supper."

"Starved. Let me show you where the root cellar is. I have smoked meat down there as well as some vegetables." Taking the shovel, Nate led the way to the back of the cabin and shoveled away the snow to reveal a cellar door. He tugged it up. "Get me the broom, and I'll make sure you don't have to deal with any unwanted guests down there either."

"I wanted to be a blessing, but I'm afraid I've been more bother than I'm worth," she said.

She gave him a grateful smile, and he felt as tall as the Texas oak in his backyard.

THE SUN WAS low on the horizon when Lucy glanced around with a sense of contentment. Nate had taken the children out to help with chores. This was her kitchen now. Now that the spiders were gone, she could enjoy her new home. Everything sparkled, even the windows. It had felt good to hear Nate's praise.

She put the potatoes on to fry in bacon grease, then cut slabs of beef for supper and put them on the stove as well. Canned green beans would round out the evening meal. While the bacon sizzled, she opened her trunk and emptied its contents onto the cot. She unpacked Eileen's belongings and laid them on the cot by the fireplace. There was a bureau by the fireplace that contained Nate's clothing: jeans, shirts, and underwear. She carried the contents upstairs and left them on a small table until she talked to Nate.

She went back to the kitchen and turned the bacon before realizing she needed more water. Surely the pump was working well, now that Nate had used it several times. With her coat buttoned to her neck, she carried the bucket out the back door to the pump. Water poured from the spout with the first pump.

She heard a man's voice call out, so she left the bucket and went around to the front of the house. A horse moved closer until she could make out the rider. Roger. When he reached the yard, she stepped off the low porch to greet him. "I'll get Nate. He's in the barn with the children."

"I didn't come to see him." He leaned back in the saddle. "Got any coffee?"

She nodded. "Come inside." What would he want with her? More insinuations that she should never have come? She led him to the tiny kitchen, then poured him a cup of coffee.

He took the cup she offered. "Sit down and quit looking like a spooked calf. I'm not going to hurt you."

She eased onto a chair and laced her fingers together. "I'm sorry we seem to have gotten off on the wrong foot."

He grimaced, then took a swig of coffee as if he needed time before speaking. He set his cup on the stained table. "I'm here to warn you."

"Warn me? Against your brother?"

He lifted a brow. "Nate is a good man. You couldn't have done better than him. No, I'm talking about our father. You're going to have to stand up to him or he'll run your life for you."

"Look, Mr. Stanton, I don't want to be drawn into your quarrel with your pa." She shuddered, imagining a quarrel with Henry. He wasn't a man to put up with much resistance to his will.

"Please call me Roger. Mr. Stanton is my pa. I see you're skeptical, but you'll find out all too soon. Pa holds everything in his fists. He never lets up. You have a chance since you just got here. If you start out as you mean to go on, you might be able to convince him to let you be your own woman."

"I *am* my own woman." His words touched a fear she didn't know she had. She'd always been the one in control. Her father had looked to her for so many things, and even Catherine had been glad to let her run the household.

"See that you stay that way. Pa will push as hard as you let him."

"I want to be part of the family. I don't want to cause turmoil."

"You'll have to cause some or you'll be sorry." He gulped the last of his coffee and stood. "I think I'm wasting my time. You're going to sit back and let him dictate what you do."

"I'll be careful." She was thankful he cared enough to warn her. "I can see Henry is a strong-willed man. Thank you most kindly for pointing out the dangers."

His smile was sardonic. "I'll let you get back to your cleaning. The cabin looks nice. Pa will pat himself on the back for picking out the right woman for Nate."

His words were more of an insult than a compliment. Lucy walked him to the door, waving until he was out of sight, then went out back to finish filling her bucket. Once it was full, she grabbed it then started toward the house.

A low growl made the hair rise on the back of her neck. A dark shape slunk from the side of the house. The gray animal had its teeth bared in her direction. Though it looked like a dog, no dog Lucy had ever seen was that threatening.

She stopped and smiled. "Hello, boy," she said in a coaxing tone. "I won't hurt you."

The animal took another step closer and snarled, showing even more of its teeth. Lucy's smile fled. She eyed the door, still twenty feet away. The beast would be on her before she could reach safety. She slowly backed up to the pump and put down the bucket. The dog or whatever it was stepped closer too.

She reached down and picked up the bucket of water. It was her only weapon, but maybe she could fling it at the animal and drive him off long enough to get to safety. She also had to warn Nate and the children.

She glanced around the yard. The privy was closer than the house. If she could get inside and shut the door, the mangy beast couldn't get to her. She took a sideways step, but the animal did too. Pace for pace, the dog kept step with her. She reached the side of the outhouse, but the door was around the corner. The animal was snarling more now, and the way its back was twitching, she suspected it was about to charge her.

She hefted the bucket in her hand and spoke to it again in a friendly voice, but it just snarled all the more. Though she hated to show such weakness, she would have to call for help.

ELEVEN

The aroma of beef and potatoes wafted across the yard. Nate's mouth watered. Usually all he managed was a meager supper, maybe slabs of bacon on bread. He rarely bothered with more than that. They were nearly done with cleaning the calf's stall.

He tossed the pitchfork into the pile of straw. "That's it, kids. Let's go get some grub." He lifted Eileen in his arms and they trooped toward the house. As they neared the house, Lucy screamed his name. "Must be another spider," he told Jed. Grinning, he set Eileen down at the front door and grabbed the broom. It sounded like it came from the backyard. Maybe Zeke had found his way back.

As he rounded the corner of the house, he heard snarling. The hair on the back of his neck rose. That was no spider. It sounded like a wolf or a dog, and he'd left his rifle in the barn. Lucy whimpered and he broke into a run.

A large mongrel, half wolf and half dog, blocked Lucy's way to the house. A bucket clutched in her hands, she stood with her back pressed to the outhouse. Nate raised the broom like a club, but before he could swing it, the animal launched itself at Lucy's throat.

Nate let out an involuntary cry, then a shape came hurtling across the yard and crashed into the mongrel in midair. Mongrel and dog rolled over together, both snarling and growling. Fur flew like blowing snow. The ruckus brought the two children to the back door.

"Get inside!" Lucy shouted to the children. She bolted away from the outhouse and ran to Nate. "Do something," she panted. "It will kill the dog."

Nate saw the children standing paralyzed by the side of the house. "Jed, get my rifle!"

The boy nodded and vanished around the side of the house. Nate propelled Lucy toward the door. "I'll handle this. You get inside."

The snarling between the dog and the wolf-dog had intensified. The two animals rolled over and over, but the wolf-dog seemed to be winning.

Lucy grabbed his arm. "That dog saved my life. You can't let that—that wolf or whatever it is—kill him."

She was right. He nodded and turned with the broom. The mongrel was atop the collie. When he whacked the wolf-dog across the head, it turned toward him, its jaws open in a snarl. It lunged at him, but the dog renewed the attack and seized the animal by its back leg. They rolled together again, snarling and spitting.

Nate brought the broom down on the wolf-dog's head with all his might, and the broom handle broke. The mongrel yelped and shook the dog off, then launched itself at Nate.

A gun boomed, and the mongrel fell at his feet. Stunned by both the suddenness of the attack and the loud crack of the rifle, he stood there a moment with the snow turning to crimson at his feet. The air was acrid with the scent of gunpowder. Turning his head, he found Lucy holding the smoking rifle. She must have run to the barn after it.

Lucy dropped the rifle and ran into the yard to the collie. The dog's ribs showed through its mangy, bloodied coat, and it licked her hand when she knelt beside it.

Lucy turned a pleading gaze to Nate. "Can you help the poor thing?"

Nate knelt beside her and ran gentle hands over the dog. It whimpered when he touched its wounds but made no move to bite him. "Good girl," he soothed. He scooped the dog up in his arms and stood. "Let's get her inside."

Lucy held the door open, and he carried the dog inside and laid her down by the fire. "I need some hot water and old rags. There should be some in the pantry."

Lucy hurried to find what he needed while he opened his tool-box and found some scissors. He cut away as much of the fur as he could and winced at the deep bites and lacerations on the dog. He washed the wounds with the water and rags Lucy provided, then bandaged the worst of the bites on the dog's leg.

"How'd you learn to shoot like that?" He felt a peculiar mixture of pride and curiosity.

"Lucy can shoot a walnut out of a tree," Jed said with obvious admiration. "Dad said she took to hunting and shooting like most women take to meddling."

Nate's mouth lifted in a smile. "Sounds like your pa had some bad experience with women."

Lucy flushed. "I never knew my mother, but he didn't have much luck with his second wife."

"I was only two when my mother died, and all I remember is the scent of her hair and her soft lap." He regretted the words as soon as he saw Lucy's face soften. He didn't want pity. He stood. "She should be all right. We'll keep her inside until she's well enough to turn outside again."

"Can I keep her?" Eileen's small hands patted the dog's head, and the dog feebly licked the little girl's fingers.

Nate hesitated. "I reckon so. I don't have a dog here since Rocky died last year. This lady doesn't look like she belongs to anyone. She's too skinny. But we should put out in Larson that we've got her. She looks to be a valuable animal."

Eileen's face clouded. "But then somebody might take her!"

Lucy hugged her sister. "I doubt anyone will claim her. What are you going to name her?"

Eileen kept patting the dog's head. "What would be a good name for such a brave doggy?"

"How about Bridget? It's Irish for 'strong.'" Lucy put a bowl of water near the dog.

"Good girl, Bridget," Eileen crooned, patting the dog again. Bridget thumped her tail on the floor, and Eileen flung her arms around Bridget's neck.

"Looks like she approves," Nate said. "Now if we're all finished with the dog, can we eat? My stomach is gnawing on my backbone."

Lucy's lips curved in a smile, and he found himself fascinated with the way her teeth gleamed and the smooth pink of her cheeks. He shook himself out of his reverie. A lucky shot with the rifle wasn't enough to get past his guard.

After supper Nate took Jed and went outside to bury the wolf-dog and to knock together some beds in the barn. He had Jed take some feed sacks in to Lucy to stitch together for mattress covers. They built two beds, one for Lucy and Eileen and one for Jed. Lucy was beautiful, but it was much too soon for her to share a bed with him, even if he wished it. And he didn't. Not yet.

As if the thought had brought her, Lucy stepped into the barn with the feed bags over her arm. "Eileen is down for the night. Could I get some straw to stuff the mattresses?"

Nate pointed to the stack of clean straw at the back of the barn. "Help yourself. You look tired. Let me help you get the mattresses stuffed so we can all get to bed."

She turned to face him. "There are many things we need to set up a home. Would your pa have extra he could share?"

Nate stiffened. "I'm no pauper, Lucy. Give me a list of what you need, and I'll get it in town."

She inclined her neck. "I would like to go with you, if I might."

Great. Now the whole town would gawk at her like she was his prize filly. He shrugged. "Suit yourself. In the morning we'll go see Pa, then take a quick run to town." He hefted an end of the bed and nodded for Jed to pick up the other end. Carrying the bed to the house, he reflected on how the day had turned out nothing like he expected.

THE NEXT MORNING, discouragement slowed Lucy's steps as she trudged after Nate to the barn. She'd gotten little sleep after reflecting on her failures the day before. Not only had she gone into hysterics over a spider, but she'd let a wolf corner her. Why hadn't she faced the animal down and forced it to back off? Instead, she acted like a damsel in distress. What would Nate think?

Climbing into the buckboard, she glanced at Nate from the corner of her eye. He didn't seem to be upset by her failure. But he had to be wondering if she was entirely too frightened and sissified to be of much use on the ranch. The Stars Above Ranch would never take its place with the big cattle empires with her slowing him down.

Nate was a fine man, and he deserved a strong wife, one who faced up to the challenges of this wild land instead of screaming for help over a spider a fraction of her size. She wished she could get over her fear of spiders, but it had dogged her ever since she could remember.

She studied her new husband as he handed Eileen up to her and waited for Jed to climb into the back. Nate's sandy hair blew in the wind, and his gray eyes looked luminous in the sun. He'd surprised her by agreeing to kill the spiders in the loft. He hadn't made her feel inadequate by asking for help either. A warm feeling enveloped her when she remembered the way he'd rushed to help when the wolf-dog was threatening her.

No other man had ever offered to protect her before. Nate's gesture baffled Lucy. She'd always prided herself on taking care of everyone else, yet her deepest longing was for someone like Nate to nurture and protect her. How could she earn his love if she wasn't all he wanted in a wife? She would have to work harder.

Eileen cuddled against Lucy's side. "Will Bridget be all right?" Her blue eyes were enormous in her pale face as she peered up at Lucy.

Lucy hugged her close. "The dog will be fine, Eileen. I left her water and some food. We'll be back in a few hours."

In a few hours it would be bedtime. Lucy's mouth went dry at the thought of the coming night. She'd fixed Nate's bed in the loft, but what would she do if he expected her to join him there? Things had been fine last night because they were all exhausted. But what if his expectations tonight were different?

She would just have to tell him the children needed her close for a while. And it was the truth. But he seemed too aloof to expect her company in bed. And he *had* built a bed for her and Eileen.

They rounded the bend in the road, and the ranch house came into view. It felt like home to Lucy already. The two-story house sprawled in several directions, and the front porch beckoned her like an old friend. Over the crest of the hill, she could see several riders rounding up cattle, and Lucy straightened in her seat. Craning her neck, she wished she could go watch them, but there was no time today. But someday she would learn just what cowboys did.

Nate stopped at the barn and got down. He tossed the buckboard reins to a ranch hand, then stepped over to help Lucy and Eileen.

Eileen planted a kiss on his cheek when he lifted her down. "I like you for a brother."

He grinned. "I think you make a pretty nice sister too."

Warmth spread up Lucy's neck. She stood to get down, then lost her balance when she started to step out. He caught her before she could tumble to the ground. Pressed against his hard chest, she caught the aroma of the soap he'd used to wash his hair. The pleasant, masculine scent, combined with his proximity, made her swallow hard.

His eyes lingered on her lips while his hands spanned her waist. Looking deep into his eyes, she felt a connection she'd never experienced. She stepped away and put a trembling hand to her hair to make sure it was still in place. Nate's hand dropped, and

Eileen took it as though he had put it down for her. Her small fingers curled around his big hand. Nate exchanged an amused look with Lucy.

"Watch it or she'll have you wrapped around her little finger," Lucy whispered.

"Too late," Nate whispered back, leading them toward the door. "I was lost when she let the calf suck her fingers. She has a lot of spirit like her sister." He glanced away. "I never did say thank you for your sharpshooting."

"It was the least I could do for making you give up your pet." A slight shudder passed through her frame.

"You replaced Zeke with Bridget."

"At least Bridget looks good with hair."

Nate grinned. "Zeke would be offended that you didn't care for his haircut."

"He's lucky I didn't have my way. If I had, he would have been bald and flattened."

Nate chuckled. The door swung open, and Doc Cooper let himself out. His lean face held a trace of worry, and Lucy tensed with concern.

The mirth left Nate's face as well, and he reached out to touch the doctor's arm. "How's Pa?"

Doc pressed his lips together. "Weaker than I'd like to see him. He had another spell a few hours ago."

Nate's face went white. "I should have been here."

"No, no. Percy fetched me, and your pa is resting comfortably."

"We'd better stay here instead of at my place."

Doc nodded. "Couldn't hurt, providing the old coot will let you coddle him a bit. I'm not telling you anything you don't know when I say your pa is the most stubborn man I know."

A ghost of a smile lifted one corner of Nate's mouth. "He's orneriest than a newly branded calf when he's sick. I'm not sure my—my wife is up to this."

The doctor's eyebrows went up to his hairline. "I wondered who this pretty lady was, Nate. Where you been hiding her?" He turned to Lucy and nodded. "These cowpokes have needed a woman's hand for a long time. It's a big job, though, missus. I'll be prayin' for you to withstand the strain."

Lucy laughed and took hold of his hand. "Until you've faced matrons determined to fit into clothes two sizes too small for them, you don't know what strain is, Dr. Cooper. I think I can handle two cantankerous men. But the prayers would be most welcome."

The doctor guffawed and slapped his hat on his leg. "You've got your work cut out for you handlin' this little woman, Nate. I wish I could be a fly on the wall and watch." Still grinning, he went toward his buckboard. "Send Percy if you need me." He climbed into the seat.

Sneaking a peek at Nate, Lucy caught his stare fixed on her with an expression on his face she couldn't read. "I'm sorry, Mr. Stanton. I didn't mean to cause you embarrassment," she whispered. "When will I ever learn to watch my tongue?"

"I thought you handled yourself right well. Doc's sense of humor can be pretty intimidating. I was proud of you."

A lump grew in Lucy's throat. No one had ever told her that. Nate's pride—for she recognized that emotion on his face now—was heady stuff.

TWELVE

The warmth of the fire welcomed them. Nate strode straight toward the hall to the bedrooms. Lucy and the children trailed behind him.

Before they reached Pa's bedroom, he could hear his father's voice raised in disgust. "Look at this food, Percy. It's not fit for man nor beast. Bring me some of that soup I smell cooking. A man needs more than this thin broth! I'll waste away to nothing."

"Doc Cooper thinks you need to shed a few pounds, Boss. This is good for you. He told me not to let you have none of that soup just yet," Percy said. "Besides, it's for supper. The meat is still stringy. You gotta wait."

Lucy crowded behind Nate to peer into the bedroom. Pa turned his head and saw them at the door. "Give me that spoon." He snatched it from Percy's hand. "I'm not so far gone I can't feed myself. Get in here, all of you. Don't stand there gawking."

Lucy followed Nate into the room and went to the bed. "Can I help you, Mr. Stanton?"

He waved a hand. "I've had all I can take of Doc and Percy

treating me like an old woman. Tell me about your day yesterday. How do you like your new home?"

What would she say? Nate hid a grin as he waited to see if she'd tell his father about the run-ins with the spiders and the wolf-dog.

"I didn't get much of a chance to see it until I cleaned it," she said. "Your son is not the best housekeeper."

Nate pulled up a chair and propped a booted leg on it. "She didn't cotton to Zeke. I had to take him to the back forty and let him go." He shot her a glance and was gratified to see slight amusement on her face.

His father huffed. "Good for her. I never did understand why you had a spider as big as a dinner plate wandering around your place."

Nate shrugged. "Oh, and Lucy saved my hide when she shot a mongrel wolf aimed straight at my throat." He would carry that picture of her holding that shotgun the rest of his days. It was about as big as she was.

Pa sat up a bit straighter. "I told you our Lucy would make you a fine wife, Nate. Sometimes your old dad knows what he's doing."

Nate's amusement vanished. His pa was determined not to admit he'd had no business finding a wife for him. "We've got other problems too, Pa. Rustlers." Too late he realized he probably should have kept the information from his father. He was so used to reporting to his pa. With his pa's gaze on him, he had no choice but to tell him what he'd found.

His father put down his cup. "Rustlers, eh? You find them yet? How many head? You tell Roger yet?"

"Don't know how many yet. I think at least a hundred and

fifty are gone. And our bull." Nate shrugged. "I'm going to look around on the way to the feed store though. I didn't see Roger on the way in. Where is he?"

"Said he was going to Larson, but I thought he'd be back by now."

"I'll check with Percy," Nate said. "We're heading to town after a while. I can track him down there if he hasn't returned."

His father yawned and his eyelids lowered. "Guess I'll sleep now."

Pa's disinterest told Nate more than anything else. If his father were himself, he'd be climbing out of the bed and going to search for the rustlers himself. "You rest," Nate said.

"You didn't eat your broth." Lucy fluffed his pillow and helped his father ease back against it.

Pa seemed already half asleep. His eyelids were half closed. "Stuff's nasty. I want a man's meal. Some of that soup Percy's cooking."

Lucy pulled the sheet up around his father's shoulders. "I'll try to make you something tastier for supper. Soup's a little much." She stepped away. "We'll be going now, Mr. Stanton. There are some things we need in town."

"We'll be back for the night in a few hours," Nate said.

His father's eyes opened. "I thought you were going to stay at your place," he grumbled.

"We will when you're better."

Pa pointed a bony finger at Nate. "You'll do no such thing. I won't be coddled. When the good Lord calls me home, I'll go, but until then I intend to get on with my life and have you get on with yours. If you want to do something for me, produce me a grandchild before I die."

Nate inhaled at his father's boldness. He stole a glance at Lucy and saw her drop her gaze to the floor. She didn't look at Nate.

She lifted her head and smiled at her father-in-law. "You rest, Mr. Stanton. We'll check in on you tomorrow."

"Do you think you could bring yourself to call me Pa or at least Henry?"

She peeked at Nate as if to ask permission. When he nodded, she smiled. "All right, P-Pa."

His father relaxed against the pillows. "You're a good girl, Lucy. If I were thirty years younger, I would have married you myself. Lucky for Nate I was too old to compete with a young buck like him."

"And I might have been interested if you were thirty years younger." A dimple appeared in her cheek.

He waved his hand. "The rest of you get out of here. I want to talk to Lucy."

Nate lifted his brow, then shrugged and left the room, closing the door behind him.

LUCY HAD THOUGHT of little else since Roger had warned her of Henry's penchant for controlling his family. What should she do if he tried to tell her how to deal with his son or tried to interfere? The fact that he wanted to speak to her alone alarmed her. "Is there something I can do for you, P-Pa?" She settled on the chair by the bed.

Henry fixed a stare on Lucy. "My son treating you right? I thought he might send you packing as soon as we showed up."

"You should have warned me."

He waved off her censure. "I didn't want to scare you off. What do you think of him?" He flashed her a sly grin.

"Nate's a hard worker."

Henry barked a laugh. "That's all you got to say? Nothing about his looks?"

"What matters is what a man is inside." Besides, she wasn't about to say Nate was the handsomest man she'd ever laid eyes on. Or that her mouth went dry every time he looked her way. "He's older than I expected. He's about thirty?"

Henry nodded. "He's a good son, but you're right. He's getting past marrying age. That's why I had to take charge. Once a man gets set in his ways, it's hard to make room for a wife and family." He looked out the window where the sunshine illuminated the prairie. "Take a gander out there, girlie. Someday we'll own as far as you can see."

She shivered at the barren landscape peeking through the melting snow. "I thought you did already."

"Not yet." His jaw flexed. "I aim to own all the land between here and Wichita Falls. I'll be the biggest land baron Texas has ever seen. If I have anything to say about it, your sons and daughters will *be* someone in this state."

Heat scorched her cheeks at the mention of children. "I just want any children we have to be happy."

He snorted. "Happiness is up to them to take hold of. With your guidance, of course. And I plan to be around to offer it as well. Nothing else you can do about it but give them enough money. And land. Land is king out here."

She couldn't put her finger on why his words made her stomach clench. "The ranch seems to be providing everything you need. How much is enough? Why do you need more?"

His eyes narrowed. "I aim for the Stanton name to be known in all of Texas."

"Why?"

His lips pressed together. "It's not your worry, Lucy. Nate and I will make sure you have more than you can imagine. You'll never want for anything again."

An unnamed hunger stirred in her belly. Not for money or things but for a connection to her parents. She leaned forward. "I'd like to know more about my father's life out here. He never talked much about it. When did he leave?"

His gaze shifted and became dreamy. "He was eighteen when your mama came home from boarding school. She was the prettiest gal this town has ever seen."

"I never knew her." She fingered the locket under her gown. It held a picture of her mother when she was young. "I wish I did."

"You look quite a lot like her, Lucy. It took me aback to meet you the first time."

"My father said that once. He said sometimes he couldn't bear to look at me because I reminded him of all he'd lost." She swallowed down the familiar pain.

Henry frowned. "She didn't have eyes for anyone but your pa. He married her within two months of coming home. I thought they'd stay here. She even inherited land next to mine, ten thousand acres. Your pa was pleased, and I don't blame him."

He shook his head. "I would have bought it myself if her grandma would have sold it. We'd planned to run our cattle together. But your mama wanted city life. She was never happy here after being in Boston for school. Said the sand made her crazy. A year after they were married, they packed up and headed for Indiana."

"Did you see them after that?"

He had a faraway look in his eyes as he shook his head. "Got a letter once in a while over the years. Knowing your mama, I reckon she wanted more than being married to a store owner."

The contempt in his voice was disconcerting. What did he really think of her mother? "Was there—conflict—in their marriage?"

He shrugged. "There was conflict before they left here. But once she got her way, she was probably happy as long as there was enough money. Was there?"

She struggled to remember when things had been better. Before Catherine. But Lucy had been so young when the two married, only eight. "I don't know about earlier. We didn't have much in the last few years. I remember a nice house we had once. But then Pa married Catherine and over the years we moved to more and more run-down places until we settled at the house on Smith Street in Wabash. We lived there for ten years."

"No wonder Catherine contacted me. I was surprised to find she had abandoned all of you."

"How did she know to contact you?"

His brows rose. "I assumed your pa had talked about our friendship."

"Did you see her while you were in Wabash?"

He fussed with his sheet. "I didn't know how to contact her. I'd expected her to be at the house."

Lucy tensed. Should she tell him about Catherine's boyfriend? Before she could decide, the door opened and Nate stuck his head in.

"We need to be going, Lucy."

"Coming." She turned toward the door. "Will you be all right, Pa?"

"You young'uns get going. I'll be fine."

STILL CHURNING INSIDE from Henry's mention of children, Lucy almost flinched when Nate touched her elbow and guided her out of the room. She found the children in the parlor and had them get their coats, all the while conscious of Nate's overwhelming presence beside her. She longed to be back in Wabash, away from these confusing emotions that ravaged her.

The coming night terrified her. What if Nate took his father's request seriously and demanded his husbandly rights? She threw her cloak about her shoulders and went outside.

"Looks like we're getting back to normal weather." Nate paused on the porch. "How about we take the buckboard to town? The snow is almost melted, and we'll need the space to bring our supplies home."

"Whatever you say."

Nate went to hitch the horses to the buckboard, and Lucy turned to stare out at the land. Though the day had warmed enough for the snow to melt, the air still held a crisp edge. Would she still be here when spring finally came? She didn't know whether to pray for that or not. Taking her place as this man's wife, in all ways, left her trembling.

But she wasn't a coward. She drew herself up to her full height and marched toward the buckboard. Following behind her, Jed and Eileen were unusually quiet, as if they sensed her mood. Nate tossed Eileen up onto the second seat, and Jed joined her there.

Nate's big hands spanned Lucy's waist as he lifted her to the seat. His grip held on a moment longer than necessary, and Lucy saw the same trepidation in his eyes that she felt.

She yearned to touch his cheek with her fingertips, but she resisted the impulse. They had much to learn about one another, and she didn't want to rush anything.

The trip to town was silent. Lucy tensed as the buckboard rattled nearer the cluster of buildings that was Larson. She dreaded the pleasantries she would have to face as Nate's new wife. Just from looking at their holdings, she guessed the Stantons were a prominent cattle family.

Nate stopped the buckboard in front of the general store. "Ready?"

"About as ready as a chicken is to get its neck wrung off," Lucy muttered.

Nate grinned. "It won't be as bad as what you've already faced today. Come on, let me introduce you, and you can pick out everything you need." He jumped out of the wagon and held up his arms for Lucy.

He helped her down. "Jed, collect your little sister and meet us inside. You all need some new clothes, so we might as well get them while we're here. Get three of whatever you need. Skirts, blouses, a nice dress for Sunday."

Lucy stopped in her tracks. "I'll not have you buying us all these things, Mr. Stanton. People will say I married you for your money."

"That's pretty accurate, though, isn't it? If you'd had enough money, you wouldn't have agreed to my father's plan. You would have found some other way around it."

What he said was true. She would have spurned Henry's offer

if she'd had any recourse. "I didn't want anything for myself. Only to protect the children."

Nate held up a hand. "I didn't mean to insult you, Lucy. What's done is done. I don't want people thinking I'm not able to take care of my wife and dependents. I'm not poor. So get what you all need or I'll pick those things out myself."

"Very well." The words were hard to say.

"We have to see if we can work this marriage out so we're not at each other's throats like Bridget and the wolf. Are you ready to be introduced as my wife?"

Lucy nodded. She drew in a deep breath, pinned a smile in place, then took hold of his arm. Nate led her into the general store, milling with people, mostly women. The familiar scents of cinnamon and mint mingled with leather and perspiration. It smelled just like the general store she frequented back in Indiana, and a wave of homesickness gripped her.

The chatter in the store ceased as they stepped to the middle of the large room crammed with everything from foodstuffs to notions to tools. Every gaze in the room pinned Lucy to the floor. Gathering her courage, she managed to smile as Nate waved his hand.

"While you're all here, I'd like to introduce you to my wife, Lucy."

A collective gasp went around the room, and Lucy couldn't help noticing the way several women turned to look at a tall woman standing near the glass jars of candy. Her thick red hair was caught carelessly in a tail at her neck, and she wore leather boots similar to Nate's under her heavy skirt. She exuded an animal magnetism that held Lucy's attention.

At Nate's words, the woman's head snapped back as though

she'd been slapped. Her deep green eyes, mesmerizing and compelling, looked almost feverish. Hectic spots of red in her cheeks, she held her head high as she stepped forward with an outstretched hand. "I'm Margaret O'Brien, your neighbor to the south. Congratulations, Lucy. You've succeeded where so many of us have failed. We thought Nate here would die a bachelor."

Margaret's handshake was firm, almost like a man's. Lucy's heart sank like an anvil in water. She felt like an incompetent child next to her. No wonder Nate was upset. This woman could have been his partner in every meaning of the word. Lucy would never manage to fill those boots.

"Pleased to meet you," Lucy choked out.

Margaret raised her gaze to meet Nate's. "I wish you well, Nate." Then her composure failed and a hint of pain flickered in her eyes. With a muttered apology, Margaret fled the store with an almost palpable wave of sympathy behind her. Lucy felt small and mean that she had hurt this woman, even unknowingly.

Once the store door slammed, the glares from the other women should have cowed Lucy, but she couldn't let them. Too much depended on her fitting in here. She managed a smile. "I do hope you'll feel free to call on us whenever you can. I look forward to learning much about ranching from you."

Several of the women looked at one another, then one by one they grudgingly welcomed her to the community. After a pause bordering on rudeness, they scuttled out the door, no doubt to find Margaret and commiserate with her. And who could blame them? Lucy was an interloper here.

THIRTEEN

The hem of Margaret's blue dress disappeared around the corner as Nate walked across the street to the sheriff's office. His spirits were low after seeing Margaret's obvious distress. It had taken a lot of strength for her to keep her composure as long as she had.

He frowned. His father had encouraged him to think about Margaret as a possible wife and yet had gone out and brought Lucy home. When Nate had a chance, he was going to ask his father why he had done it. If anyone was to blame for Margaret's upset, it was his pa.

He heard a familiar voice and went that direction where he found his brother on a bench outside the saloon. Roger's voice carried on the wind, and he told the men gathered around about the wonders of San Francisco.

Roger saw him and the animation faded from his face. He nodded at Nate. "Looks like my brother has something on his mind. I'll meet you for poker later."

The men glanced at Nate, then dispersed back to the saloon and down the street. Nate joined his brother on the bench. "Pa had another spell."

Roger bolted to his feet. "Is he going to be okay?"

"I hope so. He's resting now. We need to take as much strain off him as possible."

Roger sat back down. "He'll use this to control you. But not me. I'm shoving off."

"I need you, Rog."

"No, you don't, Nate. You have all you want right here. A big spread, a pretty little wife. But it's not for me. If you need help, hire it. You're not poor. Pa is already trying to tempt me with a new horse, responsibility on the ranch. But I see through him. When are you going to wake up?"

Roger had always had a chip on his shoulder about being told what to do. This was an old argument. Nate took off his hat and ran his fingers through his hair. "I guess there's no more to say, then. When are you leaving?"

"Tomorrow. First thing in the morning."

"You ever coming back?"

Roger hesitated, then shook his head. "I doubt it. This time was a mistake. Pa hasn't changed."

And neither have you. Nate bit back the words. "I wish you well, brother." He rose and put his hand on Roger's shoulder.

Roger stood and embraced him. "I'll write when I have an address." He released Nate, then turned and strode toward his horse.

Nate watched him go with a sense of regret and futility. He stepped onto the boardwalk in front of the sheriff's office and pushed open the door. Sheriff Borland wore a harried expression as he turned from the board where wanted posters hung. He tugged at the pants that drooped low on his hips and straightened when he saw Nate.

Stepping to his battered desk, he pointed to the wooden chair on the other side. "I reckon you're here about your cattle?" He pulled out his chair and settled into it.

"Mostly my bull. You ask Larson?"

"Yep." Borland leaned back in his chair and frowned. "He claims you're harassing him. And I didn't find any cattle on his property. No bull, either."

Though he'd expected Larson to deny it, Nate had hoped the sheriff could uncover some clue. It was clear Borland thought Nate was accusing Larson unjustly. "He's done it before," Nate said. "Last year when he was working for O'Brien, he rounded up some of my cattle."

Borland nodded. "He gave the cattle back, though, and apologized. O'Brien said it was an honest mistake."

Nate didn't believe it for a minute, but he could tell by the expression on the sheriff's face that Borland wanted the matter to drop. "What about the man Larson hired? He tried to burn down my barn."

Borland shrugged. "Larson said he didn't hire him. That he just saw the fellow by the side of the road and stopped to talk. It's your word against his."

Nate stood and headed for the door.

The sheriff called after him. "Where you going?"

"Home. It's clear I'll have to protect my property by myself."

His temper was just simmering under boil when he exited the office into the sunshine. He motioned to Jed, who was waiting for him on the bench outside the general store. When the lad joined him, they headed for the feed store. Nate stopped in the doorway when he saw Margaret's father inside. Before Nate could backtrack, the man turned and saw him.

Paddy O'Brien's florid face went redder. His lips flattened and his nostrils flared. "What's this nonsense I hear about you being married. It's not true, is it?"

Trapped, Nate stepped into the store. Four other men turned to stare. "It's true, Paddy. Lucy is yonder at the general store."

"Who is she? Your pa never said a word about you keeping company with a woman. I just saw him last month, and he asked after Margaret."

Nate felt Jed's stare and didn't want to dishonor Lucy by revealing the truth. "Lucy is from Indiana," he said finally. "You wouldn't have met her. This is her brother, Jed."

O'Brien glanced at Jed and seemed to deflate a bit. "I don't know what I'm going to tell Margaret."

"She knows," Jed blurted out. "She was at the general store."

O'Brien scowled. "I 'spect dinner will be burned and she'll be moping around. What did she say?"

Nate did not want to discuss this in front of everyone. Did Margaret's father have no sense of propriety? "You'll have to talk to her about it."

"You should have given us warning," the older man said. "It wasn't fair to Margaret. Or to me."

The man was more worried about his bottom line than his daughter. Nate hadn't seen this side of him before. His respect for his neighbor went down. But he couldn't tell O'Brien that he hadn't had any warning himself. "Sorry. It was a little sudden."

O'Brien grabbed his bill of sale and headed for the door. "See you around, *neighbor*." He glared at Nate as he passed.

LUCY WANDERED THE aisles with Eileen's hand in hers. Eileen fingered some crystal beads that caught the light, and Lucy wished she had the money to purchase them for her sister. The child loved bright, shiny things. Lucy's arms were already full of articles of clothing. She'd chosen the least expensive prairie dresses for herself and a pale blue dress for Sunday that seemed well made and inexpensive. The same for Eileen. She'd picked dungarees and simple shirts for Jed.

Nate and Jed had gone down to the feed store, and she couldn't help but wonder if he'd really gone after Margaret. No one could have missed how stricken the woman had been by the news. All Lucy's earlier hopes of making this marriage work had taken a setback when she'd seen the kind of woman Nate should have married. What had Henry been thinking to match the two of them? They were so different.

She pushed her misgivings aside and perused the tables of fabric and ribbons. She had a few coins of her own, and when Eileen begged for a bit of blue ribbon, she hesitated, longing again to indulge the child. What if she needed it later for something more necessary? She shook her head, then froze in the aisle when she saw a man staring at her. The man had a shock of graying hair that fell across his broad forehead above hazel eyes and an aquiline nose. His eyes widened the longer he stared at her.

He took a step closer to her. "Jane?"

Her mother's given name. Lucy forgot to breathe as she stared into the man's face. Her mother's eyes were the same shape and color, at least according to the locket around her neck.

"Drew, your supplies are ready," the shopkeeper called.

Drew. "My name is Lucy. Are you Drew Larson?"

He rubbed his head. "I'm sorry to disturb you. You look so much like my deceased sister that it took me aback."

"I'm Lucy, Jane's daughter. I do believe you're my Uncle Drew."

He went white and took a step back. "Jane's girl, Lucy? You were three the last time I saw you." His hand trembled as he pointed at Eileen. "She looks like you did. She's your daughter?"

Lucy shook her head. "This is my sister, Eileen. My brother, Jed, is outside helping my husband load the wagon."

He glanced around the store. "Is your father here too?"

He hadn't gotten the letter. Her eyes burned as she took his hand. "Pa died in a buggy accident. About three months ago. I sent you a letter, but it was only a few days ago. I didn't find your address at first."

The eagerness in his face vanished. His fingers tightened on hers. "I'm so sorry."

Lucy clung to his hand and tried not to let her tears spill. "Thank you."

With a visible effort, her uncle composed his expression. "What are you doing here?"

"I—I married last week and will be living here now."

"Who is your husband?"

"Nate Stanton."

His eyes narrowed and his mouth tightened. *"Stanton."* He said the word as if it were a curse.

"You know him?"

He hooked a thumb in his belt loop. "He's been a thorn in my skin for years. How did you end up with him? To my knowledge, he's never left the county."

"It's a long story."

"I have time," he said in a clipped tone.

She bit her lip, then told him how she'd met Henry and the offer he presented. Uncle Drew's face grew more thunderous as she went.

"So you married him sight unseen. You should have come to me instead."

"I dislike burdening anyone with my problems. And quite honestly, I wasn't sure your address was still accurate."

"We're family. The Stantons are enemies."

She searched his forbidding expression. "Why? They've been nothing but good to me and the children."

"They gobbled up land that rightly belonged to me. Nate has besmirched my name in the county with lies about my character."

She winced. "I detest lying above all else," she said when he paused, obviously waiting for a response from her.

"You'll soon see that husband of yours is not a man to be trusted. If you need haven, my home is always open to you."

She'd been around Nate only two days. So far he'd been merely gruff and taken aback at her arrival as any man would have been when a wife appeared unexpectedly. "Perhaps it is merely a misunderstanding between the two of you. My arrival could be the bridge to bring the two of you to a better relationship."

His scowl deepened. "I want nothing to do with the Stantons unless he gives me back my land."

Could there be any truth to her uncle's accusations? She liked Henry, but she didn't know him well. He was obsessed with land, land, and more land. But would he swindle someone for more? It grieved her to realize she didn't know.

Her husband's voice spoke from the doorway. "Lucy, I'm ready."

He hadn't seen them yet. She pressed her uncle's hand. "I shall be in touch." Stepping away from Drew, she answered Nate. "Coming."

Nate smiled when he saw her, but his grin quickly faded when his gaze went over her shoulder. With his lips pressed together, he glared at Drew. "He been bothering you?"

She grabbed his arm and tugged him toward the door. "Not at all. I've got everything on my list, but we need to hurry home. I need to get dinner on the stove." *Please, Lord, don't let him make a ruckus.*

He walked toward the door with her. "Percy will have it under control."

"We aren't eating at the main house. Your father was insistent we stay at the cabin."

Nate shrugged, and they stepped out onto the rough board sidewalk.

Lucy peeked back at the general store. She breathed a sigh when her uncle didn't follow them outside. Drew had said the relationship was irreparable, but she would do all she could to bring peace between the two men. It was likely a misunderstanding. Then she remembered poor Margaret. Maybe Lucy didn't know any of the Stantons well enough to make a judgment on the truth.

FOURTEEN

The wagon, laden with food, fabric, and planks of wood, lumbered along the road. Bits of mud, left from the melted snow, flew up from the wagon wheels. Nate risked a glance at Lucy. She hadn't said much, and he had to wonder if she was angry. She didn't look angry though. She looked tired and sad.

Though she was a tiny thing, her courage facing the wolf had startled him. She was a tiny Titan, and he was beginning to question his initial assessment of her. But the thing that stuck in his craw was that he hadn't picked her for himself. A man wanted to choose his own wife. Not that she wasn't attractive. Maybe that was half the trouble. Being around her made his palms sweaty.

Nate cleared his throat. "I thought me and Jed would build some more chairs with this lumber. Anything else you can think of, Lucy?"

"That's a good start," she said, her tone distant.

"You mad about something?" he asked, when she didn't look at him.

When she finally turned her stare his way, her expression was cold. "What promises did you make that poor woman?"

He should have realized Margaret's pain would bother her. "I never promised Margaret anything. I never even asked to call on her."

"Then why was she so upset?"

"It was assumed by our families that we would someday join our spreads into one. A merger, if you will," he admitted. "But though she would have been willing, I wasn't so sure."

After a long moment in which he held her gaze, she nodded. "I see that's true. Poor Margaret."

Nate had to wonder about this woman who was his wife. He would have felt rivalry toward another man, but Lucy seemed to see right to a person's heart and feel something that mattered. She truly was sorry about Margaret's pain.

Eileen nestled her head under his arm, and Nate looked down in surprise. The little girl's long lashes lay soft against her pink cheeks, and his heart softened. His life was changing already, and parts of it felt mighty good. He wrapped his arm around Eileen and pulled her close so she didn't jerk so badly when the wagon hit the ruts in the road.

Lucy brushed the blond hair back from Eileen's face. "She's tuckered out. I think we all are."

"I shouldn't have made you come to town so quick."

"I had to face them all sooner or later."

"Later would've been better. I should've given you time."

"It wasn't your fault. I'm the interloper, the one who snatched a handsome, eligible man out from under their noses."

Nate stared at her. Was that really the way she saw him? A warm glow of pleasure spread through his chest. Women had flirted with him before, but he'd always thought it was simply because he was a Stanton. Those women had wanted something from him—it seemed all women did.

He hunched his shoulders and stared ahead at the road. Lucy's words were likely a ploy to make sure he didn't send her packing. Or were they? Lucy had been nothing but honest with him, and for that matter, with everyone she'd encountered. Maybe she wasn't a manipulator. How could he know for sure?

The cabin looked cold and forlorn when they stopped at the barn. This probably wasn't what she expected when Pa told her of all their holdings, but she hadn't faltered when she saw it. What did that say about her? Was he wrong about her?

Clouds gathered overhead, and cold drops of rain splashed onto Nate's face. The wind freshened, and he squinted at the sky. "Storm's coming, but at least it's not snow."

He jumped to the ground and held out his arms for Eileen. Lucy passed her down to him, and he held the little girl close to protect her from as much wetness as he could.

"Jed, help your sister down, then see to the animals," he said. "When you're done, start bringing in the supplies. I'll be right out to help you."

"Yes, sir." Jed jumped from the wagon. He helped Lucy down, then led the horses inside the barn.

The rain began to come down in earnest, hard droplets that chilled him instantly. Holding Eileen in one arm, Nate took Lucy's arm, then they ran toward the house, splashing through the rivulets of mud that were already beginning to fill the yard.

He threw open the door and followed Lucy inside. It wasn't as cold as he had expected. Heat still radiated from the last of the fire. The rain drummed on the tin roof as he handed Eileen to Lucy then went to stir up the embers.

As he poked at the fire, Lucy hummed in a low voice as she rattled pans at the cookstove. It was a homey sound that he rather liked. He spent little time here, usually only sleeping on his pallet after a hard day with the cattle. The cabin was changed already after just a few hours.

LUCY COULDN'T STOP thinking about what her uncle had told her. Could his accusations be true? She didn't want to believe she'd married a man who would do what Uncle Drew had accused him of, but she needed to know the truth. Who could she ask? Nate was sure to defend himself. She didn't know anyone except the Stantons and Percy.

She began to peel potatoes for supper while Eileen played with her doll. When she heard a horse whinny, she glanced through the window. A woman climbed down from a buggy and came toward the door. Mrs. Walker. Lucy's heart leaped at the thought of talking to another woman, even if it was Henry's cousin. She threw open the door and hugged the woman.

"Lucy, my dear, is something wrong?" Mrs. Walker said when Lucy finally released her. "You're hugging me like I'm your last hope."

Lucy wiped her moist eyes. "I'm just so glad to see you. I've been surrounded by men since I got here. Come in. I'll put on some tea."

Mrs. Walker removed her gray bonnet and smoothed her hair as she followed Lucy to the kitchen. "I quite understand, dear girl. And Henry especially can be a bit overwhelming. My cousin likes his own way." She pulled out a chair at the kitchen table and settled into it.

Lucy put the tea in the pot and poured in hot water from the water reservoir on the woodstove. While it steeped, she got out the cups and saucers. She carried her potatoes to the table so she could continue to peel them while they talked. "Can you stay for supper?"

Mrs. Walker shook her head. "I'm on my way to check on Henry and thought I would pop in for a moment and see how you're adjusting."

"I'm so glad you did. It's been an upsetting day."

"Oh dear, what's gone wrong?"

"Henry had another spell. I assume you heard about that?" When the older woman nodded, she continued. "When we went to town, I ran into Drew Larson." She eyed Mrs. Walker. Should she tell her that they were kin? When the woman's expression didn't change, she decided to trust her. "He's my uncle."

Mrs. Walker took the strainer and poured tea through it into the two cups. "I see. Does Henry know this?"

Lucy hadn't considered it, but it had to be true. From the beginning, he'd known her mother's family. "I would assume so. He knew my parents."

"How interesting."

"In what way?"

Mrs. Walker stirred sugar into her tea. "He deliberately married you off to his son, knowing that you were part of a family that hates the Stanton name and everything it stands for. What is that man up to?"

"You think he wanted the marriage to heal the rift?" That thought brightened her mood a bit. She didn't want to be part of a war.

"I've seen no evidence that Henry is distressed by the conflict." Mrs. Walker sipped her tea. "But that's not all that's bothering you. I can see it in those eyes of yours."

Lucy wanted to hug the woman again. "My uncle accused Henry and Nate of taking his land. There seems to be so much that I don't understand."

"Ah." The woman cleared her throat. "I can understand Mr. Larson's bitterness."

"What happened?"

"They were friends once, Henry and Walter, Drew's father. Walter was a mentor to Henry. He idolized Walter. Then Drew killed a man."

Lucy gasped. "What happened?"

"He was young and got involved with some bad characters. They were drunk one night and shot up the saloon. The bartender fell into the mirror and died. They were lucky the town didn't lynch them."

"So how did that destroy the friendship?"

"That bartender was Henry's brother."

Lucy hadn't been expecting that. It felt odd to hear these tales about a man she'd barely known existed. Her father never talked about family, though she'd pressed him. She sat back and exhaled. "Oh dear."

"Precisely. Henry was determined Drew would pay. Walter was adamant about keeping his son out of jail. Drew ran off and joined the army before he was able to stand trial. Walter fell apart. He let the ranch go. Took to drinking away everything he had. Finally the land went on the auction block and Henry bought it. Walter died a week later. Some say he died at his own hand."

This was her grandfather. Lucy couldn't quite wrap her mind around these facts about a family she didn't know. She wasn't sure how she should feel. Had her father-in-law destroyed her grandfather, or had he destroyed himself?

"It's quite horrible. Why did Henry choose me for his son? I would have thought he wouldn't have wanted anything to do with the Larson family."

"I can't pretend to understand my dear cousin. I suspect he saw your goodness, Lucy."

"He barely met me before he was trying to persuade me to marry his son. I think it was to heal the breach, even if he didn't quite realize his true motives. I will do my best."

"I'm sure you will. You're very much like your mother, you know."

Lucy's pulse pounded in her throat. "You knew my mother?"

"Of course. She lived here all of her life, after all. That is, except for the four years she was in Boston at school. She couldn't wait to get out of here though. Your parents moved after their first year of marriage."

Lucy sipped her tea. "I never knew her. What was she like?"

"Full of laughter and fun. She loved a good time. At every dance she was surrounded by men. At one time I thought perhaps Henry would be the winner of her hand. He so wanted to be part of her family. Sometimes I think it was for the Larson name. The town was named for their ancestor and Henry seemed to desire that validation of his worth."

Lucy gasped. "He *did* court her? I wondered."

Mrs. Walker nodded. "Oh yes. He was quite distraught when she chose your father."

"Did it break their friendship?"

"Nothing could do that. Those two were two frogs. When one jumped, the other followed. I was with Henry when he heard that your father had died. He was quite devastated."

"So maybe he really just wanted to help my father's children."

Lucy's heart warmed even more toward the man who was her father-in-law.

"I'm sure that played a part. As did your own sweet self, Lucy dear. What do you think of your new husband?"

Lucy's cheeks heated, and she stared at her teacup. "He's quite handsome."

"Is he treating you well?"

Lucy nodded. "He's very kind. Most of the time."

"Most of the time?"

"He was not pleased when I showed up so unexpectedly."

Mrs. Walker laughed. "Knowing Nate, I can only imagine."

"What do you mean?"

"Nate is rather set in his own ways. I'm sure you shook things up like a small tornado. But change can be good."

"I hope Nate comes to see that," Lucy said, smiling.

FIFTEEN

By the time Nate joined Jed in the barn, the lad had already curried the horses and unloaded the wagon. The house supplies were stacked in one corner, and he'd put the feed in the grain bins. Rain still pattered on the metal roof, and the rhythm was comforting.

"Good job, Jed."

The boy flushed and his eyes brightened. "Thank you, sir."

"You don't have to call me sir. Call me Nate."

"Does that mean you're going to keep us?" Jed's voice was anxious, but he held Nate's gaze without looking away.

Nate hesitated. What did he say to that? He really didn't have a choice. Pa's health wouldn't take any more upheaval, and the marriage was legal. The best thing was to make do with the situation as best he could. And he had to admit having a pretty wife to come home to might not be such a bad thing.

Jed's face fell as the silence went on. "Don't blame Lucy for us being here, Mr. Stanton. We were in a bad situation."

He studied the boy's downcast face, then touched his shoulder.

"Pa is a pretty good judge of character. If he thought you would make good Stantons, then I reckon he's right."

When Jed raised his head, his eyes were glistening with unshed tears. "You won't be sorry, Mr. Stanton. Mrs. Thomas at the dress shop was always going on about how quick she was to learn something new. She'll learn to help you here at the ranch. And I'm strong." He flexed the muscles on his arm. "See here? I can heft a bale of hay by myself. And me and Eileen will try to stay out of your way as much as possible so you can have time with Lucy."

A lump grew in Nate's throat. Lucy inspired a lot of love in her brother. He squeezed Jed's shoulder. "I'll be glad to have the help. You don't need to stay out of the way. I don't have much experience with young'uns, but I'll try to be a dad to you as well. Tomorrow I'll start teaching you how to rope and brand. We'll be taking the cattle to market come summer, and I'll need all the hands I can get."

Jed's lip trembled, and the tears spilled over onto his cheeks. He scrubbed at his face with the back of his hand. "I'm not a bawl baby, Mr. Stanton. I'll work hard and make you glad you married us. Lucy's worked so hard to try to keep us together. Now it's my turn."

Us. He reckoned a package deal was what it was too. He had a ready-made family. It was a little overwhelming. Nate cleared his throat. "How about helping me carry this stuff to your sister? She may be a miracle worker, but she has to have something to work with."

"Yes, sir!" Jed hefted a sack of flour to his shoulder and marched toward the house. He looked back at Nate. "Uh, Mr. Stanton, I'd sure be glad if you didn't say nothing to Lucy about our talk. She hates for people to say nice stuff about her."

"She does?"

Jed nodded vigorously. "There was a guy hanging around all last summer who went on and on about how pretty she was. She finally got fed up and told him the only beauty she was interested in was that on the inside, and since all he could see was the outside, he'd best mosey on down the road."

Nate squelched a grin. "I'll keep mum."

"Thanks, Mr. Stanton." Jed started for the door.

"Jed."

The boy stopped. "Yes, sir?"

"Call me Nate. Mr. Stanton is my pa."

Jed's eyes grew bright. "Yes, sir. I mean, Mr. Nate." He was still grinning as he dashed out into the driving rain.

Nate grabbed a gunnysack full of food and slung it over his shoulder. Lucy was quite a remarkable young woman. How many women would have worked so hard and sacrificed so much for their siblings? His respect for his new wife went up a notch.

When he got to the house, Jed was jabbering excitedly while Lucy listened. "I'm going to learn to rope a steer and brand, Lucy. Maybe I'll even get to go on the cattle drive up north. You know how good I can ride."

"We'll see, Jed. That's a big job, and you're not hardly old enough."

"Old enough to do a man's job." Nate set his burden on the floor. "Jed's going to be a fine ranch hand."

Lucy put her fists on her hips. "He's only twelve, Mr. Stanton."

"I was ten when I went on my first cattle drive."

Lucy's eyes narrowed. "He's my brother, and I'll decide what's best for him."

Nate's warm feelings toward Lucy evaporated like the morning dew. She would make a sissy of the boy. "You want Jed to turn into a man or a young hoodlum?"

Lucy's face whitened, and she held up her hand as if to ward off a blow. Jed made a small sound of protest, and Nate realized he'd said too much. "I'm sorry, I didn't mean that. Jed is a fine boy, but he's almost a man, Lucy. You have to let loose those apron strings a tad."

Her sober blue eyes regarded him for a moment, then she nodded. "You may be right. But Jed and Eileen are my whole life. I couldn't bear for anything to happen to him."

"You have to trust someone, Lucy. I'm your husband now. I'll take care of Jed."

Her eyes examined him again and she bit her lip before turning back to her task of stashing the supplies without answering.

He eyed her stiff back. She wasn't giving an inch yet. Maybe he'd been a little too interfering. He needed to move a little slower, gain her trust. Things were different out here, and she didn't know how different yet.

EMOTIONS CHURNED IN Lucy's stomach. Anger and jealousy—of her brother, of all things! For so long she was the one Jed looked up to, the one whose approval he sought. The adoring look Jed gave Nate had hit her hard. For a moment she felt adrift. Without a needy brother and sister giving her life purpose, what would happen to her?

Eileen stirred from her pallet on the floor beside Bridget. The little girl sat up and rubbed her eyes. "I'm hungry, Lucy," she said plaintively.

At least Eileen still needed her. "Supper will be ready in about half an hour. Why don't you take Bridget outside until it's ready? The best thing for the dog's hurt leg is some exercise. Otherwise it will stiffen up."

The dog wagged her tail at the mention of her name. Smart dog. She'd figured out they were talking about her.

"Do you need me for anything right now?" Jed's gaze followed Eileen and the dog longingly.

"No, just keep an eye on your sister," Nate answered before Lucy could. Jed followed Eileen and Bridget outside.

Outrage churned again. It was her job to give or deny permission. She looked down at the biscuits she was making. *Help me, Lord. My attitude is not worthy of you. I should be glad Nate is taking an interest in the children. Help me to let go.* Even though she'd prayed, she didn't feel a bit better. This was *her* job. She was used to being in control. No one knew the children as well as she did.

Her heart still racing, she patted the dough, then used her knife to cut it into square biscuits. Transferring them to a baking sheet, she slid them into the oven and closed the door.

Lucy didn't dare meet Nate's gaze. She was acting like a shrew, hardly the type of helpmeet she'd wanted to be. She had longed for someone to help her carry the load, so why was she now resenting it when Nate offered to share some of her burden? Tears blurred her vision.

She heard movement behind her, then Nate put his hands on her shoulders and turned her to face him. His fingers tilted her chin up, but she stubbornly kept her eyes fastened on his shirt.

"Don't fight me, Lucy. If this marriage is going to make it, we have to work together."

Her heart jumped. He almost sounded as though he wanted them to work things out. She dared a glance into his face. His gray eyes were gentle.

"What are you saying?" she whispered.

He took off his cowboy hat with a swipe of his big hand. "I'm saying that I'm willing to be friends if you are." He gave a heavy sigh. "We haven't gotten off on a very good start, but it seems this marriage is square and legal. We may not love each other, but we can at least be friends. I like you, Lucy. You've got guts, even if you are small and spindly."

He grinned, and she smiled back feebly. She wet her lips. "What do you expect of me?" Against her will she glanced at the ladder leading to the loft.

"Not that," he said hastily. "Not yet, at any rate. You stay with Jed and Eileen. Jed can help in the field while you and Eileen take care of the house."

"I thought you wanted a wife who could rope and shoot as well as a man."

He grinned. "You sure shoot as well as any man I ever saw."

Her cheeks burned, and she ducked her head. "It's not very womanly."

He laughed out loud. "I don't think either one of us knows what we want in a mate. We're going to have to discover that as we go along. You willing to try?"

Her throat felt tight, and she struggled not to cry. "I'll try, Mr. Stanton," she managed.

"Like I just told Jed, Mr. Stanton is my pa. Think you can see your way clear to calling me Nate? Seeing as we're married and all."

Her gaze searched his, and she nodded. "I'll try, Nate."

"I will too." His gaze was soft and roamed down to her lips. His grin widened, then his eyes grew sober. "Can I kiss you, Lucy?"

Her heart fluttered like a frightened bird. She'd never been kissed, and she wanted to wait until she felt more than mere liking for a man. But this was her husband. How did she refuse him such a natural request? Before she could answer, his fingers tightened on her shoulders, and he bent his head. His lips grazed her cheek.

Her stomach felt funny, all nervous and jittery. Then he pulled away.

"That's all for now. When you're ready for a real kiss, you let me know." He sauntered to the door with a smug grin as if he knew her knees were almost too weak to hold her.

When the door closed behind him, Lucy sank into a chair. If a kiss on the cheek affected her like this, what would a real kiss do?

THE CHILDREN SLEPT nearby on their cots. Nate watched the shadows from the fireplace dance in the room. The wind had picked up outside and howled around the chimney. He watched Lucy squint over her sewing in the dim light of the lantern. She sure was a pretty little thing, and it felt good to be snug in the house with a family while the storm raged.

"That a quilt?" he asked.

Not looking up from her work, she nodded. "Jed is going to need one."

"I think there are extras at the ranch."

"I like to keep busy."

He glanced at Jed, sleeping soundly. "I need to talk to you about something."

She looked up, then put down her sewing. "Is something wrong?"

He nodded toward the boy. "Young Jed told me he is afraid someone might have followed you here. Or at least, might show up."

She clasped her hands together. "Who?"

"He didn't know, but he told me about the intruder at the apartment. I'm trying to come up with a reason for someone to break into a house where he'd find no money or anything of value. Do you have any ideas?"

She shook her head. "None. The man said, 'Where is it?'"

"What was the 'it' he was looking for?"

"I don't know. I haven't had much time to think about it. I had to pack and come out on the train immediately. Quite honestly, I thought he had the wrong house."

He frowned. "What can you tell me about your parents?"

She looked down at her hands. "You already know our father died three months ago. I never knew my mother. She died when I was tiny. Your father knew her though. He told me more about her than I'd ever heard."

Her voice held melancholy, and he wondered what his father knew about her mother. That would keep, though. "Jed said your father told him to keep some kind of secret. That someone might show up looking for something."

She gasped. "Jed's never said a word about this to me. Are you sure you didn't misunderstand him?"

"Very sure." He watched her twist a long strand of hair around her finger and bite her lip. "What did your father do?"

"He owned a pawn shop."

Ah, maybe a motive. "Anything valuable in the shop?"

She shook her head. "There was a break-in the night his buggy overturned. The thieves took everything of value."

"Everything? Nothing was left?"

"Nothing."

"Relatives?"

She looked at him finally. "Actually, I have an uncle in this area. I saw him in the mercantile."

Something stirred in his gut at her expression. "Maybe I know him. Who is it?"

"Drew Larson. My mother's brother."

"Larson!" He studied her downturned face. There was more she wasn't saying. "I know him," he said grimly.

"I know. And you don't like him. It's written all over your face. Plus, you were quite rude about him in town. Mrs. Walker told me about the feud."

"He's a cattle rustler," he said, not caring if the truth upset her.

"Cattle rustler! He said . . ." She frowned as she broke off whatever she'd been about to say.

"You've spoken to him?" He thought back to that moment in the general store. She'd been walking away from Larson. "You lied to me."

Her chin came up. "I did no such thing! You didn't ask if I'd been talking to him. You asked if he was bothering me. He wasn't."

He fixed a glare on her. "Did you arrange to meet him here? Was this marriage some kind of agreement between the two of you?" More questions raced in his head. All the stirring dreams he'd had about the future came to a halt. He should have known Lucy was too good to be true.

She held his gaze. "It was the first time I'd seen him since I was three. I knew he lived in the county, but that's all."

He wasn't sure whether he believed her or not. "Does he know you're married to me?"

She nodded. "I told him."

"Bet that set him back on his heels."

She looked down at her hands. "He was, um, surprised."

He kneeled to poke at the fire. "I'm sure he had plenty to say about me."

"He said you took some land that belonged to him."

Nate threw the poker to the floor and stood to face her. "That's a bald-faced lie! His father went bankrupt and the land went on the auction block. Pa paid a fair price for it. Larson was away in the war when it happened, and he's never gotten over it."

Her eyes were sorrowful. "Did my grandfather kill himself over it?"

He hadn't been thinking about the relationship that existed. Old Larson was her grandfather. "Some around here thought so. Any fool knew better than to cross the Red River in flood stage."

She flinched. "What happened when Uncle Drew got back from the war?"

"He wanted to buy the land back, but Pa was already running cattle on it. And Drew didn't have the money anyway. He wanted Pa to sell it on land contract. Pa told him he wasn't a bank."

Nate wished he knew what she was thinking. Her blue eyes were faraway and contemplative as though she saw something he didn't.

She finally sighed. "It's quite a tangle. I'd hoped the misunderstanding could be easily resolved."

"There *is* no misunderstanding. Larson knows exactly what happened."

"He seemed to dislike you personally, not your father. Why is that?"

He'd been right—she was perceptive. "Pa transferred the land to my name last spring. Larson asked me to sell it to him as well." He shrugged. "I can't afford to do it either. Pa has worked hard and poured all his money, sweat, and blood into building this ranch. I can't piecemeal it up and give it away."

She didn't say anything for several long minutes. "Did you pray about it?" she asked finally.

Had he? It was too cut-and-dried in his mind so he didn't think he had. "No."

She sat back in her chair and picked up the quilt piece. "Don't you think you should?"

He managed to hide his outrage. "What's to pray about, Lucy? My pa bought the land fair and square. We did nothing wrong."

"No, you did nothing wrong. But that doesn't mean God wouldn't ask something sacrificial of you."

Sacrificial? He didn't like the sound of that. "I'd better finish chores." There was no arguing with her. She didn't understand the economics of ranching yet.

SIXTEEN

The fire crackled in the fireplace and threw out light. Lucy heard every stamp of the horses' hooves outside, every whistle of the wind through the eaves. It would take awhile to get used to the new sounds. Ranch noises were far different from the clop of horses along Wabash streets. When the rooster crowed outside the window, she finally got up as quietly as possible and grabbed a dress in the dark.

It was her mother's fancy dress, the one she'd worn for courage to meet Nate. As she started to lay it aside to get one for everyday use, she heard something clunk. The firelight revealed nothing on the floor. What had made that metallic sound? She held the dress up and examined it. The buttons were small and made of pearl. Again she noticed how heavy the dress was. She laid it on the bed and felt the fabric. When her fingers reached the hem, there was something hard under the material. Her sewing kit was under the cot, so she pulled it out and extracted her scissors. The stitches in the hem were uneven, almost as though a child had done them. Once the threads were snipped, she unfolded the hem. A silver coin winked in the firelight.

Lucy picked it up and laid it on the bed, then snipped the rest of the hem. She found a total of twenty coins hidden in the hem of the old dress. Staring at them, she could hardly breathe. It was incomprehensible.

Who had put them there? Surely not her mother. They would have been in this dress for twenty years. She tried to remember if she'd ever seen Catherine rummaging in the trunk, but as far as she knew, the woman had never set foot in the basement. She was terrified of mice.

"Lucy?"

She turned to see her brother rubbing his eyes. His red hair stuck straight up. He was staring at the coins on the bed. The expression on his face caused her stomach to drop. She held out her hand with several coins in them. "Jed? What do you know about these coins?"

He licked his lips. "I—I hid them for Dad. He asked me to put them in a safe place."

"He *asked* you to hide them? They belonged to him?" Her brother nodded. She pointed to the end of the bed. "Sit down and tell me what this is all about."

"I'm not supposed to," he whispered. "He made me promise." He stepped closer, still staring at the coins.

"I've found the coins now, so you have to." She pointed again, and the springs squeaked under his weight as he sat with obvious reluctance. "Where did these come from?"

He couldn't seem to tear his gaze away. "A man brought them to the shop the week before Dad died."

"He pawned them?"

Jed nodded. "For forty dollars. He told Dad it was a fair price." It would take her months to earn forty dollars. So while it wasn't a fortune, the man had received what appeared to be a fair price for twenty coins. "So why hide them?"

Jed leaned forward. "Dad found out they were worth a fortune. Then in the paper, Dad saw that the man had been murdered." Jed shuddered and hugged himself. "That night someone broke into the shop. Dad was sure he was someone after the coins, but Dad had taken them home with him for safekeeping. The next day he told me to keep them safe. And that I wasn't to tell anyone that we had them."

Lucy wanted to shudder herself, but she didn't want her brother to see her fear. "Did he go to the police?"

Jed shook his head. "I can't remember, Lucy."

"You think someone ran you off the road deliberately?" She'd always assumed it was an accident, and Jed had been in no shape to be questioned following the tragedy.

He bit his lip. "I don't know."

"I think that's what that man wanted the other night at our old house. He was after the coins."

"How do you know that?"

"I saw someone when I took Eileen to the privy. I thought it was one of my friends, so after I took her back inside, I went out again. He grabbed me and asked me where the dollars were. It was the night the guy broke in."

She remembered the night the intruder came in. He'd growled, *"Where is it?"* Was he after the coins? Lucy picked one up. It warmed quickly in her hand. She held it under the light. "What's so special about these?"

Jed stared in fascination. "Dad said they were rare."

"And worth a fortune? How much of a fortune?" Ten thousand? Twenty? The coin shimmered in the light.

"Over a million dollars." Jed's voice was hushed.

A million dollars? Lucy's response stuck in her throat. It didn't seem possible there was that much money in the world. She rolled the coin around in her hand. "For the lot?"

Jed nodded. "There's one that's worth half that all by itself." He studied the coins on the bed and picked one up. "This is it." He dropped it into Lucy's palm.

"It's just a silver dollar."

"Dad said it was a Dexter draped bust coin. There are only eight in the world."

Would someone kill to possess this coin? She shuddered at the thought that her father might be dead because of someone's determination to have this.

"I don't know what to do," she whispered. "Who do we give the money back to? It's not ours."

"Dad said the owner was dead."

"His family might still be alive. I wonder if the police would know about this."

Jed bit his lip. "Dad said it was dangerous to tell anyone."

"I have to do something about these coins. I can't just put them back in the hem and forget them."

"Dad didn't know how much they were worth when he bought them. The owner was happy with the money too. But Dad still didn't feel right about it. He wanted to make sure they weren't stolen. That's why he wanted to talk to the police. He wasn't going to give them to the police, though, unless he found out they were stolen. He wanted to keep them."

"And the shop was broken into. *Someone* knew how much they were worth."

"Dad said maybe someone who knew their worth had been planning to steal them and found out where the owner had pawned them. He said to keep them safe until he found out, because if it was all fair and square, the money would help all of us."

She gathered up the coins. "I'll put these away for now and think about it."

"Be careful, Lucy." Her brother touched her arm. "I think they killed him. I get so scared when I try to remember that night."

Lucy waited until her brother went out to start chores, then looked around for where she could hide the money. Under the mattress was too obvious. She carried them into the kitchen and glanced around. The root cellar. She grabbed the lantern, then stepped outside and opened the door to the cellar. In the cellar she opened a barrel of pickles. After wrapping the coins in an oilcloth, she stuffed the package deep into the bottom of the barrel.

That part was easy. Deciding what to do next would be much more difficult.

NATE HAD HEARD every sound in the room below him all night long. Jed groaned several times in his sleep. Lucy was up taking Eileen to the outhouse several times, and he heard soft weeping at one point near dawn. He thought about climbing down from the loft to see who it was, but he didn't have the right words to fix the problem if it was Lucy. He'd finally fallen into a heavy sleep when he'd known he should just get up.

The rooster crowed. He rolled over and punched his straw pillow into shape. It was prickly and uncomfortable. He was used to the feather pillow now propping Lucy's head. Their conversation last night and the threat to his new family had kept him awake until the wee hours.

And Lucy was related to Larson. He didn't care for that knowledge at all. He'd been ready to trust her and work on a relationship, but what if her pretty face hid something darker? He grimaced, remembering the fear he'd seen in her face when he asked to kiss her last night. She obviously thought he intended to claim his husbandly rights. Her blue eyes had been huge, and she looked as though she wanted to bolt for the door. Those soft cheeks had bloomed color like the first rosy blush of dawn. He smiled at the memory. He'd like to make her blush again.

A rooster crowed again from the chicken coop out back, and Nate sighed. Those cattle weren't getting herded into the south pasture by themselves. In spite of having little sleep, he had to get up.

As he swung his feet to the floor, he heard the rattle of pans in the room below. He raised an eyebrow. Who was up so early and why? He pulled on his boots and climbed down the ladder. Jed yawned at the kitchen table while Lucy, her glorious blond hair still hanging down her back, poked life into the cookstove fire. She was already dressed in a faded blue gingham dress.

Jed saw him first. "Morning, Mr. Stanton."

"Call me Nate, remember?" he said, his eyes on the way the lamplight lit Lucy's hair with shimmering lights.

"Yes, sir."

Lucy turned and caught his stare. A becoming bit of color raced up her cheeks, but she bravely met his gaze. He saw the muscles in her neck move as she swallowed, then she spun around and took some eggs out of a bowl.

"Jed and Eileen got me some eggs this morning. I hope that's all right," she said without looking at him. "He did chores."

"I didn't break none," Eileen put in with a big smile.

He smiled at Eileen and put his hand on her head. "I wasn't

expecting any of you to get out of bed so early. You had a busy day yesterday."

Lucy stirred the gravy. "So did you. I heard you tossing and turning all night."

"You didn't seem to get much sleep either," he pointed out. He glanced at Jed. "We have a full day's work ahead of us. You ready for it?"

"You bet!"

He grinned at the boy's enthusiasm. "We'll be working by the big house, so I expect we'll be late tonight."

"No lunch?"

He shook his head. "We'll let Percy feed us." Bridget nosed his leg, and Nate looked down. "You want out, girl?"

The dog whined, and he went to the door and pushed it open. Bridget gave a deep bark and wobbled out the door. Barking furiously, she limped to the road and planted her feet wide as she growled and barked at a figure by the gate.

Nate squinted through the dim light of predawn. A rider on a horse. Not willing to take any chances, he shut the door and stepped to the back door, where his rifle leaned against the wall. He checked to make sure it was loaded, then swung open the front door.

Drew Larson waved his hand. "Put the peashooter away. I didn't come to see you."

Scowling, Nate tightened his grip on his rifle. "I've got nothing to say to you, Larson. And if you're here to see Lucy, I'll ask you to stay away from my wife. You tried to burn down my barn. The next time I'll shoot first and ask questions later."

Drew gave a derisive laugh. "You don't have the guts, Stanton. Now your pa, that would be a different story, but I got nothing to fear from you." He touched his hat, his gaze again on Lucy. "Morning, Lucy. I thought maybe you'd want to have lunch with your old uncle. My sister would like to meet you."

"You have another sister?" Lucy took a step onto the porch. "I have an aunt?"

"You do. And some nieces who are eager to make your acquaintance."

Her glance slid sideways toward Nate. "I should like that. But not today, I'm afraid, Uncle Drew. I have so much to do getting settled in."

Larson shrugged. "Another time, then."

"Where does she live?"

"In town. At the end of Main Street. I'll tell her you'll be along soon." He turned his horse around and rode away.

Nate let out the breath he didn't even realize he was holding. His jaw hurt from clenching it, and his heart was stuttering like a faulty steam engine. He went back inside with Lucy on his heels. Her brother and sister flanked her.

He pulled out a chair at the kitchen table. "I could use some of those flapjacks I smell cooking."

Lucy blinked as though she had forgotten what she was doing, then blushed and turned back to the stove. "The gravy is done, and the eggs will be ready in a minute." She flipped a pancake, then faced him. "I want to meet my family."

He opened his mouth, then shut it again at the entreaty on her face. "I'd rather you stayed away from him."

"I'd rather you solved your differences."

"That's not possible."

She sighed. "Very well. But I'm not going to ignore the only family I have still living."

She had a point. How would he feel if someone told him he couldn't see his family? "Fine. But I don't want him here."

"As you wish." She turned to flip the bacon in the skillet. "Jed fetched some clean water for you to wash up in."

He stared at his hands. "I don't need the water. I'm reasonably clean."

Lucy whirled and pointed a spatula at him. "Nate Stanton, this may be Texas, but where I come from, we wash up for meals. I won't have dirty hands at my table."

"My hands are clean. See?" He held them out for her inspection.

She didn't look at his hands but stared him in the eye and pointed to the bowl and pitcher. "The soap is there as well. Your father wants some genteel manners brought to this spread. You'll wash your hands, or you'll go without breakfast."

His stomach growled in answer. Nate eyed her rigid back, then grinned. Snatching up the cake of soap, he lathered his hands, then poured water over them. "Satisfied?" He held them up.

She put the plate on the table. "Thank you, Nate. Please sit down and say grace. You'll want to eat your breakfast while it's hot."

Her voice was composed, but he could see a hint of a smile on her lips. "That's what I wanted to do an hour ago," he muttered.

He caught a glimmer of a grin on Jed's face. "You have something to say?" he asked the boy.

"Nope," the boy said hastily, stuffing a flapjack into his mouth.

"Jed, what have I told you about talking with your mouth full?" his sister said. "And I didn't hear either of you pray."

Nate exchanged a commiserating smile with Jed. At least he wasn't the only one in hot water. He bowed his head and thanked the Lord for the good food.

At the conclusion of his prayer, Lucy glanced at her brother. "Would you quote your Bible verse, Jed?"

Jed turned scarlet. "Uh, I forgot it, Lucy."

"Psalm 51:2," she prompted.

"Oh, I remember. 'Wash me thoroughly from mine iniquity, and cleanse me from my sin.'"

A smile played around her lips and she glanced at Nate.

"I like Matthew 15:19 and 20. 'For out of the heart proceed evil thoughts, murders, adulteries, fornications, thefts, false witness, blasphemies: These are the things which defile a man: but to eat with unwashen hands defileth not a man.'" He grinned back at her.

Instead of replying, she lifted a sweet voice in song. *"I need Thee every hour, most gracious Lord; No tender voice like Thine can peace afford.'"*

To Nate's surprise, Jed's voice joined in as if he were used to singing every morning at the breakfast table. Eileen's sweet little voice stumbled along. The song swelled in Nate's heart too, and he had to sing along with them.

As the music warmed the kitchen, he found it warmed his heart even more.

SEVENTEEN

Lucy felt a little cranky. Maybe she had come off too pushy over the washing up, but she wasn't about to start off this marriage by letting a man eat at her table without washing his hands. She'd worked for years to get Jed in the habit, and Nate could destroy all her hard training in the blink of an eye.

She had her work cut out for her. Nate was used to being around only men, and he had no concept of the niceties of life. But she would set such a good spread for him that he would be willing to do whatever he had to do to eat her cooking.

Lucy heated water on the stove to wash the dishes, then got out the ingredients to make bread. She kneaded it with practiced hands, put it on to rise, then went through the cabin and collected all the dirty clothes. She'd noticed a pile of Nate's clothes in the pantry, of all places, so she hauled in wood and water to do laundry. She set Eileen to helping hang the clothes up to dry on some string Lucy strung up by the fire.

Humming as she worked, she baked a raisin pie, then rolled out noodles and left them on the table to dry. What a blessing it was to have chickens and eggs in the backyard. God had truly blessed her. As she'd tossed in the night, she came to that conclusion. Nate was a fine man, a bit rough around the edges, but he just wasn't used to women. She would be patient and be the helpmeet she was created to be. Nate would be glad for his father's meddling in the end. She would be everything he needed. She could do this.

She glanced at the watch pinned to her dress. Ten thirty. She'd gotten a lot accomplished in a short time. What if she went to her aunt's? It wasn't that far. She could be back in time to fix the evening meal. She'd made it clear to Nate that she intended to meet her family. Why not now?

"Let's go visiting," she told her sister. She washed Eileen's face and led her to the door.

"Where we going, Lucy?" Eileen rubbed her eyes.

"To visit our aunt."

The little girl's eyes widened. "We have an aunt?"

"We do." With Eileen in tow, Lucy went to the barn and hitched the buggy up to the horse. A niggle of guilt stirred her insides. Nate wouldn't be pleased when he heard she'd gone without telling him. But this was something she *had* to do. This was her mother's sister. The closest Lucy would ever come to actually knowing her mother. By the time she reached the end of Main Street, she'd successfully rationalized what she was doing.

The house was a neat bungalow with a large porch and flowers blooming along the brick walk. The door and shutters were painted green and so was the porch. Lucy tied the horse to the hitching post, then took Eileen's hand and walked to the door on trembling legs. She knocked on the door and waited. In moments it was opened by a young woman about Lucy's age. Her hair was dark, but her eyes were the same blue as Lucy's.

She eyed Lucy and Eileen. "Hello. Can I help you?"

"I-I'm Lucy Stanton."

The young woman took a step back, then flung open the door. "Cousin Lucy!" She threw her arms around Lucy in an extravagant hug. "I can't believe you're here. Come in." She held open the screen door.

Lucy stepped inside as a portly woman in a gingham dress rushed out of the doorway on the right, presumably the parlor. The lady wore an apron over her dress. Her arms were outstretched as she rushed forward, nearly stumbling over the tabby that lay sunning itself on the hall rug.

The woman stopped a couple of feet from Lucy. "Jane?" She rubbed her hand over her forehead. "No, not Jane. But you look so much like her."

"You're my aunt?"

The woman hugged her. "I'm your Aunt Sally. This is my daughter, Fanny. You two could be sisters. Her hair is darker, but you both have the Larson nose." She linked arms with Lucy. "Come into the parlor, my dear. Fanny, bring some tea and cookies in if you would. And milk for the little one. Eileen, is it?"

Lucy kept step with her. "Yes, this is my sister, Eileen."

Modest furniture atop a threadbare rug graced the parlor. Though a bit worn, everything was spotlessly clean. Lucy sat in a chair. An ache spread through her chest as she stared at her aunt. A desire for a mother's love was so sharp it hurt.

"What is it, dear? You look as though you're about to cry."

"I'm just so glad to meet you. Would my mother have looked like you if she had lived?"

Sally smiled. "She might not have been so portly. We did look a great deal alike. She was a year younger than I and quite gregarious, while I was much more quiet. Oh my, the men in town followed her!" She smiled at her daughter, who entered the room with a tray of tea and cookies. "Thank you, my dear."

Lucy accepted the cup Fanny handed her. "You are about my age."

Fanny set the tray on the table and arranged her skirts as she sank onto the sofa. "I'm twenty."

"A bit younger," Lucy said, smiling. "I'm twenty-two. I'm so pleased to meet you."

"And I, you." Fanny sipped her tea. "You married Nate Stanton. Uncle Drew is quite irate about it."

Lucy glanced at her aunt. "How has all this affected you? Grandfather losing the ranch land and all."

Sally shrugged her plump shoulders. "Not at all. I married before Father died. I was never in line for any of the land. My husband was my provider. Of course, he is gone now, and if Drew owned the ranch, he could provide for me and Fanny a bit. But we're getting by. I take in laundry, and Fanny does some sewing to help out."

In spite of her aunt's disclaimer, Lucy squirmed when she realized her own husband had contributed to her aunt's impoverished condition. She had to figure out some way to help them.

JED RODE BACK to the cabin. He turned and glanced back at Nate several times. Nate waved and Jed waved back. He'd always wanted a big brother. Anxiety gnawed at his belly. Even after several days here, Jed kept watching. The man was coming. He knew it. No one would let that much money go without a fight.

He avoided a mama quail and her babies as they scurried away at his approach. Picking up his pace to finish his errand and return to the safety Nate provided, Jed crested the hill and rode toward the barn to pick up the lasso Nate needed. The one they'd taken with them had broken. As he neared the yard, something moved behind the cabin. Couldn't be Bridget. Though healing nicely, the dog had stayed back with Nate.

Jed squinted at the shadows. Was Eileen or Lucy outside? When the figure moved again, he realized it was a man peering in the back window. His gut clenched, and he reined in his horse. What should he do? If he rode back to get Nate, the man might harm his sisters.

There was a shotgun in the barn. He'd seen it hanging on the wall by the door. Crouching low over the neck of his horse, Jed rode to the back of the barn and dismounted. He slipped into the back door of the barn and went straight to the gun. Checking it, he found it was loaded. He exited the back door and crept around the side of the barn farthest from the end of the house where he'd seen the man.

Studying the landscape, he saw no movement. He darted forward and dove for the cover of a shrub in the side yard. Nothing moved. He heard nothing but the wind and the thundering of blood in his ears. The taste of dust was on his tongue.

Crawling forward under cover of the bushes, Jed reached the back edge of the cabin. He listened for a moment before cautiously poking his head around the end of the building. A man stood at the open back door. He wore a blue shirt over chambray pants and muddy boots. Under his Stetson his blond hair flopped onto his forehead.

One foot was already inside. Jed had to protect his sisters.

Brandishing the gun, he leaped up and shouted, "What do you think you're doing?" He pointed the gun at the man. "Step out of the door. Keep your hands up." The gun wavered in his hand, but he kept his finger on the trigger.

The man turned to face him with his hands in the air. His handlebar mustache quivered in a smile. "Easy, kid. I'm not doing anything. Just looking for a drink of water."

Jed didn't smile back. "Then why didn't you go to the front door and knock?"

Holding out one hand, the man took a step nearer. "Put down that gun, boy, and let's talk. You're not going to shoot me."

Jed swallowed hard. "I will if I have to." He jabbed the gun in the man's direction when the fellow took another step. "Stay right where you are." His voice squeaked.

The man laughed. "What's your name, son?" He sidled nearer.

Jed backed up. What was he going to do? The man must have seen the indecision on his face, because he rushed toward Jed and ripped the gun away from him. The next thing Jed knew, the gun was pointed his direction.

"You're Jed Marsh, aren't you?" the guy snarled, his easygoing demeanor gone. Jed nodded, his throat too tight to speak. The guy grabbed his arm and pushed him toward the door. "I want the coins."

Jed had known the intruder would find them here, but he'd thought they would have more time. "Coins?" he asked, stalling for time. He smelled the strong odor of hair tonic.

"Don't play dumb with me, kid. You were with your pa. You know all about the coins." He shoved Jed through the door into the laundry room. "Get them. Now."

Jed struck the wall and the washboard fell from its hook. "I don't have them."

"Where are they?"

Jed wetted his lips. "Did you check my dad's shop?"

The man's scowl deepened. "You know I did. They weren't there. You were the only other person in that shop. You have to know where they are."

"My dad took care of the business. I just helped him out, back in the storeroom and all. I didn't do anything with the merchandise but store it."

The man poked the barrel of the shotgun in Jed's chest. "Where did he stash the coins?"

Jed knew the fellow wouldn't hesitate to shoot him. He couldn't tell the man his sister had taken possession of the coins. As he sought for a way out of the mess without lying, a whistle pierced the air, then Percy called from outside.

"Yahoo, in the house! Anyone home?" Percy's fist thumped on the door.

"Don't say a word," the intruder growled. He kept hold of Jed's arm and dragged him back toward the door. "Make a peep and you and the old fellow are both dead."

The man must have checked out the situation if he knew Percy's age. Jed knew he had to do something to save Percy, but what? He was skinny and just a kid. This fellow was big. Massive muscles bulged under his shirt. As Jed was dragged toward the door, he glanced around for anything he could use as a weapon. Nothing but a puny broom that would be no match for a shotgun.

"Lucy? Nate!" Percy's voice came again, louder this time.

Jed prayed the old cook wouldn't come inside. This fellow would shoot first and ask questions later. He stumbled over the threshold of the door as the man thrust him forward. He lost his balance and fell onto his knees. The man was walking so fast that he was unable to stop his forward momentum. His boot struck Jed's leg, and he tumbled over the top of Jed's back and sprawled onto his belly. The gun went flying into the dirt.

Jed scrambled to his feet and leaped for the gun. He got there first and his fingers wrapped around the barrel. He yanked it up. Rolling to his back, he pointed it toward where the man had been, but the intruder was on his feet and rushing for his horse tethered to a tree in the backyard. Jed rushed toward him, but it was too late. Before Jed could shout, the fellow was riding away.

Shaken, Jed lowered his gun and went to find Percy, but the cook had left without realizing the danger Jed had been in.

WHERE WAS THAT boy? Nate glanced at his pocket watch and shook his head. He'd told Jed to hurry, but the lad had been gone over an hour and a half. Nate had gotten the cattle moved to the next field over without the lariat he needed, and it was time to move on to the next field. He didn't dare do that until Jed returned because the boy wouldn't know where to find him. He dismounted and waited for Jed.

"Took you long enough," he said a little while later when the boy got close enough to hear him.

"Sorry," Jed said, his voice strained.

Nate stared at Jed's white face. "What's wrong? Is Lucy all right?"

"She wasn't home."

Nate mounted his horse. "Did she leave a note?"

"I—I didn't look."

There was a rip in Jed's pants at the knee. "Did the horse throw you?"

The boy's head came up, and indignation settled on his expression. "No."

Nate pointed to Jed's pants. "You fell somewhere."

Jed bit his lip. "I fell in the yard."

"You're rattled. What happened, Jed?"

His chin trembled. "There was a man there," he blurted out.

Nate straightened in the saddle. "Larson?"

Jed shook his head. "A stranger. He was looking for the coins."

"What coins?"

Jed held his gaze. "I told you someone was after us but that I couldn't talk about it."

Nate was about to shake it out of the lad. "I think you'd better if we have intruders to deal with."

"I'm trying to!"

The boy looked like he was about to cry. Nate quelled his impatience. "I'm listening. I won't interrupt again."

"Dad told me not to tell anyone, but Lucy found the coins." Jed heaved a sigh.

Nate listened as Jed told him a long tale about pawned coins and an accident in the rain. "So you think your dad was *murdered*?" Jed's eyes filled, and Nate wanted to embrace him, but since it was impossible on horseback, he settled for reaching over and gripping Jed's shoulder. "Did you see who ran the buggy off the street?"

Jed rubbed his forehead. "The doctor said I had amnesia from the accident. I think I'm almost going to remember everything and it goes black. It makes me so *mad*!"

The boy must have seen something that frightened him. Nate squeezed his hand, then released it. "So what about the man?"

"He said he wanted the coins. So he's tracked us here, Nate. He was big and mean."

"You managed to get rid of him. I'm proud of you. You're sure he didn't hurt Lucy or Eileen?"

Jed shook his head. "He was looking in the window when I got there, and they were already gone. I think he was checking to see if the cabin was empty before he searched it."

"Then he demanded the coins. Where are they?"

"I don't know. Lucy has them."

She hadn't said a word to him about it this morning. Didn't married people share their problems? She'd smiled and seemed unconcerned about anything when he got up. Surely that wasn't *hurt* squeezing his chest. "Do you know how much they're worth?"

Jed stared at him as if trying to decide whether to tell him. "Dad said they were worth over a million dollars."

"What?" Nate laughed and shook his head. "That's not possible. For coins?"

Jed nodded. "They're rare. Collectors pay a lot for them."

"I need to see them," Nate said, humoring him. "Let's get chores done, then we'll talk to your sister."

EIGHTEEN

❧

"Meeting you is cause for celebration," Aunt Sally said. "Shall we celebrate by going to Emma's for lunch?"

Lucy hated to think they would spend money on her when they could use it themselves. "How about we fix lunch together here, then go for a walk and see the flowers?"

Relief settled over her aunt's face. "Splendid idea. Fanny made some vegetable soup this morning, and I'm sure it's ready by now."

"I like soup." Eileen was sitting on the floor serving pretend tea to a china doll Fanny had gotten out for her.

"The bread is still warm," Fanny said, rising from the sofa.

"Let me help you."

"I'll let you two girls do the cooking while I get to know Eileen better," Aunt Sally said.

Lucy followed her cousin into the tiny kitchen dominated by a massive woodstove. The soup bubbled in a kettle and filled the room with a delicious aroma. She stirred it with a spoon Fanny handed her. "Have you lived here all your life?" she asked Fanny.

Fanny began to cut thick slices of bread on a board. "Oh yes. In this same house."

"And your father?"

"He went away a year ago. I still miss him most terribly. Mama says he's watching out for us in heaven and finding us the best mansion."

Lucy smiled. "I like the way you said he 'went away.' It reminds me that Mama and Dad aren't gone forever. They've just gone on ahead. Do you have any brothers and sisters?"

"Just one brother. Mama said she wanted a houseful, but the Lord didn't think she could handle that many. My brother, John, has a small ranch about five miles west. When Mama heard you were here, she told him to come to Sunday dinner and we'd try to get you here too."

"I'd like that." Nate would never agree to sit down to dinner with Uncle Drew. She would worry about that later. "Fanny, do you have a beau?"

Color stained Fanny's cheeks. "Not really. I was engaged once, but he went away."

"Y-You mean he went on to heaven too?"

Fanny shook her head. "Sorry, no, I mean he left town without a word. It's been a year, and I still don't know what happened to him. He didn't leave a note or anything." Her voice thickened, and she swiped her eye with a finger.

"I'm so sorry."

Fanny cleared her throat. "It's all right. I'm over him."

Lucy doubted the truth of that statement, but she didn't say anything more about the young man because her aunt came into the kitchen with a box in her hand. Eileen scampered behind her.

Her aunt's smile was bright. "I knew I had this somewhere, but I didn't say anything because I feared I'd have trouble finding it. This was your mother's. It has some mementos and a photo-graph or two, I think. I thought you'd like to see them."

"I'd *love* to see them!" Lucy wiped her hands on a towel and reached for the box.

"Sit here at the table. You may keep it, my dear."

Lucy's throat tightened. "Thank you, Aunt Sally. I have so little of my mother's. Just this locket, a watch, and the dress she was married in, really."

Her aunt sat beside her and patted her hand. "Let's see what's in here."

The box was made of wood and shaped like a small chest. Aunt Sally lifted the lid and laid it back on its leather hinges. The pungent odor of old wood wafted to Lucy's nose as she peered inside. "A dance card?" She lifted the item from the jum-ble inside.

"That was from the dance where she saw your father for the first time in four years. My, he was a handsome sight that day. All the girls sighed after him, but he never had eyes for anyone but Jane from that day on."

Lucy stared at the dance card. Her father's initials were scrawled on every space. "It appears he didn't give her the opportunity to slip away," she said, smiling. "Dad had a way of taking charge."

"I think you are a little that way yourself."

"Perhaps." Lucy laid the card to one side and dug into the box again.

She found an autograph book and began to thumb through it. Several girlfriends had written flowery compliments. She found her father's bold signature and smiled. Sorting through the memo-rabilia made her parents seem closer. Pushing aside a jumble of ribbons, she found a locket.

"Our father gave that to her for her sixteenth birthday," Aunt Sally said. "Her picture is inside."

Lucy fumbled with the catch and opened it. A young woman stared back at her in the typical, nonsmiling pose. Lucy caught her breath. "It's the same picture I have in my locket. I look much like her."

"Indeed. No wonder Nate snatched you up. He succeeded where his father failed."

Henry again. "Was Mr. Stanton upset when Mama married my father?"

"Oh yes. The men resorted to fisticuffs. He bloodied your father's lip before it was all done. It was at the dance when their engagement was announced. But a week later Henry was engaged too. To Mary Bristol. She'd loved Henry all her life. Everyone knew Henry was just trying to save face. He hated to lose at anything." She smiled. "Though I will say the two men didn't let their disagreement change their friendship."

"I can see that about Henry. He was most insistent . . ." She broke off, aware she'd said more than she wanted.

"Insistent?"

What could it hurt to tell her aunt the truth? "My marriage to Nate was by proxy. Mr. Stanton persuaded me to marry Nate sight unseen. I'd just lost my job and we were about to be evicted from our home. I had nowhere to go, so I agreed."

Her aunt and cousin wore identical expressions of horror. Fanny was the first to speak. "I wish you the very best."

"Nate is very kind. I'm sure we'll get along quite well." Did they dislike Nate so much? "And your father, Aunt Sally? I heard such a sad story about his death."

"Unfortunately, the story is quite true. There is much bad

blood between your husband's family and mine. Though I harbor no such unseemly emotions."

Lucy's love for her aunt grew. "I hope to bring healing someday."

Her aunt smiled. "I wish you well in that endeavor, my dear."

FLOWER BOXES ADDED a splash of occasional color as Lucy strolled with her cousin along the dusty street. Eileen had fallen asleep after lunch, and Aunt Sally had offered to stay home while the child napped so the younger women could have some time.

"I'm so glad you're here," Fanny said when they paused outside the millinery shop. The picture window displayed hats lavish with lace. "I hope you won't take this amiss, but you're not at all what I expected. I believe we shall be great friends."

Lucy's attention had been caught by the hats that were in last year's fashion. She turned from the window to embrace her cousin. "I think so too," she said, smiling back. "What were you expecting?"

Fanny stared at her. "When Uncle Drew said you weren't coming, I thought you were too uppity to associate with us. Or that you intended to take up the feud between our families."

"I would like to heal it." In Lucy's dreams she saw them all gathered together for Christmas dinner. A true spirit of love and union between both families.

"I'm not sure that's possible. Uncle Drew will never rest until he possesses that land again."

"Is it so very valuable? I don't understand why it matters so much."

"Our grandfather's death changed Uncle Drew," Fanny said. "I remember how fun-loving he used to be. He feels people don't treat him the same. It's a badge of honor to him that the town was named after our family. He feels he's lost status without the land."

"Is that true?"

"I don't feel it. The townspeople are very friendly to us anyway." Fanny pointed to the bench outside the café. "Care to sit a moment?"

Lucy's shoes were pinching her toes, so she nodded and followed her cousin to the wooden bench. As they neared the café, a man exited the building. He was in his twenties and was dressed in the latest style of a cutaway morning coat over his trousers.

The scowl he wore changed to a smile when his gaze swept over the ladies. He doffed his hat and bowed. "Ladies, you're enough to make a man forget everything on his mind." He stared hard at Lucy.

Under his intent gaze, Lucy's cheeks heated. "Good afternoon."

"I don't believe we've met," Fanny said. "Are you a newcomer to our town?"

"Ah, you've caught me." He replaced his hat. "I just got to town yesterday. Rolf Watson at your service."

Since she was the matron, it was Lucy's duty to take charge. She rose and extended her hand. "Pleased to meet you, Mr. Watson. I'm Mrs. Lucy Stanton, and this is my cousin, Miss Fanny Donnelly."

"The pleasure is all mine." He bowed over her hand, then pressed his lips to the back of it.

The man was smooth. Lucy could tell Fanny was interested in the handsome stranger. His blond hair fell across his forehead, and his eyes were a deep blue. Lucy couldn't tell if the glint in his eyes was mockery or genuine admiration.

"You're new to town yourself, I hear, Mrs. Stanton."

"How did you know that?"

He shrugged. "Small towns only have small interests to talk about."

She didn't like the derision in his voice. In fact, she didn't like him very much at all. The stare he kept shooting at her sent prickles down her spine. She shouldn't be so silly. Her fear was just a reaction to the discovery of the coins.

She took Fanny by the arm. "Well, we must be going. Nice to meet you, Mr. Watson. I hope you enjoy your visit here. What was your purpose, by the way?"

"I didn't say," he said, an edge in his voice. "Quite boring business, I'm afraid."

"How long will you be in town?" Fanny fluttered her lashes at him.

"However long it takes for me to conclude my business," he said. "I wonder if I might call on you, Miss Fanny? Would you agree to take supper with me tonight?"

Say no. Lucy gave a light squeeze to her cousin's arm, but it was no use. Fanny lifted her head and smiled. Her eyes were bright and her dimples flashed again. Lucy could have groaned.

"I should like that, Mr. Watson," Fanny said. "But my mother will have to give permission."

"I'll stop by and introduce myself," he said smoothly. "About five?"

"That will be splendid," Fanny said breathlessly.

Lucy watched him tip his hat and stroll down the street. "I wish you wouldn't go with him, Fanny."

"You sound like you're fifty instead of twenty-two." Her cousin's face suffused with color. "There's not a man in town who interests me. It's about time we had some new and interesting men appear. I liked him. Why didn't you?"

Lucy considered the question and didn't know how to answer. He'd been perfectly polite. How did she tell Fanny that it was intuition? "Didn't you find him much too forward?"

Fanny shrugged. "He's obviously from the city. Perhaps they are used to seeing something they want and going after it."

"If he wants you, I'm even more alarmed."

"Don't be such a matron. Let's get back to the house so I can tell Mama about Mr. Watson. I'm sure she'll be delighted."

Lucy gripped her cousin's arm when Fanny turned to retrace their steps. "Fanny, he didn't ask where you lived. It was as if he already knew."

Fanny's expression clouded, then cleared. "I'm sure someone inside the café told him. You know how people talk."

Lucy followed Fanny slowly. Something about the entire conversation seemed off.

THE SUN WAS touching the tops of the trees as Nate and Jed rode back into the yard. Lantern light spilled from the kitchen window, and he smelled the woodstove. "Bet your sister has supper ready for us."

"You going to tell her?" Jed's freckles stood out on his white face. He looked tired.

"Yep."

Jed shifted uneasily. "She's gonna be mad that I told you."

"I'm her husband and your brother. We're all in this together."

Jed's smile came then. "I always wanted a brother." He looked down at his hands. "I tried to be the man of the house, but Lucy wouldn't let me. She still thought I was a kid."

"She's like your mama. Mothers are like that. So I hear."

"Lucy always seems to know what to do."

"I've noticed that about her." For a little lady, she had a will of iron. He wondered where it came from.

"She's more like a mom than my real mom." The lad dismounted and led his horse toward the barn.

"Hang on." Nate leaped to the ground and handed his reins to Jed. "Curry them and do the chores. I'll be inside."

Jed straightened and smiled as he realized Nate was giving him full responsibility. "Yes, sir. I mean, thanks, Nate!"

Still smiling, Nate knocked the mud off his boots at the door, then entered the cabin where he caught a whiff of something that made his mouth water. "Beef stew?" he asked when he saw Lucy at the stove.

She turned and wiped her hands on the checkered apron that covered her blue dress. "It's nearly ready. Where's Jed?"

"Doing chores. Where's Eileen?"

Eileen's face peeked around Lucy's skirts. "I'm here."

"Want to help Jed with chores?"

"Can I get the eggs?"

"Yep. Be careful not to break them."

"I'll be careful," she promised.

Lucy grabbed the egg basket and handed it to her. Once the door slammed, Nate pulled out a chair. "Coffee?" He hated to launch into questions. It would do his heart good if Lucy would willingly take him into her confidence.

She poured him a cup of coffee and set it in front of him. "Is something wrong?"

"You tell me. Jed came back to get me a rope about midday."

She flushed. "I know I said I wasn't going to meet my family today, but I changed my mind."

He hadn't even been wondering where she'd gone. "You went to Larson's?"

"No. I went to see my Aunt Sally. I met Fanny too. My uncle wasn't around."

At least she hadn't spent any time with Larson. "Your aunt is a sweet lady. It's not her fault that her brother is the way he is."

"You're not mad?"

He shook his head. "Your uncle and I are at odds, but I have no quarrel with your aunt and cousin."

He took a sip of his hot coffee. "Jed interrupted an intruder."

She'd started back to the stove, but she whirled to face him again. "Was he hurt?"

"He got the gun out of the barn and ran him off. I was proud of him. He found the guy peering in the back window, then stopped him as he entered the back door."

"D-Did Jed know what he wanted? Maybe he was looking for food?"

She wasn't going to tell him about the coins. But why would she? They were still strangers. She had to wonder if some of the lies Larson had told her might be true.

He held her gaze. "You know what he was looking for, Lucy."

She went scarlet, then white. "He was from Indiana?" she whispered.

He nodded. "He tried to get Jed to tell him where the coins were."

"Jed told you."

"I wish you would have."

Her blue eyes pleaded for understanding. "I didn't want to worry you until I figured out what to do."

He took her hand. Soft yet so competent. "We're married. It's a husband's duty to figure things out and shoulder the burdens. You need to let go a little of that iron control."

"I've always been the one to decide how to handle problems. Asking for help doesn't come easily."

Stubborn woman. Even now she wasn't admitting she should have come to him. "Where are the coins?"

She hesitated. "Safe."

He pressed his lips together. "I'm not going to steal them, Lucy."

"Of course not. I-I'd rather leave them where they are."

"And where is that?"

She caught her lower lip between perfect white teeth. "In the pickle barrel."

A bark of laughter escaped his throat. "Only a woman would put something that valuable in pickles."

"I thought I'd talk to the sheriff and see if he could telegraph the Wabash police. Maybe we could find out who they belong to."

She didn't want to keep them? He studied her transparent expression and saw only concern to do what was right. "It sounds as though they belong to you. Your father purchased them for a price the owner was willing to sell."

She turned back to the stove and stirred the stew, then turned toward him again. "I've been thinking about that. What if the man who sold them to my father had stolen them? And the real owner is trying to get them back?"

"There's one hole in your theory. If whoever is after them is the legitimate owner, he would have shown up with the police and would have proven his ownership."

Her expression fell. "I didn't think of that. So whoever broke in today knows their value and wants to steal them. But how would he know?"

"I don't know. I'll see what I can find out."

"You'll go with me to talk to the sheriff?"

She still didn't trust him to take charge. He suppressed his irritation. "I don't trust the sheriff. He's friends with Larson. This needs to be kept very quiet or you'll have every thief in Texas creeping around in the dark."

She shuddered. "Then what?"

"I'll talk to Pa and get his advice. Let me handle it, Lucy. Just let go of your worry."

She chewed her lip. "I'll try."

NINETEEN

⚬❧❧⚬

Lucy could almost feel the coins vibrating from their place in the cellar.

Eileen and Jed were both asleep, and the lantern's dim glow left shadows dancing in the small room. She cast surreptitious glances at Nate as he sat reading his Bible by the fire. She'd seen his disappointment in her failure to tell him about the coins. How did she make it right? This problem involved events that had happened long before she'd ever met him. He shouldn't have to shoulder a burden like this. She wanted him to like her—to think she was capable and strong. Asking for his help undermined her competence.

She chewed her lip and sighed. Maybe she needed to bend a little here. Without interrupting him, she went to the back porch and lit a candle. Holding it aloft, she went out the back door and lifted the cellar door.

Descending into the darkness with only a small flame was like walking into a black hole. The dank odor rushed at her and left her feeling off balance. She reached the bottom of the rickety stairs and held up the candle so its puny light pushed back the shadows. The pickle barrel didn't appear to have been disturbed.

She set the candle on a shelf, then pried off the barrel lid and thrust her hand into the pickles. The pungent aroma filled her nose. For a moment she feared they were missing, then her fingers snagged the oilcloth. She pulled it up and unwrapped the cloth. The coins were all there.

She heard the stairs squeak and whirled. A large shape moved toward her. "Who's there?"

His figure loomed in the shadows. "It's me. What are you doing?" Nate's voice was husky.

"Getting the coins."

"No need. They're safe where they are for now."

The steps groaned one last time, then he was beside her. She held them out to him, but he closed her fingers back over the coins. "You don't have to give them to me."

"I want to. I'm sorry if I made you feel I didn't trust you." She stared at the money in her hand. "I'm beginning to realize I am much too fond of being in charge."

"We have a lot of adjusting to do. It's not going to happen all at once."

Nate's presence made the cold air feel warmer. Though the cellar was hardly a romantic spot, Lucy found herself wanting to move closer. To rest her head on his chest. To relinquish her solitude. Was that what becoming one meant? When one bled, the other cried out? Though she loved her siblings, she'd never felt that sense of union.

"Last chance." She held out the coins.

He gave them a cursory glance. "Put them back. It's too dark to see them anyway."

She turned back to the barrel and replaced the coins, then dropped the lid back into place. She wiped the vinegar from her hands on her apron, then took the candle in her right hand.

His warm hand gripped her left one. "Let's get out of here. There are better places to talk."

His tone was so prosaic that she couldn't help the disappointment that shot through her. Did he have no desire to hold her, to brush his lips across hers? "As you wish," she said, keeping her voice impersonal. She left her hand in his and allowed him to lead her up the stairs. He so unsettled her that she lost her balance until he steadied her.

"Careful." He gripped her hand. "I need to build new steps. These tilt. I don't want you to take a tumble with your hands full."

At least he cared a little. Enough that he didn't want her hurt. In the yard she tilted her face up to him. "Why don't you want to at least see the coins? After all, they are worth a fortune."

The moonlight illuminated his grin. "Maybe I should have looked at them. Jed says they look like regular silver dollars. Nothing that special. I can't imagine someone paying that kind of money just to put them in a drawer somewhere. That kind of hoarding doesn't make sense."

"When does acquiring more and more land translate to hoarding?" she countered. As soon as the words were out of her mouth, she wanted to snatch them back.

He stiffened and dropped her hand. "Land has a use. We can run more cattle and expand our business."

"Why?" She tried to ask her question in a genuinely curious tone without any condemnation. "If we have enough to live, why do we need more?"

He opened his mouth, then shut it again. "Good question,

Lucy. Pa has always drilled it into my head that the Stanton spread is going to be the biggest cattle ranch in Texas."

"So it's all about power?"

"Maybe. More land meant more cattle. More cattle meant more jobs for men and a productive life. I've never analyzed it."

She started to ask him if he didn't trust God to provide when it struck her that she was the same way. If she was going to talk to him about his trust issues, she needed to work on her own first.

NATE STILL CAUGHT a whiff or two of vinegar from Lucy's small hands even though she'd washed them the minute they got back inside. He poked at the fire and added two more logs before joining her on the rug in front of the fire. "Why aren't you in the chair?"

She sat watching the flames with her knees hugged to her chest. "I like to sit on the floor. It feels more homey." She scooted over to make more room for him.

He stretched out his legs and leaned back on his elbows. The braided rug was rough against his palms. "You miss Indiana?"

The firelight illuminated her pensive expression. "Not really." She hesitated. "It feels like we belong here. I know that sounds odd when we're still strangers to the area, but it was like coming home."

He sat up and scooted around to face her. "You asked me in the cellar why I wanted more land. What are your dreams, Lucy?"

Her eyes widened and she caught her lower lip between her teeth. "I've never had time to have a dream. I tried to keep my brother and sister safe from one day to the next, to feed and clothe them and make sure they were content."

"I think something more than their welfare pushed you to agree to my father's suggestion. If you dare to uncover it." He studied her expression as he issued his challenge. So beautiful and yet he still hadn't learned much about her.

She pulled her knees more tightly to her chest and propped her chin on them. "I want a family," she said after a long pause. "I love Jed and Eileen, but they will go off on their own someday. I've never felt as though I belonged anywhere. I want a family and a home where I belong."

He absorbed her words. "You've never felt you were in a place of permanence?"

Her eyes brightened. "That's it exactly. I've felt that whatever state I'm in is bound to change soon. The very uncertainty has made me long for security. For a place that is all mine. A family I can nurture and love." She swallowed.

Her words stirred something inside him, a nameless longing for what she talked about. "I've only had my father and my brother. Three grumpy men trying to rub along together as best as we could."

She released her knees and knelt in front of him. "We want the same thing then, Nate. I think we can find it together if we try. We're both—lonely."

With a shock, he realized she was right. He'd always had his father around, but there weren't many moments when he'd felt connected on more than a work level. "I didn't realize I was lonely until you said it. How did you know?"

"I saw it in your eyes the first time Eileen took your hand," she said softly.

"She's too sweet to ignore."

"You haven't been around children much, have you?"

He shook his head and glanced toward the little girl, sleeping peacefully on her cot. One small fist was curled under her cheek. His heart contracted. "Only in the most casual way at church or the neighbors'."

"You're older than Roger?"

"By a year. We grew up together and were rounding up stray calves by the time we were eight."

"I was cooking and cleaning like an adult by about that age myself." She leaned a little closer. "Have you ever seen a real family in action? Both parents, children around the dinner table, everyone supportive of each other?"

It was difficult to think with her so close. He couldn't look away from the intent expression in her blue eyes. "I don't believe I have."

"I saw a touch of it at my aunt's house today. Though her husband is gone, his presence was felt. And my cousin is so close to her mother. I didn't want to leave them."

The O'Briens were his closest neighbors, and Margaret hardly had an ideal relationship with her father. On the other side were the Larsons, and he vaguely remembered going to dinner there when he was a youngster. The table had been full, but conversation had been stilted. The children were expected to keep silent, and they'd eaten quietly, then were shooed outside to play.

"Do you think we can do a better job?" she asked, her voice wistful. "I read *Little Women* a few years ago, and I realized I wanted a family like that. One that laughed and played together."

"*Little Women*? Is that a novel?"

She nodded eagerly. "I brought my copy with me if you'd like to read it. It's about four sisters during the Civil War. I wanted to be part of that family. Even though they were as poor as me, they were rich in family. And their last name was March. That was close enough to Marsh to make them feel like my own sisters."

"I'm not much of a reader. Other than the Bible." He cleared his throat. "Though I'd read it if you'd like me to."

"We're going to do this, aren't we, Nate? Become a family?"

"We are. It won't be easy though. We're still strangers. But I want to remedy that." He glanced toward the table beside her chair. "I'd like us to start by reading the Bible together as a family in the evening."

Her eyes went wide. "Oh, I'd like that! Where shall we start? Proverbs 31?"

He smiled. "I think the Bible has things to teach both of us, not just you. Let's start in Ephesians."

"I don't quite remember what all is there. It's about families?"

He nodded. "Husbands are told to love their wives. I'd like to learn to love you, Lucy. I don't think it will be hard to do."

Her face was only inches away. Her lips parted, and he caught a whiff of her sweet breath. A strong urge to kiss her overtook him. He didn't realize his arms were on her shoulders until he felt the fabric of her dress under his palms.

He pulled her closer and bent his head. His lips touched hers and he inhaled the scent of lavender that surrounded her. She was soft and warm in his arms, and he drank in the sweetness of her kiss.

TWENTY

⸎

P a didn't look as bad as Nate had feared. He was sitting in
the rocker on the porch with the cat on his lap when Nate
helped Lucy down from the buggy. Cowboys stared as the
sun lit her face. Nate moved to block their view. How long would
it take to get used to the way other men stared at his wife? She sure
was a pretty little thing.

"Take your sister to see the kittens in the barn," he told Jed.
"I'll have Percy call when chow is ready." The boy nodded and
led Eileen off toward the barn. Several puppies with round bellies
rolled together in the grass by the porch as he offered his arm to
Lucy and escorted her to the house.

"You kids are a sight for sore eyes." Henry pushed the cat to
the porch. "Sit down and tell me what you've been up to."

Nate noticed he didn't get up. His dad's color was still a little
off too. He pulled two other chairs close to his father's. "How you
feeling, Pa?"

His father waved a big hand in the air. "Better than I can convince Percy. He's about to drive me crazy. I'm not an invalid. He's

been fussing over me like I'm a newborn calf." He stared at Lucy. "My boy treating you okay, Lucy?"

She arranged her skirts and looked up with a smile. "Of course. We're getting settled in. I have the cabin cleaned and organized."

His pa stared at her with an intent expression. "Good, good."

Nate stretched his legs out in front of him. "Listen, Pa, we have a problem and we need your advice."

"You haven't had a fight already, have you?"

Nate grinned. "We're fine. At least for now. But we had a break-in yesterday. Luckily, Lucy wasn't home. I think we need to find a good private investigator."

His father straightened. "Investigator?"

"Lucy, you want to explain?" he asked. She nodded, and Nate sat quietly as she went over how she came to be in possession of the coins.

His father didn't speak until she was done. "I don't see what the problem is, girl. Your pa bought them fair and square. The coins are part of his estate now. They belong to you."

She shook her head. "They might not, though. What if the man who sold them to Dad got them illegally?" She glanced at Nate. "I was thinking about what you said, Nate. About how if they'd been stolen the true owner would have shown up with the police. But what if the man who sold them to my father was part of a gang and sold them by himself? His partners might be the ones trying to get them back."

"If that were true, he wouldn't have taken such a paltry sum for them. He would have known their worth."

She chewed her lip. "I hadn't thought of that. Perhaps you're right."

His father leaned over and patted her hand. "It's admirable

that you don't want to possess illegal goods, Lucy, but don't worry about it. I'm sure the law is on your side. Think what we could do to expand our holdings with that kind of money."

"It's Lucy's property, Pa. She can do what she wants with it."

His father's expression turned thunderous. "Ridiculous," he muttered. "A man knows what's best for his family."

Nate stared at his father. He'd never seen him take such a contemptuous tone toward women. But then, they hadn't been around women much. "It's Lucy's say."

"Is it the *right* thing to do?" Lucy asked. "I'm more concerned with what's right than what's legal."

His father's scowl deepened. "What will satisfy you? We will get this settled, then you can spend that money without qualms."

Lucy glanced at Nate then back to his father. "To find out if anyone has reported them missing. That would help. And to see if the Indiana police know anything about the man who was killed."

His father glanced at Nate, and Nate nodded. "That's why I need a good investigator."

"Or the police," Lucy put in.

"You sure don't want to talk to the sheriff here," his pa said. "I'll see what I can find out. An investigator might want to see the coins and take imprints so they can be identified. Can you bring them to me?"

Lucy tensed and Nate realized she didn't want to unearth the coins. "Let's see what the investigator has to say first. He might just need to know what they are. Jed said their father said they were 1804 Dexter dollars. That might be enough to track them."

His pa's lips tightened. "It might take a few days to hear back."

His father was used to having his every command obeyed. He

and Lucy were sure to tangle at some point. Nate wanted to be around when that happened. Two such strong-willed people couldn't get along forever. "Thanks, Pa. Let us know what you hear." He glanced at Lucy, who sat with her hands folded in her lap.

She held his gaze, then turned hers to his father. "I met my aunt and cousin yesterday."

His father bristled. "I hope you didn't allow them to smear your new name."

"Of course not. They are much too genteel to air their grievances."

"They have no grievances. Not against me or any other Stanton. I bought that land fair and square."

Nate decided to change the subject before his father had another heart attack. "Any news on our bull?"

The older man shook his head. "I reckon we won't get him back. Best be looking for a replacement. I hear Zeller has a strong bull with good lines he might be convinced to sell."

"I'll check it out. How much do you want to spend?"

His father shrugged. "Use your own judgment. We want our brand to mean something. If that means we have to pay big bucks for a proper bull, we will."

Sure as the world, Nate would buy a bull, and his father would find fault with either the bull or the price. "When you're feeling better, we'll look at him together. I might go to Dallas and look at some at auction next month."

"We need a replacement sooner than that."

Nate started to argue, then decided against it. His father was determined to be obstinate today. Was it because he saw his strength slipping away and wanted to exercise his control to compensate? Sympathy stirred in Nate's chest. Someday he would be older and weaker too.

HENRY FOUND AN investigator but had said nothing more about needing to see the coins. Lucy tried not to think about them in the cellar for a few days. The men were out in the fields today but close by, so Lucy decided she would fix a nice noonday dinner for them. They were going to be cutting calves so they'd be tired and hungry when they came in. She set a chicken on to boil at eight, then cut noodles to dry.

Dinner was ready by one. Lucy kept glancing worriedly through the window but saw no sign of her menfolk. By one thirty she was becoming angry, and by two she was downright livid. In fact, if the men didn't come in soon, the noodles would be over-cooked and the chicken would be dry as chalk. It was the height of inconsideration to let this fine food go to waste.

"We might as well eat without them, Eileen."

Lucy lifted her sister onto the chair, then ladled up rubbery noodles and stringy chicken. It tasted as bad as it looked. Eileen picked at her plate, and Lucy finally gave her a piece of warm bread spread with butter and jam. By the time she put Eileen down for her nap, Lucy's anger was white-hot. She rehearsed all the things she would say to Nate when he got in. And Jed. He knew better.

She started to dump the remains of the meal into a dish to give Bridget when she got back with the men, then stopped and stared at the food. They would just have to eat it. Where she came from, food was a precious commodity. If it was not the best now, maybe that would teach Mr. Nate Stanton to be on time for a meal next time.

Lucy put the pan back on the stove to stay warm, then felt the clothes hanging around the cabin. They were dry, so she took them down and folded them. She carried Nate's up the ladder to his room. His bed had not been made, and she clicked her tongue at her forgetfulness. She would have to remember tomorrow.

She threw the covers up over the bed, and her foot hit something under the bed. Curious, she knelt and peered in the darkness. A battered metal box, about six inches by eight inches, was the only thing under there. She laid a hand on the cool surface and pulled it to her. For a moment she hesitated. Maybe it was something private. But she was his wife, and they should have no secrets from one another.

She inched open the lid. Inside were a journal and a daguerreo-type. Lucy picked up the photo. It was of a young woman holding a baby. She had a look about her that reminded her of Nate. Lucy was looking at Nate's mother. She was lovely, with a cloud of thick, dark hair and Nate's stubborn mouth and expressive eyes.

A lump in her throat, Lucy dropped the picture back into the box and picked up the journal. It looked old, too old to be Nate's personal journal. The battered leather cover felt loved and worn in her hand, and the pages smelled old and stale.

She opened the first page. Mary Elizabeth Stanton. His mother's journal. Tears stung Lucy's eyes. Poor motherless boy. This was all he had of his mother, all the experience he had of women as well, just some brief memories of a long-dead mother. No wonder his father was determined to find him a wife.

She read several pages. Mary had a gentle heart, and it appeared Henry had ruled the house tightly. There was a mention of his anger when she'd burned chicken one night. On another page Mary said he'd sold her favorite horse to pay for a new bull. She'd grieved that he'd done it without asking her. But in spite of having an autocratic husband, Mary had sprinkled her journal with bits of poetry, verses of Scripture, and hints of her sweet spirit.

Lucy wished she could have known the woman. Had Nate ever read this and seen his father through Mary's eyes? Roger's warning had begun to make a little more sense. Lucy would have to find the line between respect and keeping up necessary boundaries. It wouldn't be easy without talking to Nate about it.

She put the journal back into the box. She shouldn't have read it, not without Nate's permission and knowledge. It was too private, almost sacred. Her anger mostly evaporated, she finished making the bed, then dropped the freshly folded clothes into a box that served as Nate's chest.

She had just finished putting the clothes away when she heard a horse neigh in the yard. Compressing her lips, she glanced out the window. Jed was still mounted, but Nate jumped to the ground and was opening the barn door.

Lucy lifted the watch that hung around her neck. The watch had belonged to her mama and offered her some comfort as she checked the time. Four o'clock, almost time for supper, and the uneaten dinner sat congealing on the stove. Her anger raged again, and she went down to meet them.

NATE WAS BONE weary, and his stomach was gnawing on his backbone. Jed had made several pointed comments about dinner around one o'clock, but Nate had ignored him. The lad needed to grow up and realize that a man didn't go running home when his belly got a little empty. He didn't go home until the work was done, and there hadn't been a good time to take a break, even though he'd told Lucy they would be home for lunch.

"Help me curry the horses, and we'll see if Lucy can rustle us up some grub."

The boy's shoulders drooped, and Nate almost relented, then remembered he was supposed to be teaching Jed how to be a man. He was responsible for Jed now. He shoved open the sliding door to the barn and led his horse inside. They quickly curried the horses and turned them out into the stable. Nate tossed a pitchfork full of hay over the fence, then clapped Jed on the back.

"You did a man's work today, Jed. I was mighty proud of you."

Jed's chest swelled, and if his grin were any bigger, it would have split his face. "Thank you, sir."

"You as hungry as I am?"

Jed nodded. "Lucy is probably wondering where we are."

"She knew we were working." Nate started toward the house. "I'm sure she figured out we were busy when we didn't make it back."

A strange aroma wafted toward him when he opened the door. It smelled like something charred and a bit like glue. Whatever it was, it didn't smell appetizing. Still, Nate would put a good face on it and force it down. He was hungry enough to eat whatever she threw at him.

He forced a smile. "Smells like something's cooking."

Lucy stood and put her fists on her hips. "Something *was* cooking. Now something is burned. But help yourself." She made a sweeping gesture toward the cookstove. "If you dare." Her eyebrows lifted in challenge.

Nate looked at Jed, and Jed looked at Nate. Nate knew he wore the same expression the boy did. A look of panic and dismay. He sidled over to the stove and glanced in the pan. It might have been chicken and noodles once, but now it more resembled a sticky gob of glue.

"Uh, looks good," he said lamely. Lucy almost visibly swelled, and he was reminded of an outraged mother hen.

"It was good around one o'clock. Even at two it was still edible. Now it looks—it looks like porridge!" Lucy stalked toward the fireplace and sat beside Eileen. Even Lucy's back and neck looked outraged.

Nate scratched his head. The boy's eyes were round and pleading as he stared from the mess on the stove to Nate.

"Do we have to eat it?" he whispered.

"I heard that, and the answer is yes." Lucy jumped to her feet again. "Maybe it will help you remember to come home in time to eat tomorrow."

Nate frowned. This was not going the way he had pictured the evening. He'd planned to eat a hot, home-cooked meal, then take the buggy over to the main house and check on Pa.

"I see I need to explain the way a ranch works."

"No, I need to explain the way a cook works," Lucy said. "When food is ready to be eaten, the men come and eat it. Jed is a growing boy. He needs to eat three square meals a day. Look at him, Nate. He's skinny as a pitchfork and needs fattening. Providing for my family is one reason I agreed to marry you. And you need to eat three meals a day yourself. If you can't be bothered to come home for dinner, then you need to tell me, and I'll pack you a lunch or bring it to you."

She was right. His heart clenched at the boy's thinness. He

looked back at Lucy. Her cheeks were rosy and her blue eyes sparkled. He grinned. "A bit riled, aren't you? You sure look pretty that
way. Maybe we'll have to try this again tomorrow, Jed."

Her brother grinned, though his eyes were still anxious. He'd
obviously been made to toe the line by his sister before.

For a moment the color in Lucy's cheeks deepened. Then the
corner of her mouth lifted and her dimple appeared. "Don't think
fake compliments will make me forgive you." Though her tone
was severe, her eyes smiled.

He held up his hands and turned to the boy. "She has me, Jed.
I should have realized you would need to be fed. But we'll take our
punishment like men, what do you say?"

Jed gave a doubtful glare at the mess in the pan. "Do we
have to?"

"Are you a man or a rabbit? Come on, this will taste better
than it looks." He grabbed the ladle and tried to scoop some out
of the pan. It stuck to the spoon and refused to drop to the plate.

"I think I'll be a rabbit today," Jed said.

Lucy sighed. "Since you're truly contrite, I'll see if I can find
something edible for you."

Nate shook the spoon again. The glob clung steadfastly to the
spoon. He dropped it back into the pan with a sigh of relief. "Jed
and I will rise up and call you blessed, won't we?"

"If I don't have to eat that slop, I'll even tell everyone she's the
prettiest woman in Indiana," Jed said.

"Indiana, my foot! She's the prettiest woman in the Red River
Valley—in Texas even." Nate caught Lucy by the waist as she
sashayed past him. She smelled good, kind of like fresh-baked
bread. "Do you forgive us?"

"I forgive Jed. I haven't decided about you yet." Her lashes lowered to her cheeks, then she raised them, and he was dazzled by the light in her eyes.

He wished the kids weren't here. How was he supposed to woo his wife with a constant audience? It would be a challenge, but for the first time Nate realized he intended to do just that. Almost against his will, his hands tightened around her waist, and he pulled her against his chest and rested his chin on her head.

"You're staying right here until you tell me I'm forgiven," he said softly.

She struggled to get free for a moment, but then her arms circled his waist, and she stood content in his arms. "I'm not complaining," she said too softly for the kids to hear. She pulled away. "I need to tell you something."

He studied her troubled eyes. "What's wrong?"

"I saw your mother's journal in your room. I must confess I read a few pages. She was a lovely woman, Nate."

His throat tightened. "You can read it all you like, Lucy. I'd like to think my mother is looking down and is happy I have a good wife."

Her eyes filled with tears and she nestled her face against his chest.

His heart soared. She must find him attractive. Maybe even as attractive as he found her. The Bible admonished him to love his wife. He was beginning to realize that might not be too difficult.

TWENTY-ONE

The days sped by in a blur of busyness. Lucy had so much to learn she felt her head must surely explode with the knowledge she stuffed in. She and Nate were still wary around one another, but they were slowly learning about each other. They had begun evening devotions with the children, and he'd given her his mother's journal to read.

Spring had finally come to Texas. Wildflowers brought welcome bits of color to the landscape, and the air was filled with the fragrance of new life. Lucy carted her washtub outside and scrubbed the clothes while Eileen occupied herself "planting" her own small garden, though the seeds were way too deep. Lucy would have to fix it when Eileen wasn't looking.

Lucy rubbed at a spot on Nate's dungarees. Her hands were red and chapped, but who would have thought she would find such satisfaction in caring for a man and his belongings? Nate's prediction about the softness of her hands had proven true, but Lucy didn't mind. Her rough hands were proof of the effort she was putting into this marriage.

She hung the clothes on the line Nate had put up for her and went to the house to start dinner. Nate had told her he would be in the south pasture all day and had asked her to bring the meal to him. Since that one missed meal, he had been conscientious about keeping her informed of his mealtime activities. She allowed herself a small grin at the tiny victory.

"Eileen, it's time to come in."

Lucy went inside and took the bread from the bread box. She cut thick slices and made egg sandwiches, then wrapped them in cloth and put them in a box. She added cheese and the pie she'd made earlier in the day.

She cocked her head and listened. Eileen still hadn't answered her. She went to the back door. "Eileen, come in now!" There was still no answer, so Lucy stepped outside. She sighed when she saw no sign of her sister. Eileen was probably in the barn petting the calf.

Lucy hurried across the yard to the barn. They would have to hurry, or Nate would accuse her of ignoring his mealtime. She shoved open the door and stepped into the dimly lit barn. A shaft of sunlight illuminated the dust motes, and the straw made her sneeze.

"Eileen?"

The only answer she got was the snort of the horse in the far stall and the rustle as the calf shuffled in the hay. Beginning to be alarmed, Lucy turned and ran back to the front yard. "Eileen! Where are you?" She raced around the house several times before she could admit the obvious to herself.

Eileen was nowhere to be found.

Her heart was racing like a runaway train, and her mouth was dry with panic. Shading her eyes, she stared out at the horizon. Where could Eileen be? Lucy was torn between wandering out to find Eileen herself and going for help. Her heart screamed for her to find her sister now, but wisdom dictated finding Nate. He knew the area.

She threw the sidesaddle on Wanda and clambered atop the mare's broad back. Digging her heels into Wanda's sides, she clung desperately to the pommel as the horse broke into a canter. Within minutes she was in sight of the herd of longhorn and could make out Nate's familiar broad shoulders.

At the sight of her husband, tears sprang from her eyes and she began to sob. "Nate!" she screamed. The sound that came out of her mouth was closer to a croak.

Nate's head came up, and he kicked his horse into a run, with Jed right behind him. "What is it? What's wrong?" His gaze darted past her. "Where's Eileen?"

"She's gone! I was doing laundry, and she was playing outside. When I called her for lunch, she was missing." Aware she was beginning to babble, Lucy took a deep breath. "I didn't know where to look."

Nate turned and whistled. "Bridget, come here, girl!" The dog came bounding to him.

The dog. Lucy dared to hope. "Do you think Bridget can find her?"

"She loves Eileen. She'll find her."

They turned and rode back to the cabin. There was no sign of a small blond head anywhere. Lucy fought the tears that wanted to fall. "She's still not here."

"I'll look around just to make sure," Nate said. "Did you check the privy?"

"Yes, she's not there. Let me check again." Lucy rushed to the privy and threw open the door. Empty. Her shoulders drooping, she followed Nate as he strode around the yard and then checked the barn.

He knelt and took Bridget's head in his hands. "Find Eileen, Bridget." He released her. "Go, find Eileen!"

Bridget barked and began sniffing the ground. She circled the privy, then went around to the front. She paused at Eileen's small garden plot and then tore off toward the north.

"Quick, get the horses, we'll follow her!"

Lucy wanted to just run after her, but she'd never keep up with the dog. She grabbed Wanda's reins and managed to mount by herself. Nate and Jed were already ahead of her. She bounced hard in the saddle as Wanda strove to catch them.

She could hear Bridget barking as she made her way toward a meadow by the river. Eileen loved water. Her heart in her mouth, Lucy bent low over Wanda's neck and smacked her hand on the horse's rump. "Eileen!"

Nate and Jed reached the grove of trees, and Lucy got there a moment later. Panting nearly as hard as Wanda, she looked around for her sister. Nothing.

"We'll check the river. You check the area." Nate's voice was grim, and Lucy's eyes filled with tears as she watched him and Jed stalk purposefully toward the river. She could hear the rushing water from here. The Red River could be deadly this time of year.

Then Bridget gave a joyful bark. The dog was leaping happily into the air. Lucy looked closer and saw the still form of her sister on the ground. She rushed to Eileen and reached her just as the little girl sat up and rubbed her eyes sleepily. Bridget licked her face, and Eileen began to cry.

Lucy scooped her into her arms and hugged her fiercely. "Here she is," she shouted.

"Lucy, you're hurting me."

Lucy wanted to loosen her grip, but she couldn't let go. "I thought I'd lost you," she whispered. "Don't ever do that again, Eileen. You know better than to go off without telling me."

Jed and Nate came running. Jed's face was streaked from tears, and Nate's eyes were bright with relief. Jed took his sister from Lucy, and she wrapped her arms and legs around him.

"I looked for you, Jed, but you was hiding," she said reproachfully. "I walked and walked, but you weren't there."

Nate held out his arms for Eileen, and she went to him. He set her on the ground and knelt beside her. "Eileen, what did I tell you about watching out for Lucy?"

She hung her head. "You said to stay close to her all the time, so's I could see her."

"That's right. What did you do today?"

Eileen started to cry. "I just wanted to find you and Jed. I wanted Jed to see my flowers."

"I know, sweetheart, but you disobeyed me. You know what that means, don't you?" Nate's voice was gentle but firm.

"I . . . have to be punished?" Eileen's tears flowed in earnest now.

Nate nodded. "Afraid so."

"Nate, no! I'm just glad to have her back safe and sound."

He took Lucy's hand and led her away from the children. "Eileen knew the rules, Lucy. If we let her get away with it this time, she might not remember how important this rule is the next time. The next time she could drown or Indians could find her first. I'm responsible for her now, and this is the way it has to be."

Lucy's eyes burned from all the tears she'd shed. "You're right. I've never had to punish her before."

He turned and went back to Eileen. He picked her up and went to his horse. "We'll discuss what the punishment will be when we get home."

Lucy mounted her horse and followed Jed and Nate home. She knew Nate was right, but that didn't make it easier. It had always been hard for her to discipline Eileen, who was so small and engaging. But this had been willful disobedience. She knew she wasn't to leave the yard.

They reached the cabin, and Jed took the horses to the barn. Nate carried Eileen inside while Lucy followed, her footsteps dragging. He sat on a chair and pulled Eileen onto his lap, then motioned for Lucy to be seated next to him.

"What do you have to say, Eileen?"

"I's sorry," she wept. "I shouldn't have gone out of the yard. I knew I wasn't s'posed to."

"Lucy was very sad when she found you gone. And we didn't make the rule to be mean. You remember when the mongrel wolf came?"

Eileen nodded. "Lucy shooted it with the gun."

"Another wolf could have come when Lucy wasn't there with the gun. There are Indians and snakes too. All kinds of things that could hurt you. We make a rule because we love you. And Jesus is sad when we disobey. Do you want to tell him you're sorry too?"

Eileen nodded again and clasped her little hands together. "Jesus, I's sorry," she sobbed. "I didn't want to make you sad, and I didn't want to worry Lucy. Help me be a good girl next time. Amen." She sniveled and wiped her nose with the back of her hand.

Tears burned Lucy's eyes. Wasn't that good enough?

"Am I going to be punished now?" Eileen's voice was pitiful.

"Do you think you should be?" Nate stroked her hair.

Eileen hesitated. "You have to 'cause you said. I wouldn't want God to think you was a liar."

Lucy thought she saw a hint of moisture in Nate's eyes. "No supper, then," he said. "And you'll have to stay on your bed the rest of the evening."

"Nothing for supper?" Eileen asked. "Lucy fixed dumplings."

"I don't want to discipline you, Eileen. Just like God doesn't like to discipline us. You can have bread and milk but no dumplings."

Tears streaming down her face, Eileen rose. Nate looked at Lucy helplessly. She could see the toll this was taking on him.

He knelt beside Eileen and hugged her. "I love you, sweetheart. Let's pray and promise God we'll try to obey next time."

Eileen wiped her eyes, then wound her arms around his neck and kissed him. "I love you, Nate. I'se glad you married us."

"So am I," Nate said, his gaze meeting Lucy's.

SUNDAYS WERE ALWAYS spent at the big house, but as Lucy rode in the buggy toward the ranch after church, she wished she could prepare Sunday dinner on her own. Though the cabin was small, it was home now after two months. Maybe she would bring it up today.

Nate stopped the buggy in front of the house. "Someone's here." Nate helped her down from the seat.

Birds were singing from the bushes and trees as her shoes hit the mud. She eyed the other buggy. It had a cover and looked new. "Who is it?"

"I don't recognize the horse." He lifted Eileen from the seat and set her down beside Lucy. Jed vaulted over the side to join them.

Lucy took his offered arm and skirted the worst of the puddle from last night's rain. The air smelled fresh and clean. After living in the cabin, the main house looked impossibly expansive and lavish. Nate held open the door.

Voices carried from the parlor, and she recognized her aunt's voice. "It's Aunt Sally!"

Lucy hurried across the polished wood floor to the first room on the right. Her aunt was sitting on the horsehair sofa with Fanny. She held out her arms for Eileen, and the child rushed to her lap. Lucy's smile faded when she saw the man in the chair near Fanny. Rolf Watson. He must have been keeping company with Fanny since they met him last week. The smile he turned on Lucy was entirely too smug for her liking.

She nodded stiffly. "Mr. Watson." Ignoring him, she hugged her aunt and cousin. "I didn't expect to see you here." Far from it. She'd had no idea they socialized with her father-in-law.

"Henry asked Rolf to dinner, and we tagged along." Sally's smile turned droll as she glanced at Henry.

Lucy finally dared to peek at him herself, but his expression betrayed no dismay. His smile was expansive as he gestured to the chairs. "We were just talking about you, Lucy. Your aunt would like to invite us all to Sunday dinner next week."

Lucy wanted to accept immediately, but she glanced at Nate. He was studying the male visitor, and she thought she saw speculation in his eyes. She beckoned to her cousin. "Fanny, if you wouldn't mind, we should see if Percy needs any help with dinner."

Fanny rose, and the two women went to the kitchen where

they found Percy heaping fried chicken on a platter. He eyed them. "Don't need no help, ladies. Dinner's about ready."

"We just thought we'd check. We can set the table." Lucy grabbed blue-and-white dishes, then handed her cousin the table-ware caddy.

"You didn't really need my help, did you, Lucy?" Fanny's blue eyes held amusement as they began to arrange the dishes.

Lucy set down a plate. "No. What are you doing with Mr. Watson? Why did Henry invite him here?"

Fanny arranged cookies on a plate. "It appears Rolf is a private investigator. Henry has hired him for some reason and wanted an update."

Lucy's cheeks heated. "He was in town before I asked Henry . . ."

"You hired Rolf?"

"No." Lucy didn't want to say more. Not yet. While she trusted her cousin, she still didn't trust Rolf. He was in town before Henry had known about the coins. So what was his real purpose? Could whoever was after the coins have hired him to track her down and Henry had blindly fallen into the man's plans?

"Lucy?"

She shook herself out of her reverie. "How did Henry meet Rolf?"

"I believe Henry heard about him and requested him to come by. Rolf asked if he might bring me and Mama to dinner."

"Rather brash," Lucy said. "Especially considering the tension between our families."

"Rolf didn't know about that."

Lucy wasn't so sure. There was a lot going on behind the man's handsome face. She feared for Fanny. "I'm sure it was innocent." She picked up the tray and followed her cousin back to the parlor.

The men were hotly debating the results of the presidential election between Hayes and Tilden. Though Hayes had been inaugurated, Henry claimed it all illegal. They fell silent when the women stepped back into the room.

Henry rose. "I'll leave you ladies to chat while I discuss business with Rolf and my son. I'm sure Percy will have dinner ready soon."

"You never responded to my invitation for Sunday dinner," Sally said.

Henry fell silent for a moment before nodding. "I have no quarrel with you, Mrs. Donnelly. I assume your brother will not be in attendance?"

Sally shook her head. "He will be out of town next week. Maybe next time." Her voice held a bit of hope.

Henry didn't answer that. "Nate, Rolf, Jed. In my office, please."

Lucy glanced at Nate and he nodded at her. "We'd be delighted to come as well, Aunt Sally," she said. "Can I bring dessert? I have pecans, and I can make some pies."

"That would be lovely, my dear."

When the men were gone, Lucy glanced at her cousin. "How much of Mr. Watson have you seen, Fanny?"

"He's been to dinner twice a week." Her dimples flashed. "What do you have against him, Lucy? Don't bother to deny it. You've set your affections against him from the first moment."

"Did you ever find out how he knew where you lived?"

"I didn't ask him, but it's a small town. There's no reason for your distrust."

Lucy wanted to believe Fanny. She wanted her sweet cousin to find happiness, but something about the man put her off. "I hope you're right. What is your opinion, Aunt Sally?"

Her aunt smiled. "I want Fanny to be happy, of course. My preference would be for her to marry a man from our area so I could continue to see her, but I don't want to be so selfish to deny her a chance at happiness just because I want her nearby. Rolf seems a good man. He's quite polite and well spoken. He dresses well. I asked my brother to examine his background and see if he has the means to care for Fanny."

"What did Uncle Drew find out?"

"He hasn't gotten back to me yet, but I expect a report soon. In the meantime, Fanny has a handsome man to squire her about."

"Have the two men met?"

"Of course. I arranged for them to meet at once. Fanny has no father to look out for her, and Drew fulfills that responsibility whenever I need him."

"Did Rolf say why he came to town?"

"I didn't ask."

Lucy opened her mouth, then closed it again. What was there to say when all she had to go on were feelings?

TWENTY-TWO

❦

Nate never felt at ease in his father's library. There wasn't a good place to sit with the stacks of papers on every available chair. He moved a pile of folders and settled into the chair closest to his father, leaving Watson to do the same with the chair by the door. Something about the fellow put Nate's back up.

Henry motioned to the chair Watson stood by. "Set that stuff on the floor and pull your chair closer. I want a report."

Watson did as directed, scraping the chair legs along the wooden floor. "In order to find the owner of the coins, I'd like to take them back to Indiana with me for verification."

"That won't be possible," Nate said at the same time his father nodded.

Henry's brows gathered together in a stern frown. "It makes sense that he would need someone to examine the coins, Nate."

"No. Sorry, Pa, but we don't really know this man. I'm not giving him anything." He stared at Watson. "If you find the owner, you can let us know and we'll see about returning his property. Until then, the coins stay with us."

The man shrugged. "I hope you have them safe in a vault somewhere."

Was the guy fishing to find out where the coins were? Nate didn't trust him. "They're safe."

"I'd like to at least look at them myself. Have a photograph taken."

"No. And I'm a little concerned about your intentions regarding Fanny."

Watson's brows rose. "I hardly see where that's any of your concern."

Nate wondered himself at his prodding, but he knew Lucy was concerned. It had been all over her face. "She's my cousin by marriage and has no father to look out for her."

"I'm here about business, Mr. Stanton, not my private life."

"Does she know you don't have any serious intentions?"

Red swept up Watson's face. "I have merely taken her to dinner on occasion. That hardly constitutes a marriage proposal."

The guy was going to hurt Fanny. Nate wanted to throw him out on his ear, but he rose when he heard Percy whistle. "Sounds like dinner is ready." He opened the door and let Watson exit ahead of him. Fanny would need to be warned.

His father stood from behind the desk. "Nate, what's gotten into you?"

"Pa, you don't even know this guy. Why would you trust him?"

"He has an excellent reputation."

"Well, I don't believe he's all he says. He's too slick. He can make general inquiries first."

His father came around the side of the desk. "Maybe you're right. We'll see what he finds out first."

SHOPPING DAY ALWAYS lifted Lucy's spirits, and the early June weather was so fine, she was especially happy. She left Jed and Nate at the feed store and walked down the boardwalk with Eileen by the hand. A woman's voice called her name, and she turned to see Mrs. Walker hailing her from the front porch of a neat two-story home.

"I've been wondering how you've been getting on," Henry's cousin said when Lucy reached the porch. "Do you have time for a visit?"

"I'd love to chat," Lucy said, removing her bonnet. "And I wouldn't turn down some tea. All those men drink is coffee, coffee, and more coffee." She and Eileen followed Mrs. Walker into the kitchen. A starched linen covered the table, and there were vases of bluebells in the room. One on the windowsill and one on the table.

Mrs. Walker put the teakettle on the woodstove. "Tell me what you've been up to." She fetched a tiny set of teacups and teapot for Eileen.

The little girl squealed with delight when the older woman pointed out a tiny table in the corner and set the items on top of it. Eileen took her dolly to the small set to play.

"Mostly just cleaning the cabin and putting things in their place." Lucy hesitated. "We had Sunday dinner at Henry's yesterday. Rolf Watson was there with Fanny and Aunt Sally."

"I've seen him squiring her around."

"You sound as though you don't approve."

The older woman shrugged. "It's not my place to approve or disapprove, but I fear young Fanny is going to get her heart broken. I've seen his type before."

"She seems to have seen his true nature." Lucy watched her get out the tea strainer and cups.

Mrs. Walker sniffed. "That man could charm a honeybee from its hive. All the girls in town are after him. It's no wonder Fanny was taken in."

"Do you know what he's doing in town in the first place?"

Mrs. Walker set down her teacup. "I've heard he was hired to track down the owner of some land O'Brien wants to buy."

"Are all landowners so determined to own the entire state of Texas?"

"I'm afraid so, dear. Why are you so interested in Mr. Watson?"

Lucy didn't know how to answer the question. "Curiosity for my family's sake," she said finally.

Mrs. Walker smiled. "Your cousin has to make her own mistakes. You can't control her love life."

"I merely wanted to ensure she wasn't getting involved with some kind of shyster." Lucy's cheeks burned. She remembered the woman's comment on the train about Lucy's need for control. That wasn't it at all. She merely wanted Fanny to be happy.

The older woman patted her hand. "Honey, I'd hoped you were learning to let go of that desire to make things right for everyone."

Lucy's face burned even more when Mrs. Walker shook her head, then picked up a cookie and nibbled on it. "It's no sin to want the best for the people I love."

"No, it's not. But the best you can do is pray for them. Let God lead them. Do you feel you have the wisdom necessary to advise your cousin about a matter in which you yourself are woefully inexperienced?"

"I have prayed for Fanny." Every night and with great fervency.

"And I expect the prayer has been for her to see through the scoundrel."

Lucy wanted to deny the charge, but they both knew it was

true. She clearly remembered praying exactly the way Mrs. Walker had said. How did she know when they were virtually strangers? "I *do* want her to see the truth."

"And what if God has other plans? You don't know that man's heart. Perhaps he's not the womanizer you think."

"*You* thought so too!"

Mrs. Walker laughed. "I'm an old woman. I might be wrong about him myself. I've judged people in the past and been wrong. We can pray we are both wrong this time."

"Then what should I be praying?"

Mrs. Walker picked up her tea. "For God to keep your heart pure and for him to mold you as he would. Anything else is out of your control. We can only change ourselves with God's help. Changing other people is not our job."

"I don't want to change Fanny."

"Don't you?"

Lucy couldn't hold to her original declaration with the woman's gray eyes seeing into her soul. "Perhaps I do feel Fanny is a little too giddy and easily swayed by a persuasive smile."

"And perhaps she is. But your responsibility is to love her with God's love and let her make her own decisions. I would imagine she has not asked you for advice but you have been quick to give it anyway."

Lucy ducked her head and nodded. "If you saw a friend about to fall off a cliff, wouldn't you step in front to save her?"

"That's a little different. The danger is clear. This is not. It's Fanny's decision to make, not yours." She nodded to the tea. "Enough of this. Let God show you how to pray for Fanny."

Lucy took the cue. "Have you seen Henry lately?"

"He usually stops by when he's in town. I checked on him

after his spasm, but he does so hate to be coddled. He told me not to come back unless I could promise not to hover. Since I couldn't promise, I stayed away."

Lucy smiled at the woman's practical tone. She knew Henry well. Lucy accepted the tea Mrs. Walker offered. "You've known Nate all his life."

"Oh my, yes. He and his brother are like my own. My William and I never had children. He was killed by a robber when we'd been married just six months."

"Oh, I'm so sorry!"

"It was a long time ago. Nate and Roger helped ease the pain. That young scamp Roger came to see me. I fear he will never grow up."

"He warned me about Henry," Lucy said. "It's clear the two of them don't get along."

"He and his father have been at loggerheads since Roger was a child. Henry has always had dreams and goals for his boys. Roger wasn't one to fall in with those plans."

"I'm still getting to know Nate. And marriage is an adjustment."

The older woman gave her a sharp glance. "You indicated when we spoke last that you found Nate handsome and he was treating you well. You're not sorry you married him?"

"Oh no, not at all. H-He's quite suitable."

Suitable didn't begin to explain how he made her feel when he looked at her.

LUCY LEANED BACK in the swing on her aunt's porch and gave it a push with one foot. "Dinner was amazing, Aunt Sally."

Her aunt beamed. "Your pies were the real hit. I must have your recipe."

Lucy glanced at Nate beside her. The meal had gone very well. The small talk had stayed on ranching and things that had been happening in town. Henry had been polite and courteous to her family. And thankfully, Rolf had not been in evidence. Maybe he'd gone to Indiana on his assignment. She could only hope he'd stay gone.

Her cousin jumped to her feet. Fanny looked very fetching today in a sky blue dress. She stood at the top of the porch steps and watched a figure walking across the street toward town.

"What's wrong?" Lucy asked.

"I-I'm not sure," Fanny said. "It almost looks like . . ."

Her mother joined her. "Honey, you're always seeing Andy around every corner."

Fanny wilted. "You don't think it's him?" She stared after the figure.

"No." Her mother guided her back to the guests. "How about some tea and coffee? You and Lucy could prepare it if Lucy doesn't mind assisting."

Lucy stood. "I'd be glad to help." She followed Fanny into the kitchen. "You thought that man was your former fiancé?"

Tears hung on Fanny's lashes. "The walk was just like his."

"Have you never tried to find out what happened to him?"

"Oh, I talked to his family. They say he's well and living in Arizona."

Lucy got out the tea caddy. "You've never written?"

"Oh yes. I never heard from him."

"Fanny, you have not gotten over Andy."

Fanny turned to face her. "You're thinking of Rolf, and I

admit I was trying to see if I could care for another man the way I did Andy. I tried. Really, I did. My heart is taken. I must face the fact it always might be."

"What about Rolf?"

Fanny frowned and put down the cup in her hand. "I saw him with another woman the other day. He kissed her. I don't believe he will ever settle down with one woman."

"I'm sorry if he hurt you."

Fanny waved her hand. "When I realized I really didn't care, I knew I was wasting my time and his. Not that he cared." She shrugged. "I overheard something though, Lucy. I'm glad we're alone. I heard him talking to a man. He said he was going to search the Stanton homestead. I assumed that meant your cabin. What could he be searching for?"

Lucy's stomach plunged. "I haven't trusted him from the first time we met. Thank you for telling me. I'll let Nate know we need to be careful." She picked up the tray. "We'd better get back. Your mother will be looking for us."

THE TASTE OF dirt clung to Jed's tongue. His muscles were getting used to riding after spending so much time in the saddle. Was he taller? He glanced at his new brother. Maybe someday Jed would be able to do everything Nate could.

"Circle around that way." Nate pointed toward the north where a stand of trees split the milling cattle in two. "I saw several strays trying to get across the river. And hurry. There's a storm coming."

Jed nodded and guided his horse toward the trees. His new

hat fit just right, and his own rope hung from the saddle horn. He was a real cowboy. He urged his horse into a trot. "Yeehaw!"

The steer nearest him lifted a lazy head and stared at Jed as if to question his right to make him move. The beast's tail swished and he swung his horns at the horse, then lumbered past the stand of trees toward the river. Jed managed to get the small group of strays over to the main herd. He sat back in the saddle and glanced around to make sure he hadn't missed any.

Nothing moved but the grass. His stomach grumbled when Nate joined him.

Nate grinned. "I heard that. Good job, Jed. You're a natural."

Jed sat taller. "Thanks."

Thunder rumbled overhead. Nate glanced at the sky and frowned. "Looks like a real bad one."

Jed stared at the black, churning clouds. Lightning flickered before the thunder came again. It was going to take half an hour to get home. Good thing he'd brought an oilcloth slicker.

The lightning bolt seemed to come from nowhere. It arced across the sky, followed by the loudest thunder he'd ever heard. The horse reared at the sound, and Jed wasn't expecting it. He found himself flat on his back and spitting sand out of his mouth.

Nate dismounted and grabbed Jed's hand. "You okay?"

Jed let Nate haul him up. "Yeah." The ground rumbled under his feet. "That's some thunder."

Nate glanced around, then grabbed Jed's hand. "That's not thunder. Run!"

Jed leaped toward the trees with Nate, though he had no idea why he was running. If there was lightning, weren't you supposed to stay away from trees? It wasn't until he glanced over his shoulder that he saw wild-eyed cattle pelting headlong toward them.

The sight galvanized him into a faster run, and he reached the first tree in seconds.

"Climb!" Nate grabbed him by the waist and hoisted him into the air.

Jed scrambled to the first limb, then kept on climbing to allow Nate room. Nate leaped up to the limb but lost his grip and fell onto the ground.

Jed's eyes widened. "Jump, Nate!"

His new brother was going to die. Jed closed his eyes. He couldn't watch.

Jed clung to the limb with all his might as everything in his world shook. In a moment he was back in Wabash with the rain driving down and his father beside him. The carriage careened and he yelled. With his eyes closed, he could almost remember what happened that night. He held his breath as the familiar fear swamped him. No matter how hard it was, he wanted to remember now.

"Jed? You okay?"

He opened his eyes. Nate was staring up at him with concern in his face. He'd made it to safety. The cattle were past the trees, and the tree no longer shook.

He hadn't been able to help Nate, and he'd failed his father in some way too. Though he couldn't remember the details, he couldn't miss the shame. He swallowed and nodded. "Yes, I'm fine. It's over?"

"We're safe."

But Jed didn't feel safe. He wouldn't feel safe until he remembered what had terrified him so that night.

NATE'S MUSCLES ACHED from the day's work as he sat at the dinner table. He and Jed had branded calves all day. The light scent Lucy wore wafted around Nate as she put the plate of food down in front of him. She smelled much more tantalizing than the salt pork and potatoes she'd prepared. A curl had escaped the roll on the back of her head, and he had to resist the impulse to twist it around his finger.

He looked down at the plate. "Smells good."

"Percy told me it was your favorite meal."

"It is." He waited until she was seated, then bowed his head. "Lord, thank you for keeping us safe today. May this food give us strength to do your work and carry out your will. In Jesus' name, amen."

"Amen," Eileen echoed in her sweet voice.

When he raised his head, Lucy's blue eyes were staring at him. "What?"

"Were you in danger today?" she asked.

"It was really cool," Jed burst in. His gaze dropped to his plate when Nate shot him a glare. "Sorry. I wasn't supposed to tell, was I?"

"No, you were not." Nate pressed his lips together. Lucy was going to be upset all evening now. "We're both fine."

She sat back in the chair and folded her arms across her chest. "What happened?" When neither he nor Jed said anything, she stared at her brother. "Jed, what happened today?"

The boy shoved food into his mouth and chewed. His panicked glance slid to Nate. Lucy's lips flattened and her finely shaped brows drew together.

"All right," Nate said. "There was a bit of a cattle stampede. We were caught in the middle."

"We had to climb a tree," Jed said eagerly. "We were just lucky it was there. It was the only one big enough to hold us both. The cattle thundered by right under us."

Lucy went white. "You could have been killed. Both of you."

"But we weren't," Nate pointed out. "God took care of us like he always does. No need to fret, honey." The word was out before he realized it, and her expression softened. He reached over and grasped her hand. The skin was soft under his calluses.

"It upsets me so much," she burst out. "Both of you out there facing all kinds of danger when I can't even see."

"What would happen if you could see us? You can't keep us safe by willing it. God will do as he sees best. Nothing we can do about that."

She looked down at her plate. "I could pray."

"You can do that anyway," Nate said.

"It's not the same."

"Life happens, Lucy. Good and bad, they come to all of us sooner or later. We can't will away the bad things. They are part of what shapes us into the people we become."

"You sound like your cousin Mrs. Walker. She preached the same thing in town on Monday."

He grinned. "That's a compliment." He watched her take a few dainty bites. This woman he'd married was so mysterious to him. He still didn't know what she wanted for herself from this marriage. Security for her siblings had driven her here, but did she have any goals of her own other than a family? What did she think of him? He wanted to know all those things.

"How about you and I go for a ride after we eat?"

"A ride?"

Nate nodded. "I'd like to show you the river by moonlight. It's only about half an hour away. Tonight is a midsummer full moon. We can watch it come up."

"But what about the children?"

"Jed can take care of Eileen. They can play checkers."

"I like checkers," Eileen said.

"You go ahead." Jed leaned back in his chair. "Me and Eileen can even do the dishes."

"As you wish," Lucy said.

They finished dinner and Nate got out his Bible. "I think we were in Proverbs."

"Proverbs 18," Jed said. "Can I read tonight?"

In answer, Nate slid the big Bible across the table to the boy. It warmed him that Jed had taken so much to this time together. Even little Eileen seemed to pay attention as she sat on Lucy's lap. He listened as the lad began to read the verses.

"'A brother offended is harder to be won than a strong city: and their contentions are like the bars of a castle.'"

As the verse sank in, Nate's thoughts jumped to Drew Larson. Though he wasn't a brother in the official sense, Nate thought he was a Christian. The rancor between the families had grown and made the barriers higher and higher. But that wasn't his fault. Was it?

Jed continued to read. "'Whoso findeth a wife findeth a good thing, and obtaineth favour of the LORD.'"

Nate's glance slid to Lucy. Her chin rested on Eileen's head. She'd brought him nothing but blessings. In his heart he thanked God for the wife he'd been given. And he'd tell her how thankful he was tonight at the Red River.

TWENTY-THREE

L ucy stood on the bank of the Red River and watched the reddish water move past. Bees hummed in the grass, and the moist scent of riverbed and moss permeated the air.

Nate stood nearby. "Not too close. It's slippery at the edge."

She lifted her face to the breeze so she didn't have to look at the intensity in his face. Had he brought her out here for an uncomfortable discussion? The sun was beginning to set, and the sky was turning orange and violet. She willed herself to accept whatever he had to say.

Curling her fingers into her palms, she turned to face him and found him standing even closer than she thought. Her nose was nearly touching the button on his shirt. "Just say it."

"Say what?"

"Whatever you brought me out here to say. Something is on your mind."

His fingers gripped her shoulders. One hand moved from her shoulder to her chin, and he tilted her face up toward his. "Listening to Jed read Proverbs tonight made me realize that though I kicked against it at first, God gave me a great blessing in you and the children. I'm finding myself quite content with having a wife around. Jed has been a big help, and I love Eileen."

Jed had been helpful. Lucy wished she could have done as much to assist her husband as her brother. "I'll try to do better. How can I help with the ranch?"

He cupped her cheek as he smiled. "I rather like coming home to a hot meal and having clean clothes without having to think about it. You're doing a fine job."

His words warmed her nearly as much as his touch. Almost. "You brought me out here to tell me that?"

"I wanted to spend some time with you. We've talked about the coins and whoever broke into the ranch house. We've discussed raising Jed to be a man, but I don't know what you want out of life other than a family. If we're going to spend the next fifty years together, we'd better start getting to know one another. What kind of house do you want me to build you? What's your favorite color so I can buy you a dress? What convenience can I buy to make your work easier?"

Fifty years together. Her mouth went dry at the thought. She hadn't allowed herself to think much beyond each day as the sun rose. What did she want? Children of her own. Her cheeks warmed. A husband whose gaze went soft when he looked at her. Friends and family around.

"Well?" he prompted, putting his arm around her.

How could she possibly say such intimate things to him? He would think her quite forward. "I like being part of your family. I want to be part of the town, to help others. I don't need *things* to be happy. And I quite like our little cottage."

"There has to be more than that. What do you want for *you*, Lucy? Not for other people but for you."

He still embraced her, and Lucy could feel the warmth of his hand through her dress. His other hand was still on her cheek and he rubbed his thumb across her lips in a most distracting way. "I don't know."

"You just don't want to tell me." He dropped his arms back to his sides. "I'd hoped you would."

The disappointment in his voice stung her. "What do you want, Nate?"

"To build a great cattle empire here in the Red River Valley. To be such a man of integrity that my children will be impacted after I'm dead and gone. I thought you'd mention children, Lucy, since you mentioned them before. Don't you want a houseful?"

"Yes, I would love children." She wetted her lips.

"I reckon we're going to have to change our living arrangements for that to happen."

There was laughter in his voice, and she swallowed the answering bubble of mirth in her throat. "I know." She was determined not to crack a smile. She wasn't ready.

He folded his arms across his chest. "But not yet."

She shook her head. "Not yet."

He took her arm and turned her to face the rising moon. "There's our midsummer moon. The next moon will be a blue moon."

"The moon will turn blue? I've never seen such a thing." He was standing so close she felt him shake his head above her, and she dared to lean back against him. "Of course, I've lived in a town all my life where I didn't notice the moon and stars."

"It's called a blue moon because it happens infrequently. It's the third moon in a quarter when there are four full moons in a season."

What was the point of bringing her out here to see the moon? It was large and full as it rose in the fading light. "It's beautiful."

He turned her to face him again. "It is and so are you, Lucy. I want you to be my wife in every way, but I have a feeling it's going to take awhile for that to happen."

At the question in his voice, she nodded. "Not yet," she whispered.

"I figured if we talked about it, you could get used to the idea."

She glanced up at the moon. "Next month is the blue moon?" When he nodded, she swallowed. "Then let's talk about it again then, okay? I think I'll be ready then."

He smiled. "My little planner. Everything neat and in order. You ever want to cut loose and do something spontaneous?" He pressed his lips against her forehead and trailed kisses down her face to her mouth.

She drank in his kiss. Spontaneous might be good if she could get used to it. Was it too much to expect to want sweet words of love? He liked her. That much was clear. But what would it take for him to love her? She pulled away and looked into his face. She felt something for him, but she wasn't going to his bed without love on his part and hers. Not even in a blue moon.

LUCY YAWNED. DAWN had barely pinked the sky. She'd awakened early, and her first thoughts had been of Nate's words last night. She'd gotten up, determined to do more to be the kind of wife he needed. She gingerly touched the cow with one hand and wrinkled her nose at the odor of cow and manure. Positioning the bucket under the cow, she grabbed the udder and squeezed. Nothing. She huffed and got a firmer grip. This couldn't be that hard. She'd already watched Nate do it for months. If he could do it, she could. Maybe if she sang to the animal . . .

She cleared her voice and thought of the words to that song Nate sang when he milked. She raised her voice in melody.

"'I dream of Jeannie with the light brown hair. Borne, like a vapor, on the summer air.'"

She felt stupid singing a love song to a cow. But Bessie seemed to like it. The cow snorted, then swished her tail, and a drop of milk squirted the next time Lucy squeezed. Heartened, she leaned her head against the cow and tried to get a rhythm going. *Squirt, squirt. Ping, ping.* She smiled. She was getting it!

Then Nate's deep baritone chimed in with her soprano.

"I long for Jeannie with the day dawn smile. Radiant in gladness, warm with winning guile.'"

His gray eyes were smiling as he pulled up a stool beside hers. Did he love her? She was beginning to think he felt something, even as this feeling grew in her own heart. Was it love? She hoped so. She wanted to love her husband. But she'd had so little experience with men. Maybe it was merely physical attraction. Whatever it was, she wanted to nurture it.

"I reckon you're getting the hang of this," Nate said. "Almost half a bucket."

"You usually get over a bucket."

"I didn't at the beginning. Once those fingers get stronger, you'll be great at it."

Her fingers did ache. She flexed them. "You want to finish? Bessie might appreciate being totally emptied." She scooted over to make room for him. His broad shoulder grazed hers, and she could smell the clean scent of the soap he'd used to wash. She wanted to lean against him and have him gather her in his arms.

The weather had turned hot. Even this early she was too warm. She and Nate were alone, a state that came so seldom she felt tongue-tied.

"I thought we'd go check on Pa today after supper," Nate said. "We haven't been over for two days. That okay with you?"

"Of course. I made some pies yesterday. I'll take one to him."

"He'll enjoy that. All he's done lately is eat, Percy says. I think Percy is getting tired of cooking for him."

"I wonder if we should take dinner to him for a few days to give Percy a break. I could go over early to cook." She almost hated the thought of leaving her little cabin. It had quickly become home. "You and Jed could join us after you're done with chores."

"I bet Pa would enjoy the different food." Nate rose and took the bucket of frothy milk. Lucy followed him, and they crossed the yard to the house. She'd opened the windows to take advantage of what wind there was, and the new yellow gingham curtains blew in the breeze.

"You've done wonders with the house," Nate said. "I never realized before how much this place needed something. Pa hasn't even seen it yet."

"He'll just say, 'I told you so.'" Lucy smiled and took Nate's hand.

He gave her a surprised glance, then laced his fingers through hers. A warm glow spread through Lucy's stomach. She prayed every day for the relationship between them to blossom and flourish. It looked as though God was answering that prayer.

"You checked on your coins lately?" he asked, still holding her hand.

She nodded. "This morning when I went to the cellar I checked them. Still there."

"I thought Pa would have heard something from Watson. It can't be that hard to track down something that rare."

"Maybe they were in a private collection."

They reached the front door, and he opened it for her. A bit of milk sloshed over the rim of the bucket, and he steadied it. "We can ask Pa when we get there. At least the fellow is gone from town."

"He'll be back. I'm glad Fanny isn't pining for him anymore."

"You two had a chat at dinner on Sunday?"

She took the bucket from him and poured the milk into the butter churn. "She is still pining for the fiancé who left and never came back."

"Love does that." A tender expression emerged on his face when he added, "So I'm told."

She had hesitated to say anything to him about her cousin's warning since his father had hired Rolf, but he really needed to know. They'd gone to town on Monday and he'd worked in the field until late yesterday. She hadn't found a time to bring it up without the children.

He was staring at her. "Is something wrong?"

"Fanny told me she overheard Rolf tell a man he was going to search the Stanton cabin."

His lips flattened. "For the coins?"

"I would assume so."

"I had a feeling he was trying to get his hands on them."

She nodded. "I thought so too, but it's possible he just wants to see them so he can identify them properly. I'd like to give him the benefit of the doubt, but I don't trust him."

"Neither do I. I'll keep an eye out for him."

She turned away and put the lid on the churn. The lantern was lit so she knew the children were up. "Eileen, want to churn the butter?" she called.

Her little sister came running into the kitchen. Nate lifted down the churn for her and set it on the floor by her feet. Lucy watched the little girl begin to churn. She would wear out soon, and Lucy would take over, but it was good experience for Eileen. When Lucy glanced up, she caught an expression of tenderness on Nate's face as he watched Eileen work at the churn that was nearly as big as she was.

He was a good man.

TWENTY-FOUR

Lucy adjusted her bonnet to guard her face from the harsh Texas sun and followed Nate outside after lunch. He helped her hitch the horse to the buggy. "Are you sure you know how to get to the main house?"

"Don't worry, Nate. We'll be fine."

"Sorry." He grinned and put an arm around her. "I can't help but worry when you're out by yourself."

The hug he gave her felt like one he'd give Eileen, and it irritated her. She wanted him to cradle her in his arms and kiss her, really kiss her. Not that light peck on the cheek he'd taken to giving her every night. How did a woman go about letting a man know she was ready for more than he was offering? Lucy gave a tiny sigh. She'd been thinking about that blue moon.

"What's wrong?"

"Nothing." She pulled away and climbed into the buggy without his assistance. She stared into his perplexed gaze and stretched out her arms. "Could you hand Eileen up to me?"

He stared at her a moment, then shrugged. He scooped up

Eileen and handed her to Lucy. "You girls be careful. Don't forget there's a rifle under the seat if you need it."

"I remember." She stared straight ahead and slapped the reins against the mare's back. "Dinner will be at six. Try not to be late."

Nate reached up and grabbed the reins. "Lucy, what's wrong? Did I do something?"

Shame twisted in her gut. It wasn't his fault she was feeling so blue and rejected. He was doing everything he could to make this work. How was he to know she was ready for a deeper relationship? She bit her lip and raised her gaze to his. "We'll talk in the blue moon."

Amusement filled his eyes. "Keep thinking about it."

He slapped the mare's hindquarters and she set off at a trot. As she guided the horse, Lucy stewed about what to say to him. Half the time she didn't know what she wanted, so how was he supposed to know? Ever since the night at the river two weeks ago, she'd realized she was about ready for a real marriage.

The recent rains had left the ground muddy. Lucy tried to keep the buggy in the driest areas, but she still got bogged down several times. Eileen fell asleep, and Lucy breathed a sigh. Now she could concentrate on where she was going and on her own thoughts. She rounded a curve and hit a deep patch of mud. The mare whinnied and thrashed in the mud, flinging up bits of muck onto Lucy's dress.

"Whoa!" Lucy pulled on the reins and clambered down. The mud sucked at her boots, and she almost fell as she made her way to the horse's head. She patted her and tried to back the horse out of the mud. The horse reared in terror, and Lucy scrambled back. She lost her balance and sat awkwardly in the mud. Struggling to get up, she fell forward. Near tears, she tried to get on all fours, but the mud held her.

She might have to send Eileen for help. She could see the smoke from the main house from here. Then a horse whinnied behind her. She turned and looked up into the smiling face of a man she vaguely recognized as the foreman at the O'Brien ranch.

He tipped his hat. "Morning, Lucy."

"That's missus," she corrected.

His grin widened. "Whatever you say, ma'am. You need some help? Looks like you're in a bit of a predicament."

His smirk raised Lucy's ire, but she was in no position to refuse help. "I would appreciate it," she said coldly.

"Say that like you mean it, and I might see my way clear to helping you." He put his hands on his hips, and his white teeth flashed.

"Sir, give me your hand!" She wasn't about to play games with him.

His eyes widened, and he stepped forward and offered his hand. She gripped it with her mud-covered one, and he hauled her inelegantly to her feet. Before she could thank him and release his hand, he gave a tug and jerked her into his arms.

"Now I'll take my appreciation." He bent his head.

Lucy didn't take time to think, she just walloped him upside the head with a glob of mud she'd inadvertently clutched in her other hand. It hit him in the eye, and he let out a yelp. He was so startled, he let loose of her, and she sprang to the buggy and wrested the rifle from under the seat.

"I won't hesitate to use this on a coyote like you. I appreciate your help, but not enough to offer more than a handshake and a thank-you. Now mosey on down the road. My father-in-law is expecting me, and his men would be rather put out to find you'd manhandled me."

The foreman's face suffused with red, and he narrowed his

eyes. "I was just helping you out of the mud. It's your word against mine." He tipped his hat. "I'll be seeing you around, Miss Lucy."

"That's missus!" she shouted after him as he vaulted to his horse and wheeled angrily away.

LUCY SNAPPED THE whip over the mare's head. "Giddyup!" She flipped her filthy skirt around her legs and hunched forward. She couldn't wait to get out of this mud-encased dress. The horse and buggy cantered into the yard. Lucy pulled hard on the reins to halt the horses, then she flung herself from the buggy and scooped up Eileen. Several ranch hands gaped as she hurried to the house. She was wet and scared, but she was determined not to let that bully cow her.

Henry, his spectacles perched on his nose, looked up from where he sat by the window with a book in his hand. His bushy eyebrows rose when he saw her condition and he stood. "Lucy, what's happened to you?"

"My buggy got bogged down in the mud." He didn't need to worry about the man. She would take care of her own battles.

"My dear girl, you must get out of those wet clothes." He went to the hall. "Percy, fetch the trunk with Mrs. Stanton's things in it." He turned back to Lucy. "I kept some of my wife's nicer things since they were all I had of her. You're about the same size. I think they'll fit."

"Oh, I couldn't wear them. An old pair of dungarees and a shirt will do until I get home."

"Absolutely not!" He gestured for her to sit. "Percy will bring the trunk, and you can take whatever you like."

"Your cushion will be soiled if I sit. I'll clean up in the kitchen." She hated to feel like she was asking for anything. She took Eileen's hand.

He followed them into the kitchen. Eileen climbed into a chair. Henry watched Lucy sluice water over her exposed skin. Flecks of mud fell to the floor and she grimaced. "I'll get it." She crouched and began to pick up the bits of debris.

"Lucy, please." At the pained look on his face, she stood. "You're not a servant here. You're my daughter. I don't want you acting like you're here on suffrage."

Tears welled in Lucy's eyes. She'd always been so used to carrying her own weight, of trying not to be a bother, that it came hard to accept what he was offering. "Thank you, Pa."

Henry colored with pleasure. He knelt beside Eileen's chair. "And I'd like you to call me Grandpa, if you'd like, Eileen."

The little girl stared into the older man's face. She put a small hand on each side of his face. "I like you. You can be my grandpa."

Henry kissed her, then fished for his handkerchief. "You've made me very happy by joining our family, Lucy. I know it hasn't been easy for you. My Nate can be like a penned bull when he feels he's being forced into something. But I've seen the way he looks at you. You two are a good match." His voice was full of satisfaction.

"I hope you're right," Lucy said quietly.

Percy came in dragging a chest behind him. He dropped it with a thump in front of Lucy. "Took me forever to find this, Boss. It was in the attic."

Henry reached over and opened the chest. Inside, shimmering silk dresses caught the sunlight.

Lucy gasped at the glorious array of color and texture. "These are far too grand to wear to cook in." She fingered a pale pink fabric.

"Nonsense, they've been tucked away too long. You heard Percy. They were in the attic not doing a body any good." He pulled out the dress she had touched. "This will look lovely on you. You might as well surprise Nate when he comes."

Lucy didn't have time to argue. "I must get busy. Thank you, Pa. I'll try to be careful of it." Holding it away from her soiled dress, she hurried to the spare bedroom. Water stood in the pitcher, so she slipped out of her soiled dress, washed, and stepped into the clean dress. It was only as she began to button up the tiny seed pearls on the bodice that she realized it was the same dress Nate's mother had worn in the picture in the box in his room.

She slid her hands over the smooth fabric. Would it bother him to see her in this dress? Maybe she should choose another. She bit her lip. There wasn't time to change. She would barely be ready for the men as it was if she didn't get started on supper. No, she would just have to wear this one.

Her boots were too muddy to put back on, so she would just stick them on the porch to dry. She could knock off the hardened mud before she went home. In her stockings she padded to the kitchen, depositing her boots on the porch along the way.

Percy stood amid the pots and pans waiting for her. Together they whipped together chicken and dumplings and apple pie using canned apples from the larder.

Percy tasted the stew. "You sure know how to cook, Miss Lucy. It does a body good to eat someone else's cooking for a change."

She smiled. At least this was one wifely duty she knew how to do. She spent the rest of the afternoon making biscuits and pies.

Just before six the door banged, and she heard the sound of men's voices. She could make out Nate's voice amidst the babble, and her heart leapt.

"I'll set the table." Percy grabbed a handful of plates and dinnerware and rushed off to the table.

Lucy picked up the pot of dumplings and followed him. The men's voices stilled when she entered the dining room. Her gaze picked out Nate from the group of cowboys. She didn't see his father. His laughter died when he saw her, and she couldn't read his expression. Was he dismayed to see her in it?

"Is that my mother's dress?" he asked, his voice soft.

"My—my dress was soiled. I fell in the mud when the buggy got stuck."

"The bad man yelled at her." Eileen slipped her hand in Nate's.

He glanced at Lucy, then knelt beside the little girl. "What bad man, sweetheart?"

Lucy hadn't wanted Nate to know until she was ready to explain it to him—alone.

"Lucy hit him with some mud. He was mad." Eileen spoke in a confiding tone as Nate lifted her into his arms.

"Lucy, what's this all about?" Still carrying Eileen, Nate stepped next to Lucy. "Did someone threaten you?"

"A man stopped to help me get out of the mud. I don't know his name, but he's the foreman at the O'Brien ranch."

"Childress." Nate's expression darkened like a lowering storm cloud. "Did he touch you?"

Before Lucy could answer, Eileen piped up again. "Uh-huh. But Lucy got the gun."

"Lucy? What did he do?"

The entire roomful of men seemed to be holding their breaths.

Lucy sighed. "He thought I ought to show a bit of appreciation for his help."

"I see. What kind of appreciation?" Nate's voice was dangerous, and Lucy shivered.

"A—a kiss was what he had in mind."

Nate ground his teeth together. "Jed, come with me. We're riding to the O'Brien ranch."

Lucy laid a hand on his arm. "Please, Nate, I handled it. I warned him off with the gun."

"A man like that will be back." He shook off her hand. "Come on, Jed."

"Not Jed!" Lucy cried out when her brother moved to go with him.

Nate paused, then nodded. "You're right. It might be dangerous."

Dangerous! Lucy's heart clenched. She couldn't bear it if something happened to Nate. It was all her fault. She should have told Eileen not to say anything, but she hadn't realized the little girl had seen so much. She had been sleeping when the man rode up.

"What about dinner?" she called.

"Keep it warm."

She knew better than to berate him this time. She began to pray that God would keep him safe.

NATE'S MUSCLES WERE strung as tight as a tanning rawhide. His hands gripped the reins, and he urged his horse faster along the muddy road to the O'Brien ranch.

Part of his anger was rage at himself. He never should have

allowed Lucy to go out by herself. This was still very unsettled territory. Even O'Brien had only moved into this area last year. Indians still roamed, burning out the occasional settler. He needed to remember he was a family man now. His wife and her family depended on him to make proper decisions. This afternoon's had obviously been a bad one.

Several ranch hands milled around the corral as he stopped at the hitching post. He dismounted and tied his horse, then motioned for his men to stay where they were while he went to the door. He pounded on it with his fist. Only silence answered his knock. He pounded again, then took a deep breath. He had to stay calm and present his case to O'Brien in a reasonable fashion.

There was still no answer at the door, so he strode to the corral and watched two men working to saddle break a young mare. Peering through the dust and commotion, he finally spied O'Brien leaning against the fence by the barn, watching the action in the corral. Clenching his fists, Nate made his way to O'Brien's side.

O'Brien jerked his head up in surprise when he saw Nate. "Nate. Margaret isn't here."

"I didn't come to see Margaret." Nate held out his hand. "I got some business with one of your hands."

The man regarded him with a sober gaze. "Serious business, looks like."

"Martin Childress manhandled my wife today."

O'Brien's mouth pressed into a straight line and his nostrils flared. "That so? Care to tell me about it?"

"Where can I find him?"

O'Brien cocked an eyebrow. "I fired him this morning."

Nate gritted his teeth. "Got any idea where he is?"

"Town, most likely. Check the saloon."

"I'll check there. I can't have my wife tormented."

"Congratulations on your marriage, by the way. I heard you got hitched, and she's a pretty little thing." O'Brien grinned and held out his hand.

Nate shook it. "Thanks. I'm a lucky man." And as he walked back to his horse and mounted, he realized how true that was. How many other wives would have drawn a gun on a man like Childress? And it wasn't just her fire and spirit that drew him or her exquisite beauty. It was something else, something that was all Lucy. Her fierce caring for her brother and sister, her determination to learn everything she needed to know to be a good rancher's wife, her moral backbone.

It had thrown him to see her in his mother's dress. He'd fingered that picture until it was about worn out. Until he'd seen her in Ma's dress, he hadn't realized how tiny his mother must have been too. No wonder Pa wasn't afraid that Lucy wouldn't make a good rancher's wife. He was always talking about how Ma had loved the ranch and how the men had adored and protected her.

Lucy had that way about her too. She drew people to her as naturally as bees to flowers. He glowered at the thought of how Childress had dared to touch her. Digging his knees into his horse's side, he headed to town.

When he reached Larson, he stopped at the saloon and pushed inside. Childress was there, as he'd expected. He was talking to Curly Milton, a ranch owner from the other side of the county.

Childress flushed when he saw Nate and the men behind him. His hand went to his holster, but he paused when Nate pulled his gun first.

"No need for gunplay." He held out his splayed fingers to show he held no weapon.

"Not this time, maybe," Nate said. "But I won't say the same if you dare come near my wife again." It was all he could do not to grab the man by the throat and throttle him.

Childress laughed, but it was forced and without humor. "I got no reason to seek out the pretty lady, Stanton. I merely stopped to help her out of the mud. If she says I did more than that, she's lying."

Rage tightened Nate's throat. He seized Childress by the collar and hauled him to his feet. "My wife doesn't lie," he snarled. "I'm giving you just one warning. Stay away from Lucy." He turned to the rancher. "This man manhandled my wife, Curly. You don't want his kind around your pretty daughters."

The man's bald head went pink and his brows drew together. "In that case, I'll take my leave of you two." He stood and tossed some coins onto the table where they rolled against the plate and stopped.

"Hey, what about my job?" Childress called.

"I'm not interested in hiring you." Curly clapped his hat on his head and strode out of the saloon.

Childress's lips drew back in a snarl like that of a rabid dog. "You'll pay for this, Stanton. You and that so-called wife of yours." He jerked out of Nate's grip and ran from the building.

Nate shouted and took off after him, but the varmint had vanished. Frowning, Nate ran for his horse. He would have to be more vigilant with Lucy.

TWENTY-FIVE

The Red River, swollen from spring rains, rushed along beside their picnic spot in a tumble of water and flotsam. Lucy watched as Nate tossed a ball with Jed and Eileen. Since he'd come back from confronting Childress two weeks ago, things had been pleasant between them. Too pleasant. His gaze was admiring and gentle, but it was as though he was waiting on a sign from her. Several times she'd opened her mouth to talk to him about their relationship, then closed it just as quickly.

They had family devotions each night, and Lucy was impressed at the amount of Scripture Nate knew and at the depth of his wisdom. She'd wanted Jed to have a godly role model, and he adored Nate. They attended worship every Sunday, making the drive to town like a normal family. But when she had looked around at the other families who filled the pews, she knew they were like none of them. She longed to be like the other wives, secure in a husband's love. She looked at Nate playing with the children and smiled. God had been good to them so far. He would bring them the rest of the way to the fulfillment of all he planned for them. She could hold on to that certainty.

Nate's sandy blond hair fell across his forehead as he laughed and feinted away from Jed. Eileen squealed and threw herself against his leg. A smile tugged at Lucy's lips. She caught her breath at the wonder of her feelings. For the first time, she loved him as a wife should love a husband. Looking at his masculine arms, she desired them around her. He looked at her, and she felt the heat of a blush on her cheeks. Did he know?

Nate reeled over with Eileen still clinging to him and collapsed on the quilt beside her. He closed his eyes. "I'm beat. We're supposed to be resting up before starting the roundup tomorrow, but I don't think this is the way to do it." He scooted over and put his head in Lucy's lap.

Lucy ran tentative fingers across his forehead, then lightly touched his thick hair. Nate's eyes were still closed, and for that she was thankful. She stroked his hair, enjoying the feel of it between her fingers. She didn't want to think about the roundup. Especially the branding. Her stomach congealed with dread at the thought. But Nate needed all the help he could get.

"What time do we start tomorrow?" she asked.

"I told the boys to meet at the south pasture at six. Lord willing, we'll be done by suppertime on Wednesday. Since we're starting so early, Pa suggested we bring Eileen to him tonight."

"She'll keep him running."

"It was either that or he'd insist on helping with the roundup. At least this way he feels useful, and Percy will help him. Eileen will be fine." Nate sat up and sighed. "I reckon we should be going. Pa is expecting us for supper, and Bessie will be caterwauling to be milked."

Their idyllic day was at an end. She gathered up the remains of their dinner, then folded the quilt. Jed carried the things to the wagon.

That night she could hardly sleep for worrying about the coming three days. What if there were spiders when they slept out on the ground? And what if the ranch hands realized she was a tenderfoot and despised her for it? She wanted Nate to be proud of her. Lucy sighed and rolled over. She could hear Nate's soft snore above her head in the loft. He obviously wasn't worried about the roundup. And why should he be? He wasn't the one on display, the one everyone would be judging. An image of Margaret, tall and competent, floated before her like a gray cloud in the sky. Margaret would know how to handle herself on a roundup. All Lucy could do was disappoint.

The rooster crowed at five, but Lucy was already awake. She hurriedly dressed in a pair of Jed's dungarees and one of his flannel shirts.

Nate's brows lifted when he saw her attire, but he grunted in approval. "Glad to see you showing some sense about it," was all he said.

She fixed breakfast while he loaded the bedrolls into the wagon. The three of them ate in silence. Lucy kept stealing glances at Nate's distracted face. He already had the cattle in his mind. After breakfast she followed him and Jed outside. The wagon was laden with the supplies for meals. At least part of her day would be spent with something she knew and loved. Bridget jumped into the wagon to join the fun.

The scene at the roundup was already chaotic. Cattle bellowed, and thick clouds of dust hung in the air. The air was fetid with the scent of cattle and manure. Lucy felt faint and nauseated, and the real work was yet to begin.

The men began to herd the longhorns together. Lucy mounted her mare and found her horse knew what to do better than she did. The mare cut and wheeled among the melee of horses and cattle while Bridget followed, nipping at the heels of the calves who tried to get away. They cut out the unbranded calves and herded them toward a corral the men had built.

Lucy took a deep breath as Rusty, the Stanton foreman, knelt to drop the branding irons in the fire. A movement to her right caught her eye, and she turned. Margaret O'Brien, her generous curves evident in her dungarees and shirt, laid her hand on Nate's arm. His head was bent attentively to her.

Jealousy, hot and unexpected, swamped Lucy. What was Margaret doing here? She looked completely at home in those clothes. She laughed and tilted her head coquettishly to listen to something Nate said, then walked toward the branding fire. Picking up a branding iron, she nodded for Rusty to ready the first calf.

The calf bucked and tried to run, but the two men holding it bore it to the ground. Margaret walked to the calf and applied the Stars Above brand. The calf bawled, and the sound smote Lucy's heart. She bit her lip so hard she could taste blood. The calf bawled again, and bile rose in her throat. Lucy turned to run, but her feet wouldn't obey her. A mist blocked her vision, and the ground rose up to meet her.

"Lucy!"

Hands shook her, but she kept her eyes shut. She didn't want to wake up. It was too early. She would just sleep a few more minutes, then get up to fix breakfast.

"Lucy, wake up."

Gradually she became aware of the hard chest she rested against and the feel of gentle hands holding her. The sounds around her penetrated her consciousness. Cattle lowing, men yelling above the din. Lucy opened her eyes and blinked. Nate's anxious face swam into focus. Over his shoulder she could see Jed, and just past him, Margaret's concerned face.

Memory flooded back. That calf, the awful bawling, and the stench of burning hair. She felt faint again and closed her eyes. Tears stung and slipped from her closed lids.

Nate's strong arm lifted her to a more upright position. "Would you like a drink of water?"

She nodded. Anything to avoid looking at the pity in Margaret's face. Pity for Nate, for the burden he carried having such a sissified wife. She sneaked a peek at his face through her lashes.

"Here, take a sip of water." He held a canteen to her lips and she gulped it, then coughed as it went down the wrong way.

"Careful." He held it to her lips again, and she took another drink before she swiped the back of her hand across her mouth.

"Thanks." She finally dared to meet his gaze. "I'm sorry, Nate," she whispered.

"Sorry for what? It's a bit overwhelming the first time. You're doing fine. I told you to stay home but you were insistent on coming."

"The calf." Lucy gulped and broke off.

"I know. But the calf is fine. Look." He pointed to the little blaze-faced calf on the other side of the fence. It nuzzled its mother, then scampered off to play with a friend.

Relief filled her, but the entire procedure still left a bad taste in her mouth. She let Nate help her to her feet. Wooziness rushed over her again, and Nate caught her or she would have fallen.

"Hey, Boss, 'spect you'll be having a little one scampering about, huh?" One of the men laughed, and heat flooded Lucy's face. If they only knew.

Nate ignored the impolite comment and escorted Lucy to

the wagon. She sank weakly onto the ground and leaned against a wagon wheel.

"You should have married Margaret," she muttered. She sensed Nate go still.

"What's she got to do with this? Are you upset she's here? She always helps with our branding, and I help with theirs. She's just a friend, Lucy." His voice was stiff. "If you don't know I'm an honorable man by now, you don't know me at all."

She winced and was suffused with shame. "It's not you, it's me. I'm useless as a ranch wife. Margaret wasn't just watching, she participated. I will never be able to do that, Nate." Her shoulders slumped, and she buried her face in her hands.

Nate knelt beside her and his breath whispered on her neck. His big hands took hers and pulled them from her face. "Lucy, I never asked you to do that. You're the one who's so determined to prove yourself. You don't have to prove anything to me."

She stared into his gray eyes doubtfully. "You said I was little and puny, that I couldn't be a good rancher's wife."

"I was angry then, and wrong. Size doesn't matter—heart does. And you've got the biggest heart I've ever seen." His eyes were tender, and his hands cupped her face.

Her heart surged with hope. Did he mean it? His face came nearer, and her eyes fluttered shut. She held her breath and lifted her face. His breath touched her face. She waited in almost unbearable anticipation.

"Is she all right, Nate?"

Lucy's eyes flew open at the sound of Margaret's voice. Nate rocked back on his heels, then stood.

He held out his hand to Lucy. "She's fine, Margaret. Thanks for your concern. I'd best get back to the men."

His warm palm left Lucy's with obvious reluctance. She forced herself to smile at Margaret. The other woman watched Nate as he strode back to the dusty, noisy scene. She tore her gaze from Nate's back and smiled distractedly at Lucy.

"I'd better get back too." She dashed off without waiting for Lucy to reply.

Lucy turned her back on the commotion and began to sort through her supplies. She would not watch the woman ogle her husband. God would not be pleased at her jealousy. Nate said he was happy with her the way she was. She would cling to that.

Dinner was nearly ready when a buggy came rolling across the field. Shading her eyes, she waved at Henry and Eileen. Henry stopped the buggy at the chuck wagon and hoisted his bulk to the ground. Lucy went to get Eileen.

"Couldn't stay away, could you?" Lucy asked Henry with a teasing smile.

"In all the years we've been ranching here, I've never missed a roundup. I'm not going to start now." Henry's color was good, and his eyes were bright with excitement. "I think I'll go see if my boy is doing it right." He strode eagerly toward the men and animals.

"It smells." Eileen wound her arms around Lucy's neck and wrinkled her small nose.

"I know, sweetheart. But we'll stay here and get dinner ready." She put Eileen on the end of the wagon and stirred the stew one last time. She heard Eileen gasp and whirled to see what was the matter.

A Comanche, dressed in buckskin and moccasins, stood by her sister. His brown hand was touching Eileen's shining golden locks. Eileen's blue eyes were wide, and tears trembled on the ends of her lashes.

Lucy sprang to her side and thrust her body between Eileen

and the Indian. "Would you like something to eat?" she asked in a shrill voice.

The Indian's dark eyes narrowed, and he touched Lucy's blond hair with a curious hand. Lucy flinched away, and he frowned.

"How much?" He gestured at Eileen. "I give two fine horses for girl child."

Lucy put her sister behind her. "No! She is not for sale."

"I give you five horses." He reached around Lucy for Eileen.

"No!" Lucy knocked his hand away. Trembling inside, she was determined not to show her fear. Where were the men? Didn't they see the danger?

The Indian scowled and stepped back. He crossed his arms over his chest. "Ten horses."

"No, not for a hundred horses." She scooped Eileen into her arms and dashed toward the safety of the men and cattle. Was he following? Risking a glance back, she didn't see a rock in her path. Her foot struck it, and she went tumbling through the air. Lucy desperately tried to hang on to Eileen and to protect her with her own body.

Twisting as she fell, her arm hit the ground first, and she felt a sickening jerk inside. Crushing pain and nausea dimmed her sight to a pinpoint. She held Eileen against her with her good arm. A moan escaped.

Eileen began to sob and wail. Moments later Nate knelt beside her.

"What happened? Are you all right?"

"My arm. The Indian," she babbled.

Nate ran his hand over her arm, and she cried out when he touched her elbow. "You've dislocated your elbow. I'll have to put it back in place." He stood and waved. "Margaret, could you help me?"

Lucy gritted her teeth. They wouldn't hear her cry out. She would show them what stuff she was made of.

Margaret held her hand while Nate took hold of Lucy's arm, one hand on either side of her elbow. "Ready?" Beads of perspiration stood out on his forehead.

"Yes," Lucy whispered. She closed her eyes and pressed her lips together.

Nate jerked, and Lucy thought she would be sick. A scream hovered on her lips, but she refused to let it out. The pain was excruciating, and her vision wavered for several long moments. Then the pain began to ebb until it was a manageable dull throb.

"You're a brave woman." Nate helped her to sit. "What happened?"

Peering past his shoulder, she realized the Indian was gone. Her shoulders eased and she sighed. Eileen was safe. She told Nate about the Indian's offer for Eileen.

He sucked in his breath, and his face went white. "You're both beautiful and rather exotic looking to him. I'll have the men keep an eye out, and I want you to stay close to me."

He smiled, but his expression seemed forced to Lucy. She shuddered. He wouldn't have to tell her twice to stay close.

He stood. "You rest that elbow. Margaret can see to finishing dinner."

"I can do it." Lucy managed to get to her feet. Margaret wasn't taking over her job. She knew this competitive spirit she had toward the other woman was a sin, but she couldn't seem to help herself. Her elbow throbbed, but she pressed it against her side and hurried to finish dinner. She would prove to Nate she was a better wife than Margaret if it was the last thing she did.

TWENTY-SIX

⮾

Nate limped a bit as he walked toward the campsite. A blister had formed on his heel, his back felt like someone had stuck a pitchfork through it, and his left hand throbbed from a burn left by the branding iron. His bedroll was going to feel mighty good tonight.

The sight of the firelight on Lucy's golden hair made the glow of the campfire even more welcome. Her radiant hair fell to her waist. What would she do if he walked up and plunged his hands into that glorious mass? Scream, probably. He was filthy and he stank of cattle.

But he was blessed to call her his wife. His bemused grin faded. Unfortunately, that's all she was. A woman he called his wife. He'd watched for a sign from her that she was ready to move forward into a deeper relationship with him, but just when he thought there might be hope, she stepped back again.

She looked up as he approached. Her blue eyes were shadowed, but he didn't think it was from the pain of her dislocated elbow. She seemed to be using that arm a bit.

"I heated some water for you," she said. "Jed already washed up and went to bed."

"He worked as hard as a man today. You've done a good job with him." Nate thrust his hands into the kettle of hot water, splashing it over his face and neck. "Whew, that feels mighty good."

"I brought a piece of pie from the chuck wagon. I thought you might be hungry."

"I'm almost too tired to be hungry. But pie sounds good." He took the pie from her outstretched hand and gulped it down in four bites. All he really wanted to do was crawl into his bedroll and rest his weary body.

The air was muggy, even as late as it was. Staring into his wife's lovely face, Nate felt all thought of sleep leave him. He pushed a log over to the fire and sat on it, then patted the spot next to him. "Let's jaw awhile. I'm not as tired as I thought I was."

She came toward him and perched on the log next to him. Her arm brushed his, and the contact sent a shiver up his back. "How's your arm?"

"Better. It still aches some, but the more I use it, the better it gets." She leaned forward and poked at the fire with a stick. Tiny sparks escaped the flames and shot upward into the dark night.

Nate reached over and captured her hand. She jumped but didn't pull away. Instead, her slim fingers curled around his and returned his pressure. "I was proud of you," he said softly.

Lucy jerked her head up. "How could you be proud? I fainted at the sight of a simple branding. I ran shrieking in fear at the sight of an Indian, then stumbled over my own feet and dislocated my elbow." Her voice was low and anguished. "I'm sure the men were laughing at the boss's poor choice of a wife. I came here to be a helpmeet, but it seems all I've managed to do is to be a hindrance."

"That's not true, Lucy. I'm glad you're here."

"Truly?" She turned to face him, and the movement brought her face only inches from his own. Her breath touched his face, and he caught a glimpse of perfect white teeth in the moonlight. Her breath was sweet and enticing. Something stirred in his heart. Some new emotion had sprung to life.

He couldn't help himself. His fingers traveled up her arm to her mane of hair, and he pulled her into his arms. Nate heard her soft gasp, and it only served to inflame the passion he felt for her. She fit into his arms as though she were made for him.

Her face turned up to his, and he pressed his lips against hers. At first Lucy was stiff, then she wound her arms around his neck and returned his kiss. His heart hammered against his ribs as he tasted the sweetness of a real kiss from her for the first time. The wonder of holding his wife in his arms this way drove all thought from his head.

He wanted to go on kissing her, but she pulled away a bit. "Did I hurt you?" he muttered in a hoarse whisper.

Keeping her face turned away, she shook her head. Was she crying? Nate touched Lucy's chin and turned her to face him. Her face was wet with tears, and his throat tightened. "What is it, Lucy?"

"Now you kiss me. Now when I've failed so miserably. I don't want your pity, Nate. I want your love and your respect. You expected certain things from a wife, and I don't think I can ever meet those expectations."

"I don't have any expectations. I was wrong to lash out at you when you first came. Wrong and pigheaded."

Lucy knuckled away her tears. "You and Pa are building an empire here. An empire takes an empress, someone who can stand at your side and fight whatever comes without fear. Today has shown me how inadequate I really am."

"This doesn't sound like the Lucy I know. Where's that spunky little woman who faced down the wolf? Where's that gal who made me toe the line at mealtimes? I need you, Lucy. I just didn't realize it before." He twined a long curl around his finger.

"I wish that were true. You're so self-sufficient, Nate, a self-made man. I have nothing to bring you that you don't already have." Her chest heaved. "I want to be a blessing, but I don't know how."

He tried to pull her close again, but she stood and evaded his grasp. "You're the only blessing I need."

She relaxed against him and he tucked her into the bedroll. "Get some sleep, honey."

He wandered through the maze of bedrolls and campfires until he reached the outskirts of the camp. What had gotten into her? He didn't expect her to brand cattle. Lucy likely needed wooing, but he just didn't know how to do it, especially encumbered by her brother and sister. Not that he didn't love them, but sometimes a man needed space to say those things only a wife should hear.

All he knew were cattle and horses, and they were easily handled by a cattle dog. He was out of his element here. If one of the newfangled universities offered a course on women, he would be the first to sign up. Lucy made his head spin with all her jawing and emotional turmoil. Next time she started talking like that, he'd just pull her into his arms and kiss her until she shut up. He grinned at the thought. She would likely toss a clump of mud at his head like she did to Childress.

He flopped down under a cottonwood tree. "I could use some help here, Lord. What do I do about this?" In the stillness of the night, Scripture crept into his mind. Scripture he thought he'd never need to apply to his own life.

"Husbands, love your wives, even as Christ also loved the church, and gave himself for it."

The words wrapped around his heart. He'd admitted he cared for her, but did he love her? Nate examined his emotions.

He loved Lucy. She was the best thing that had ever happened to him.

He didn't care if she never came on another roundup or ever learned to rope a calf. He loved her fire and determination, her desire to do right, just the essence of who she was. What she did was unimportant.

A knot gripped his gut. He hadn't done a very good job of letting Lucy know that. No wonder she was all wrapped up in performance and ability. He had to tell her how he felt and make it right.

But as quickly as the notion struck, he knew that was wrong. Words wouldn't convince Lucy. Actions were the only thing she would understand now. His actions had told her she was unimportant next to the ranch. Only actions would convince her she was the most important thing in his life. She would have to see the difference in him. Then he would tell her he loved her. Not before.

LUCY'S ARM STILL ached, but it was a good sort of hurt. The kind she felt when she probed a wound and brought out a splinter. The way she felt when her stomach burned with hunger but Jed and Eileen got up from the table with full bellies. Her arm would heal, thanks to Nate.

From here she could see Margaret's strong body, could hear her robust laughter. Margaret would have bred strong sons for Nate. She could have stood at his side, shoulder to shoulder, and carved an empire out of this desolate place. Tears pricked Lucy's eyes, but she pushed them away. She would prove her worth somehow.

She kicked open her bedroll and sat down to take off her boots. Crawling under the blanket, she groaned at the hardness of the ground. She'd gotten spoiled in that soft bed Nate had made for her.

As if the thought had brought him out of the fog, Nate came through the smoke of the fire with an intent smile on his face. He said nothing, simply picked up his bedroll from the other side of Jed and laid it down beside her. He shifted it closer to her, then took off his boots and crawled under the blanket.

His arm snaked out from the covers and his fingers grasped hers. She waited for him to speak, to explain his intentions, but moments later she heard the even sound of his breathing. But even in his sleep, his hand still gripped hers.

Lucy rolled over on her side and watched his face in the moonlight. She'd longed to watch him sleep for months. Now that she had the chance, dozens of people were around. Lucy was so bewildered, she found it hard to fall asleep, in spite of her fatigue. But Nate's presence beside her eased the fear she'd had of sleeping on the ground. No tarantula would dare bother her with his strong arms next to her.

Jed and Nate were already gone by the time she awakened. Lucy sat up and rubbed the sleep from her eyes. The morning air was heavy with the promise of heat and humidity. A single spray of some kind of yellow wildflower lay on top of her bedroll.

"Nate," she murmured. She picked up the flower. What had gotten into him? He was acting almost romantic, which was totally out of character for him. She lifted the flower to her nose and breathed deeply of its fragrance. Sighing, she laid it aside and scrambled to her feet. There was a lot to do today.

She rolled up her bedroll and pulled on her boots, after shaking them first to make sure no creepy crawlies had found their way inside. She tugged her comb through her hair, then wadded her long tresses up on top of her head. Good thing she didn't have a mirror because the sight of her bedraggled state would surely be depressing.

When she made her way to the chuck wagon, most of the men were already out with the herd. She took a tin plate and scooped up a bit of the congealed gravy and hard biscuits. Lucy shook her head. If she'd awakened in time, she would have made some flapjacks. If the illustrious Margaret had made this breakfast, she wasn't as perfect as Nate thought. She winced at her own unattractive thoughts.

The mess had been left dirty, so she scraped the remains onto a plate for Bridget and heated water to wash up. The bawling of the calves made her wince, and she thought about going back to the cabin. But Lucy couldn't force herself to go. Quitting was against her nature. Maybe today would be better. Nate's gift of the flower had given her fresh hope somehow.

She had just finished the dishes when Margaret came toward her. Striding like a man, her hair carelessly braided and tossed over one shoulder, she was the picture of health and vitality. Her white teeth flashed in her tanned face, and Lucy had to smile back.

"I need a break," Margaret said. "My throat is as dry as gypsum. Any water handy?"

"Of course." Lucy grabbed a tin cup and scooped some water into it.

Margaret drank thirstily and wiped her mouth with the back of her hand. Lucy watched in fascination. She'd never met a woman who was so vital and alive. Margaret made no pretense of femininity, but she was mesmerizing in spite of it.

Margaret plopped onto the ground at Lucy's feet. "You don't like me, do you, Lucy?"

Lucy blinked. "I—I don't really know you, Margaret. I'm sure you're a very nice person."

Margaret laughed. "Nice? That's the first time anyone ever accused me of that. Overbearing, outspoken, those are terms I'm more familiar with."

Lucy opened her mouth, then closed it again. What could she say to that? It was all true, after all.

Margaret seemed amused at her obvious discomfiture. "Don't worry. You won't hurt my feelings. Your problem with me is that you think I'm after your husband. You wouldn't be far wrong. But I know when I'm licked. He's in love with his pretty, genteel wife, and someone like me will never tempt him away."

In love with her? For a moment Lucy's heart soared, then thumped back to the ground. Not likely. He felt something for her, she would allow that. But love? He loved his ranch, not her.

Margaret leaned forward. "We're going to be neighbors, and we need to clear the air between us. Yes, I was hurt when you came waltzing in the store on the arm of the man I had claimed as my own. Not that Nate realized he was claimed, mind you, but I'd staked him out just the same. But I'm now sure it's for the best. Nate and me are too hardheaded to rub along very well together. We would have always been clashing heads." She grinned. "Not that you haven't had your share of clashes."

"I—I do have a temper myself." Heat scorched Lucy's cheeks.

"You would make him a much better wife. Unfortunately, it's too late."

Margaret's eyes narrowed. "He loves you, Lucy. If you think there's anything between us, I'm telling you there's not."

She wished Margaret spoke the truth. "You're so strong. I wish I could be like you."

Margaret shook her finger in Lucy's face. "Sounds to me like you're expecting more of yourself than Nate expects from you. You need a dose of reality. Loving one another through arguments and sickness, through lean times and child rearing, that's reality. Let off trying to control all of it and just accept what comes." Margaret rose to her feet and swept her up in a bear hug. "We'll be friends one of these days, Lucy. Give us both some time to lick our wounds. I like you. You've got spunk. It's about time you showed it."

Lucy's nose was pressed against Margaret's shirt. The woman could be Lucy's friend if she could let down her defenses. Lucy hugged her back. "Thank you, Margaret."

TWENTY-SEVEN

❦

Lucy stirred the beans and then began to make cornbread for supper. The roundup was almost over, and she would be glad to get out of the dust and noise. And the smell! She wrinkled her nose. Margaret's words echoed in her mind. Did she expect too much of herself? And she had to admit she took pride in doing more and giving more than other people.

Tears welled in her eyes, but she pressed her lips together and beat the cornbread batter as if it were the cause of all her turmoil. Tears never solved anything, but lately it seemed she was on the verge of them all the time.

While the cornbread was baking, she walked over to watch the last of the roundup. A thrill of joy shot through her as she watched Nate astride his black gelding. He'd only bought the horse last week—a magnificent animal. Man and horse were well matched. Nate's powerful arms controlled the huge creature as an ordinary man would a pony, while his muscular thighs dared the horse to try to throw him.

Nate's sandy hair was already beginning to lighten from the spring sunshine. He was a man who would turn heads no matter where he lived or what he did. Margaret rode next to him. She had that same vitality and vigor Nate possessed. But Margaret said she didn't want Nate. How could any woman say that and mean it? Nate had but to crook his finger, and any woman would want him. Lucy's heart clenched. She would earn his love somehow.

He wheeled around on his horse and saw her. A tender smile accompanied the hand he lifted in greeting. Nate cantered over and looked down at her from his saddle. "You've been in hiding all day. You getting used to the noise and commotion?"

She smiled. "I just thought I'd look to see how Jed was doing." And she had a need to see her husband, but she couldn't tell him that. She couldn't get enough of looking at him lately. What would he think of that if he knew?

Nate pointed out a group of riders across the field from them. "Rusty is teaching him to rope. He's picking it up pretty well, though on his first few attempts he managed to rope the fence post instead of the calf."

"You've done so much for him. He actually likes work, and he's got a confidence I've never seen him show before. Thank you, Nate."

The tenderness in his gaze sucked the breath from her lungs. The expressions on his face and the solicitousness of his manner for the past two days had Lucy pondering. Was he really not disappointed in the bargain anymore? She was afraid to hope for that.

"Jed's a good boy. He'll be an asset on the cattle drive next week." He looked over her head. "Here comes Pa with Eileen."

Lucy turned and waved.

"I've missed her. She keeps things lively."

Lucy laughed. "I think things have been plenty lively around here."

"At least Zeke didn't show up."

Lucy gasped. "Um, just where did you turn that spider loose?"

Nate grinned. "Far from here. But spiders can travel a far piece. Want to take a walk in the moonlight tonight and look for him? He might come if I call."

In spite of herself, Lucy felt the corners of her mouth turn up. "No thanks. I might have to ask you to stomp on him."

"I'd do it for you."

His gray eyes seemed to reach into her soul with an emotion she hadn't seen there before. What was going on in his head? A lump formed in Lucy's throat. "You—you would?"

His gaze caressed her face. "I reckon I'd do most anything for you, Lucy."

How did she answer that? Before she could make a fool of herself, Eileen and Henry reached them.

"This little girl is pert near pining herself to death for you," Henry said in a booming voice. "I tried reading her a story, and Percy even offered to let her help bake cookies, which was a big sacrifice since he never lets anyone in his kitchen." He caught Lucy's gaze. "Except for you, Lucy."

Eileen threw herself at Lucy's legs and began to clamber up them like she would a tree. "Lucy, we baked-ed cookies with raisins. Percy let me put the raisins in."

Lucy hugged her, relishing the feel of her small body. "You're getting to be a big girl, sweetie. Did you thank Percy?"

Eileen nodded and her blond ponytail whipped in the breeze. She gazed up at Nate's horse. "Can I pet him?"

"How about a ride on Morgan?" Nate said. "Want to come too, Lucy?"

She glanced back at the chuck wagon. "I really should check

on the cornbread." But the thought of being next to her husband for just a few minutes was almost too enticing to resist.

"I'll watch it," Henry said. "You go ahead with Nate."

The pleased expression he wore brought a smile to Lucy's lips.

Nate held out a hand. "Pa, you hold Eileen until I get Lucy up here, then she can put Eileen in front of her."

Eileen held out her arms to Henry. "Grandpa, you want to come too?"

Henry lifted her into his arms. "No thanks, pumpkin. That horse of Nate's won't let just anyone ride him. You and your sister are special."

Eileen preened. "We're special, Lucy."

Nate slid back in the saddle, then gripped Lucy's hand and lifted her up in front of him. Henry handed Eileen up to her, while Nate reached around Lucy's waist and took the reins. He smelled of horse and leather with a hint of spice from his hair tonic. His breath ruffled her hair, and without thinking Lucy leaned back against his chest.

The shock of contact slicked her palms with perspiration, and she swallowed. Touching him just made her realize all she was missing. After taking a deep breath, she started to ease forward, but his left arm came around her waist and pulled her closer. She could feel the hard muscles of his chest against her back, and he rested his chin on her head.

"Faster, Nate!" Eileen kicked her little legs and giggled.

Nate obliged by digging his heels into Morgan's ribs. The horse broke into a canter. Eileen loosened her grip on Lucy's arm and clapped. They rode with the scent of sage and creosote blowing in their faces.

Finally Eileen tugged on Lucy's arm. "I have to go potty," she said in a loud whisper.

Lucy nodded and told Nate. He pulled on the reins and stopped beside a rocky outcropping on the far side of the men. He slid to the ground and reached up to lift Eileen down.

"Wait for your sister," he told her.

His big hands spanned Lucy's waist as he lifted her from the saddle. Setting her on the ground mere inches from him, she had to fight an urge to wrap her arms around his waist and rest her head on his chest. What would he do if she did that? His gray eyes were somber, and his hands still held her. She stepped away. Tearing her gaze from his, she turned to check on Eileen.

A rattle sounded to their right. Eileen stood only two feet from a coiled rattler. "Eileen, no!" Lucy hurtled toward her sister. A split second later the rattler struck at Eileen, but Lucy got there first. The fangs sank into Lucy's right forearm, then pulled back for another strike. Eileen was shrieking, but Lucy felt nothing at first. Then a boom sounded, and a bullet slammed into the snake, driving its still-writhing body away.

Nate was there instantly, kneeling beside her. Two tiny puncture wounds oozing blood was all the damage Lucy could see, so she didn't understand why his face was so white. She felt fine. The snake must not have had much venom.

"Let me see." His voice was terse.

She cradled Eileen with her good arm and held the right one up like a child offering a gift. Dizziness suddenly swamped her. Then the pain struck, deep, burning pain. Lucy bit her lip in an effort not to cry out. She gritted her teeth against the agony.

Nate took her arm in one hand, reaching into his pocket with the other. "Pa!" he bellowed across the field.

The rowdy, boisterous calls of the roundup faded until there was just Nate's white face and Eileen's keening cry. Lucy held on to both to keep herself conscious. She mustn't frighten Eileen. Her sister clung to her and she patted her hand weakly.

Nate scooped Lucy up in his arms. Henry took Eileen, and they both ran with their burdens toward the fire. Nate pulled his pocketknife out of his dungarees and heated it in the fire. He held it poised over Lucy's arm, an apology in his eyes.

His fingers bit into her flesh, but Lucy didn't cry out. The deeper pain of the bite was too great. She fought nausea and breathed deeply.

"This will hurt," he said softly. "I'm sorry, love." Then the knife plunged down into Lucy's arm, and he made two slits over the puncture wounds.

The pain bit into her and she cried out. Circles of blackness came and went in her vision. Nate brought the cuts to his mouth. He sucked, then spat bright blood. Again he sucked the poison from her wounds and spat it out.

Time lost all meaning for Lucy as she watched her husband battle to save her life. She felt far away, as if this were all happening to someone else. Her vision blurred and chills ravaged her. She tried to speak, to tell him not to do this. Nate was risking his own life to save hers. If he had a cut in his mouth, the poison would kill him. She had brought him no blessing. She'd been a curse instead. But the words wouldn't come. Her numb tongue was thick in her mouth. She closed her eyes and welcomed the blackness.

"YEEHAW!" NATE LASHED the whip over the horses' heads as he drove the rig toward home. Her head on Jed's lap, Lucy lolled bonelessly in the back. Nate didn't know another time he'd been this afraid. Not when the fire burned down the barn, not when the Red River flood came almost to the house. His knuckles white, he urged the horses to go faster.

Dust kicked up behind him as he jerked the team to a halt in front of the main house. He scooped up Lucy and carried her into the house and up the steps to his old bedroom. His boot heels echoed emptily on the polished wood floors. Lucy's welfare landed squarely on his own shoulders.

He laid her in the bed. "Bring me that bowl and pitcher of water," he told Jed. Jed sprang to obey and brought the washcloth as well. Nate loosened the buttons on her shirt and began to sponge her with the damp cloth.

Lucy thrashed and cried out. Nate felt helpless as he watched her agony. He wished he could take it for her. Rattler venom could kill even a hardy man, let alone a tiny thing like Lucy.

The front door banged, and moments later he heard his father's voice.

"Nate, how is she?" His father's voice was loud in the quiet room.

"Still unconscious."

"Doc will be here shortly. I sent Rusty after him." His pa stood at the foot of the bed, his big hands gripping the bedpost.

"Where's Eileen?"

"Percy has her. He'll be along with her in a few hours, once we're sure Lucy is out of danger."

He stared at his father. "Will she be out of danger, Pa? What if she doesn't make it?" The question was an anguished cry from his heart. He felt like a child again, needing assurance from the one stable thing in his life. "How did you bear it when Ma died?"

His pa was silent for a moment, his dark eyes moist and far-away. "One day at a time, Nate. I made it one day at a time." He leaned over and gripped Nate's hand. "It will be all right, son."

"We have to pray." Nate felt Jed's fingers creep into his hand, and he squeezed them with more reassurance than he felt. He bowed his head. "Oh Lord, we can only ask for your mercy right now. Don't take Lucy from us." His throat closed, and he couldn't speak. Jed gave a slight sob.

His thoughts were too jumbled to even voice out loud, but he knew the Holy Spirit was there to speak them to the Lord. Jed sniffled, and Nate raised his head. They all stared at Lucy until the door banged again and the doctor came bustling down the hall.

"How's my patient?" Doc set his black bag on the foot of the bed.

Lucy's face was ashen against the white pillow. Doc examined her pupils, then pressed his stethoscope to her chest. Nate held his breath and continued to pray.

Doc straightened. "Her heartbeat is pretty irregular, Nate. I won't lie to you. It's going to be pretty touch and go through the night. Keep sponging her off with water and try to get some water down her as well." He gripped Nate's arm and peered into his face. "How about you? Suffering any ill effects from sucking out that poison? Any sores in your mouth?"

Nate shook the doctor's arm off impatiently. "I'm fine. Do you think she'll make it, Doc?"

The doctor shrugged, his brown eyes kind. "Do I look like God, son? Sometimes I feel all I do is travel around to watch him work. It's like offering a thimble of water to help the ocean. You are already appealing to the only one who can decide that." He snapped his bag closed. "There's nothing I can do for her, Nate.

She'll likely wake up soon, but she'll be hurting some. I'll leave some laudanum here to give her. If she gets worse, send Percy for me."

Nate nodded, and Pa walked the doctor to the front door. Jed sighed and sat in the chair beside his sister. Putting his face in his hands, he gave a huge sigh. Nate put a hand on his shoulder. "We'll get through this together, Jed."

Jed raised wet eyes to meet his gaze. "What will happen to us if—if Lucy dies?" he whispered.

Nate knelt beside him. "We're a family now. I'll take care of you and Eileen no matter what. Don't you worry about anything. I love you, Jed. You and Eileen both."

He flung his arms around Nate's neck and burst into noisy sobs. Nate pulled him tight against his chest and patted his back.

"What's all that caterwauling?" Lucy's voice was weak. She struggled to sit up, then whimpered. Gasping, she gripped her stomach, and her face went a shade whiter. "Water," she whispered.

"I'll get it!" Jed rushed from the room.

Nate knelt beside the bed and touched Lucy's cheek. "Feeling pretty bad?"

"Like the barn fell on me." She tried to smile but moaned instead.

Nate smoothed the hair back from her forehead. "You're going to be fine. The doctor was just here. We'll have some rough next few hours, but you hang on."

Her fingers crept across the top of the quilt and gripped his hand. "If I don't make it, Nate—"

"Hush, don't even think that way." Now that she was awake, he felt a surge of hope, and not even Lucy could be allowed to dampen it.

"Jed and Eileen—"

"Don't worry about them. They'll be fine."

"But if something should happen, if I don't pull through this—"

Nate caressed her cheek. "Rest, love. I'll take care of Jed and Eileen."

Relief lit her face, then cramps struck her, and she doubled up in agony. Nate felt helpless watching her suffer. Remembering the laudanum, he snatched it up and uncapped the bottle. He slid an arm under her and managed to get a swallow down her. Gasping, she fell back against the pillow.

Jed brought back the water, and Nate gave Lucy a drink. Once she was sleeping again, he talked Jed into getting some rest, promising to call him if there was any change.

FOR THREE DAYS Nate sat for long hours in the chair beside Lucy, offering her sips of water between bouts of sickness and sleeping. Her chills finally eased, and a bit of color began to come back to her cheeks. Nate was bleary-eyed with fatigue, and when she closed her eyes, he dropped to the floor and rested his head against the mattress.

Lucy's fingers entwined in his hair. "There's room in the bed for you."

He raised his head and stared into her blue eyes. She'd made it over the hump. He could see it in her tender smile and pink cheeks. Without another word, she pulled back the quilt and scooted back against the wall. Nate pulled off his boots and crawled into the bed.

He stretched out his arm, and Lucy curled up against his side. The sensation of someone else in the bed was a strange one, but something he thought he could get used to pretty quickly. Her breathing evened out, and he relaxed himself. She was asleep. Now if he could do the same. His mind whirled. When she was fully recovered, they would have to have a long talk. It was time to take up their lives together in earnest.

AN UNFAMILIAR WEIGHT pressed against Lucy's waist, and she opened her eyes to find herself facing the wall in an unfamiliar room. She tried to move her arm and winced. The pain brought the memories flooding back. She looked down to see what pinned her in place and found an arm. Nate's arm.

Shock rippled through her, and she eased away and sat up. Last night his face had been tight with worry and fatigue. Now sleep had eased the lines and tension. A wave of love swept over her, and she reached over and smoothed the hair back from his face. His eyes flew open, and she stared deep into their depths.

A smile curved his firm lips. "Good morning. How do you feel?"

She responded with an answering smile. "A little sore and weak, but better I think." Much better, in fact. She felt clear-headed. And hungry.

He lifted his hand, and his fingers grazed her cheek. "You look lovely."

Heat flooded her cheeks, and she tore her gaze away. She glanced toward the sunshine streaming through the window. "What day is it?"

"Thursday. You've been out for three days."

She gasped at that news. She'd interfered with the ranch. "When do you leave for the cattle drive?"

"You eager to get rid of me?"

Her gaze flew to meet his again. "Of course not. I—I just thought you'd be gone already."

"I wasn't about to leave my wife."

The cattle drive was important, so his desire to be with her told her as much as the tender expression in his eyes. "Where's Jed?"

"In the kitchen. You want to see the children? They've been so worried."

She nodded. "Was I so terribly sick?"

He leaned closer and pressed his warm lips against her cheek. "I almost lost you, Lucy. Don't ever scare me like that again."

She smiled. "I'll try not to."

He kissed her again. "I'll send the children in. I need to see about finding another cook. Marcus broke his leg yesterday. I can see we're going to have several weeks of hardtack and poor grub, but we'll live." He tucked the quilt around her, obviously reluctant to leave. "I'll be right back." He swung his legs out of bed and went to the door.

Lucy watched him leave, but a hard rock of determination grew within her. She'd failed at the roundup, but she would prove to him she could stand toe-to-toe with Margaret. Earning his love might not be easy, but it would be worth it.

NATE SHOOK HIS head as he walked to the barn to help with chores. The gal had spunk. He was almost giddy with relief that she'd pulled through. It had been touch and go for way too long.

Eileen was in the barn playing with the kittens. She sat on the straw with six kittens tumbling over her lap. "Can I take one home, Nate?"

"Not until they're weaned from their mama." He stooped to talk to her. "Which one do you want?"

"I like the white one." She held it up to her cheek. "She has one blue eye and one green one."

"So she does."

Eileen stared up at him. Her lip began to quiver. "Is my Lucy going to go to heaven?"

He sat cross-legged beside her and pulled her onto his lap. "Not anytime soon. I just talked to her, and she ate breakfast."

The child began to sob noisily. "I don't want her to go to heaven. Not ever. My daddy went to heaven, and I never get to see him anymore. I want Lucy to stay with me."

He stroked her hair. "She's going to stay with you, honey. I love her so much that I'd fight the devil himself to keep her."

She hiccupped, then her tears subsided. "Lucy doesn't think you love her. You said she was too little. Don't you like little girls?"

He hugged her. "Little girls are my favorite. I love Lucy, but it's a secret. Don't tell her, okay? I want to tell her myself."

Her small hands patted his face. "Little girls are okay?"

"I love you, Eileen. I want to be your daddy and big brother all rolled into one. Is that okay?"

Her blue eyes were enormous as she stared at him. "Can I call you Papa?"

A lump formed in his throat. "I'd like that very much. Promise you won't tell Lucy yet?"

She held up her small hand. "Pinky swear?"

He hooked her little finger with his. "Pinky swear. I'll let you know when you can talk about it. It will be soon."

But when? If he told her before he left, he wasn't sure he could go.

TWENTY-EIGHT

◦◦◦◦

By the end of the day Lucy was longing for home. The main ranch house was lovely, but it wasn't her home. Funny how she had begun to think of the cabin as her home so quickly. She hadn't had a home her entire life, not a real home. Now she did.

Nate brought the buggy to the front of the house, then escorted her out. His steadying arm around her waist gave her a peculiar, happy feeling. Jed helped Eileen clamber into the backseat while Nate swung Lucy up onto the front seat. She felt naked without her bonnet, but it had been lost somehow in the excitement. The sun on her bare head was a welcome sensation. She still felt chilled and weak.

"Cold?"

She forced a smile. "Not really. I'm feeling much better. The sun feels good."

"At least you won't be on the trail with the dust mixing with the perspiration until you look like you're covered in mud."

They crested a hill and the cabin came into sight. A curl of smoke rose in a welcoming spiral from the chimney. "Someone's started a fire. That's odd. It's way too hot for a fire. Unless it's the cookstove."

Nate frowned. "Maybe one of the hands came over." He stopped the buggy in front of the house instead of the barn. He jumped out and lifted Lucy down. His manner was brusque and businesslike as if he had something else on his mind. He helped her to the door.

The door swung open as they reached it, and Margaret's shapely form filled the doorway. "Welcome home," she said with a smile. "Now I'm not staying, mind you. But I thought after your ordeal you wouldn't feel up to cooking. There's a roast and potatoes in the oven, and your bed is all ready for you." She stepped aside to allow them to enter.

"H-How thoughtful," Lucy stammered. Margaret's overwhelming presence and many abilities just made Lucy feel even more inadequate. She squared her shoulders and smiled at the other woman. She could learn from Margaret.

"We sure do appreciate it," Nate said. There was affection in the nod he gave her.

Nate led Lucy to the bed and made her sit down. Kneeling beside her, he slipped her boots off.

"I'm fine," she protested. "I feel better than I expected to."

"I still want you to lie down and rest. I'll get a quilt." He took a quilt from the rack and pulled it over her.

Margaret's face was filled with concern. "Can I do anything for you, Lucy?"

"No, you've done so much already. Thank you, Margaret."

"If there's anything you need, just send Jed after me." Margaret picked up her basket and went to the door. "I'll check in on you tomorrow. Doc says your recovery has been nearly miraculous. I'll be here to help while Nate is gone too. Call for me anytime."

"I'll walk you out," Nate said. "I need to talk to you anyway."

JED FIXED HER a cup of tea, and Eileen curled up beside her on the bed while Lucy read her a story from one of the books they'd brought in the trunk. The scent of the roast and potatoes began to fill the air. Eileen fell asleep beside her, and Jed went outside to practice his rope throwing. He took Bridget with him. The long-suffering dog would be his "calf."

She heard Nate overhead in the loft. Scraping and banging, he seemed to be moving furniture. Curious, Lucy eased out of bed without awakening Eileen and went to the ladder leading to the loft and climbed it. Peering over the top, she found Nate with a broom in his hand.

He saw her and gave a sheepish grin. "I thought I ought to make sure there are no spiders up here before I leave."

"Why? You're not afraid of them."

"No, but you are. I'd like you to sleep here while I'm gone." His gray eyes were intent.

Lucy finished the climb into the loft and stepped onto the rough floor. What did he mean? Her gaze probed his, and neither of them looked away.

"Then when I get back, I'd like us to share this room." His gaze never left hers as he took a step nearer.

Lucy's mouth went dry, and she was afraid to breathe. "I-It's not the blue moon yet."

"This will help you get used to the idea." He was right in front of her now. He took a ringlet and twisted it around his finger. "I reckon it's time we tried to make this marriage work."

Lucy wanted to ask him how he really felt about her, but the words stuck in her throat. Maybe he could grow to love her through the intimacy of marriage. He'd been different lately. Maybe he was already beginning to love her.

"But not until the blue moon," she whispered. "You have to be back by then. You will, won't you?"

"You and your planning." He grinned. "I'll do my best. I love Jed and Eileen, but I want our own kids too. I reckon that can't happen the ways things are right now." His thumb traced her jawline.

"I—I want children too." She barely managed to get the words out past the lump in her throat.

His fingers touched her hair again. "Girls with this pretty hair and your blue eyes."

"Strong sons," Lucy whispered. "With broad shoulders and gray eyes."

Those gray eyes crinkled in a smile, and his rough fingers caressed her cheek. "We'll take what God gives us."

His face came closer, and Lucy closed her eyes and leaned against his chest. She was almost too weak to stand.

The front door banged, and Jed's voice rang out. "Hey, Lucy, Nate, where is everybody?" His shout woke Eileen, and she began to cry.

Nate sighed and stepped back. "I can't seem to woo my wife no matter how hard I try," he muttered. "Will you stay here in my bed, Lucy?"

She opened her eyes. Unable to speak, she nodded, then went to the ladder and climbed down to see to Eileen.

"CROWN ME." NATE pushed his black checker toward Jed with an air of triumph. From the corner of his eye he could see Lucy moving about the stove. She was stronger than he'd expected and he thought she was mostly recovered from her snakebite. All evening the tension between them had grown. Should he ask her to share his room tonight, before he left for such a long trip? She'd probably bring up the blue moon again.

He mentally shook his head. She wasn't ready. It wouldn't be fair to start a new life together, then leave her. Words of love seemed trapped behind his lips. In the loft he'd wanted to tell her she was his sun and moon, the one thing he would give all his possessions for. But such romantic words would have seemed strange pouring from the lips of a cowboy like him. He was no poet. But why couldn't he manage the simple words "I love you"?

Nate had never thought of himself as a coward. But when it came to matters of the heart, he was at a loss. He dragged his concentration back to the game before Jed could notice his preoccupation.

"Supper's ready," Lucy said. Eileen put her doll into the little bed Nate had made for her.

Nate stood. "Come with me, Eileen. I'll pump the water for us to wash up." He took the little girl's hand and they went to the back door. As Nate pumped the handle and water gushed over Eileen's then Jed's hands, he was struck with how dear this little family had become to him. It wasn't just Lucy. God had surely blessed him.

If he hadn't been so pigheaded at first, would things be different now? Maybe Lucy would not feel this fierce desire to prove she was as good as Margaret. He could see that was what drove her. And it was his fault. He'd gotten them off to a wrong start by being so contemptuous of her size that first day. What an idiot. It had been cruel too.

He sluiced water over his hands and dried them on the towel that hung over the pump. As he went back inside with the children, he decided to just table all thought of his marriage until he got back. God would help him find his way through this morass of doubt.

"Did you find a cook?" Lucy asked him over dinner.

He nodded. "Just in the nick of time, Margaret agreed to go. There was no one else. We'll be well fed."

"That's good," she said, but her eyes were shadowed.

He wanted to reassure her that he felt nothing but friendship for Margaret, but she changed the subject.

After supper they had their evening devotions together as usual, and then he climbed the ladder to bed. Tomorrow he would leave for Kansas. Normally he was full of excitement the night before a cattle drive. Now he hated to leave Lucy and Eileen behind. It would be a long three weeks away from her. Maybe he should have allowed her to go, but she was so small and slight. He wanted to protect her. Surely that was a normal response for a husband. He punched the pillow into shape and closed his eyes. He couldn't worry about it now. It was too late to change anything.

The next morning he was awake before the rooster crowed. Noiselessly he dressed and slipped down the ladder. He touched Jed's shoulder, but the lad was already awake. He sprang out of bed, a smile on his eager face.

Nate looked at Lucy, still sleeping peacefully, one arm flung under her head. He knelt at the side of the bed and touched her forehead with his lips. Her eyes flew open, and he stared into the depths of her blue eyes. Every time he looked at the sky this summer, he would think of her. It would be hard to be away so long.

"I'm leaving now."

Pushing her heavy hair from her face, she sat up. "I'll fix you some breakfast."

"Don't bother. Jed and I will grab some biscuits. I'm not really hungry, and I don't think Jed could eat a mouthful. He's too excited." He leaned over and pressed his lips against hers, savoring their softness. Her arms went around his neck, and she clung to him.

"Pray for me. I'll be praying for you and Eileen."

A shadow darkened her eyes, and she nodded and averted her gaze.

He frowned. "Is something wrong?"

"No, no, of course not." She scrambled out of bed in a flurry of voluminous nightgown. "I'll walk you to the door."

At the door he took her in his arms properly and buried his face in her sweet-smelling hair. "I reckon this will be the longest cattle drive in my life with a pretty wife waiting for me at home. I'll be back as quick as I can."

She nodded, and he gave her a lingering kiss before he stepped through the door. "Come on, Jed, we'll be late." With a final wave, he and Jed went to the barn and saddled their horses.

TWENTY-NINE

⋐◆⋑

The silence was deafening after Jed and Nate were gone. Lucy had tossed and turned all night after learning Nate had asked Margaret to go instead of her. She read Eileen a story, then got her dressed. She felt surprisingly well—all traces of her weakness had finally left her.

She was a little chilly and went to her trunk for her shawl. As she rummaged through it, she noticed the bottom had come loose a bit. She started to press it back into place, but it wouldn't seat. Maybe there was an edge loose. She tugged it up a bit and peered under the bottom. There was a paper there. Stiff and yellowed. She pried on the bottom enough to be able to slip the paper out without tearing it.

She unfolded the document and stared at the faded ink. It was a deed of some kind. She studied it. It was a land deed made out in her mother's name. For ten thousand acres of land in the Red River Valley. She didn't know much about plats and surveyor's notations, but could this deed be to the land Henry had mentioned to her? And if it was, what did that mean? She had to find out before she told Nate about it.

She took the buggy to town and went to the county clerk's office. When she presented the deed, the clerk checked it against the records and told her it was legitimate. The news took her breath away. She had to tell Nate, but he would just send her home again once the news was delivered. Unless he couldn't. What if they were too far from home by the time he realized she was there? She could ride at the back of the herd and escape detection for a few days.

Lucy flew into a flurry of activity. She stuffed extra clothing for her and Eileen in a bag and tried to decide what to wear. A dress was impractical. She found a pair of Jed's dungarees he'd left behind because they were threadbare. They would have to do.

"Where are we going, Lucy?" the little girl complained.

"A great adventure! We're going with Jed and Nate."

Eileen thrust out her bottom lip. "We'll go tomorrow. And I don't like the cattle. They smell."

"If we don't go now, we won't see Jed and Nate for a long, long time. Would you rather stay with Grandpa Henry?" Lucy had been toying with the idea of leaving her anyway. It would be a hard trip for a little girl. And it would be difficult to hide Eileen from Nate's eagle eyes.

Eileen considered it, then nodded. "I love Grandpa."

Maybe she would be all right. Lucy had to make an instant decision. "All right. I'll run you over there."

She took Eileen's hand in one hand and snatched the bag with the other. She would have to hurry. She paused in the yard. The coins. Did she dare leave them unprotected for three weeks? The place would be empty and Rolf could waltz right in here and look for them. She smiled. He'd never look in the pickle barrel. They were safe.

She saddled up Wanda, then hefted Eileen to the saddle,

strapped on her bedroll and bag, then clambered up behind her. She'd never get used to riding this way. No matter how much she did it, she felt awkward and strange.

Cantering across the track, she headed for the main house. Minutes later, she pulled Wanda to a halt and slid down. Practically running, she hurried into the house. Henry was reading in the parlor.

His face brightened when he saw her, then his gaze took in her strange apparel. A smile tugged at his lips. "You're going with Nate, aren't you? I knew you had spunk. You got any more clothes than that?"

"Only a couple of dresses."

"I got a trunk of Nate's old clothes in the attic from when he was a boy. Some of them will fit you." He rose and took Eileen from her. "I reckon I'm babysitting for young Eileen here. You and me will have fun, chickadee." He tossed her in the air, and Eileen squealed.

"I really don't have time to look for more clothes," Lucy said.

"You got hours yet. The end of the herd won't pull out of here until close to noon by the time they all get rounded up and moving." He carried Eileen to the back stairway and opened the door. "It's that trunk at the top of the stairs. There's clothes going back to when Nate was a baby."

Rather than argue any more, Lucy raced up the stairs. She threw back the lid of the trunk and rummaged through it. She would have to come back when there was time. The trunk was full of mementos of Nate's childhood. Rifling through small dungarees that would fit Eileen and tiny boots that she could imagine on her own child someday, she found three pair of dungarees she thought would fit her and four shirts.

She hurried back down the stairs, then went out to her horse and pulled down the bag. Pulling out Eileen's belongings, she stuffed the things she'd found for herself into it and carried Eileen's clothing inside.

"I have to go," Lucy told Henry. She knelt beside Eileen and hugged her. "You be good for Grandpa."

"Grandpa says I'se always good." Eileen wrapped her arms around Lucy's neck. "Bye, Lucy. Don't cry. I'll take care of Grandpa."

Henry took Eileen from her and gave Lucy a slight shove. "And I'll take care of our little girl. Now run along before all this blubbering is useless and Nate is gone without you."

After one final look, Lucy ran for her horse. Her heart pounded against her ribs, and she prayed to escape discovery for a few days. She had to make this work.

THE LOWING OF the longhorn cattle and the stench they left in their wake made Lucy begin to question her decision almost as soon as she arrived. The air was thick with red dust, and it was hard to breathe. Lucy coughed and pulled a red bandanna up to cover her mouth. Her hair was tucked up under a hat.

"Hey, cowboy, over here!" A weathered man Lucy didn't recognize waved to her.

He must not realize she was a woman. She hid a grin as she rode over to join him.

"You're late, tenderfoot. You'll have to ride in the rear. You'll soon go runnin' home to mama." His face cracked in a grin, and the smile made him resemble someone, but Lucy couldn't decide who it was. "Round up them strays over there and watch to make sure they don't get away. My name's Bo, and you'll be answering to me this trip." Digging his knees into his horse's ribs, he wheeled and rode away.

Well, there was no time like the present to learn this cowboy business. Lucy set her chin and rode toward the stray cattle. They resisted her efforts to make them go the right way, and by the time she got them turned the right direction, she was wilting in the dust and heat. The sun beat down in a merciless glare, and she longed for some shade and a drink of cold water. She'd remembered a canteen, but the water was warm and brackish.

She wiped her mouth and pulled her bandanna up again and got back to work. At times she felt as though she was barely clinging to the pommel as she grimly fought to do what was expected of a cowboy. Once she thought she saw Jed in the distance, but she pulled her hat down lower over her face and went the other direction. She couldn't risk even Jed's discovery.

It still amazed her that the cowboys hadn't realized who she was. Divine providence perhaps?

When night fell, she was so stiff she almost fell from the saddle. Now she knew why cowboys walked bowlegged, she told herself with a grim smile. Hunkering down around the fire, she got her plate of beans and bread and retreated to the shadows again.

She wolfed down her food, then unrolled her bedroll and crawled under the blanket. She should wash up, but she couldn't find the energy. Lucy fell asleep to the sound of the men laughing and singing camp songs.

Morning came way too early. "Breakfast, tenderfoot."

A hard boot in the ribs roused Lucy from sleep. She groaned and tried to sit up, but every muscle in her body cried out in pain.

Bo prodded her with his boot again. "Get up, or you can just head on back where you came from. We don't need no lazy boys on this trip. You're awful puny. I'm surprised your mama let you out to come with us. You're no bigger than a grasshopper. What's your name?"

Her name. She tried to pitch her voice low. "What should I do first, sir?" she asked, hoping he wouldn't ask her name again.

"Sir. I like that. You are learning. For now, just get your lazy hide out of bed and get your breakfast. We pull out in half an hour." He walked away without waiting for an answer.

If she could just escape detection for one more day, she should be safe. Nate wouldn't waste that much time to send her back. She forced herself to her feet and went to find breakfast.

The second day was a repeat of the first, with Lucy growing more confident on the back of the mare. She watched the others and learned to cut a steer out of the herd and how to drive strays back to the main group. Feeling rather smug, she stopped to take a swig of water and noticed a man driving two steers behind a rock. Thinking they would exit the other side of the rock, she watched, but they didn't emerge.

Alarmed, she rode over to see if something was wrong. A man was tethering the cattle together behind the rock. It was Childress, the man who'd attacked her. In a flash Lucy understood what was happening. He was stealing Nate's cattle. Anger gripped her, and she started to pull her rifle from its sling on her saddle, but then her hand stilled. What rustler would be afraid of a boy by himself, rifle or not? She wheeled her horse around.

But her movement had caught the rustler's attention and he turned his gun her direction.

A bullet whizzed over her head, and she bent low over Wanda's neck. Another bullet whined by close to her cheek, and then she was out of range. Shaking, she saw Bo on the other side of the herd and made her way to him.

"A rustler!" she gasped.

Bo jerked his head up. His eyes narrowed as he stared at her. "Where?"

"Behind that rock." She pointed. "It's Childress. He has two cattle tied up. He shot at me."

His lips thin with rage, Bo rode off to where she pointed. Before he got there, a man on a horse tore out from behind the rock. He lashed his horse ferociously as he tried to get away. Bo shot over his head, and the man hunched down.

Another cowboy rode to intercept the rustler, then another. Within minutes, he threw down his gun and surrendered. Bo drove the rustler on, pausing long enough to give her an approving nod. Lucy swelled with pride. She'd done well today. Wait until Nate heard about it. Margaret herself couldn't have done better.

It was nearly dark when Bo rode back. He made his way to her side. "The boss wants to see you."

Lucy barely contained her gasp. "What for? It's bedtime."

"When the boss calls, there ain't no bedtime, kid. You head on over there now." Bo's voice brooked no argument.

"I'll go in the morning."

Bo grabbed Lucy by the collar and raised her to her feet. "You'll go now. You got a lot to learn and this is the main lesson. When the boss says jump, you ask how high." He released her, and she fell to the ground.

She rose, dusting herself off. "Yes, sir." There was no help for it. She lifted her chin in the air. Nate wouldn't send her back, not now. Her heart beat loudly in her ears as she saddled her horse and rode to the front of the herd. Maybe she had proved herself today. That was all she could hope for.

She found Nate outside the chuck wagon with Margaret and six men circling him. Pulling her hat over her brow, Lucy dismounted and walked toward them. Staying in the shadows, she listened for a moment. They seemed to be reading the Bible. Nate was having a Bible study?

"You mean no matter how good I am, God won't let me into heaven?" Margaret's voice was indignant. "I've proven my worth to anyone who dared question it, Nate Stanton!"

Several of the men nodded and frowned as if they didn't understand either.

"God loves us for who we are. We can't work our way to his love. That doesn't work here on this earth either. You either love someone for who they are, or you can forget it. Love that is earned is no love at all. It won't last."

Nate's words struck at Lucy's heart like an anvil. Was that what she'd been trying to do all her life? Even with God she tried to be good, to be worthy of his love. She tried to control things because she wanted to prove her worth. He loved her in her sin. Why wouldn't he love her always?

And now with Nate . . . she'd tried to work her way to his love as well. He either loved her or he didn't. And with Nate's words, she realized she desperately wanted to be loved just for being who she was, not for being like Margaret or anyone else. Just for being herself.

Her blood surged. She would find out now where she stood. If Nate chose to love her, wonderful. If not, she would go on being the best wife she could, but with the gifts God had given her, not the ones he had given Margaret.

"You wanted to see me?" Lifting her head, she was ready to let him see her face.

"I reckon I owe you some thanks, young man." His attention was on the Bible he was closing as the other men stood and began to wander away. "You've got sharp eyes."

"That's more than I can say for you, Nate." Margaret laughed. "That's no lad—that's a girl." She rose and knocked the hat off Lucy's head.

Lucy had wrapped a bandanna around her hair to keep it from falling out while she worked and while she slept. She whipped the bandanna off and let her hair flow free. "Hello, Nate."

"Lucy!" Nate rose to his feet. "What are you doing here? And where's Eileen?"

"I left Eileen with your father. I wanted to come with you, but I was afraid you'd send me back, so I tried to stay out of the way for a few days."

"I think it's time for me to get another cup of coffee," Margaret murmured. She rose and left Lucy staring into Nate's eyes.

"This was very foolish," Nate said with a frown. "You're in no shape for this trip. I'll have to send you back."

"I'm fine. Really. We've come too far. If you do, the drive will be delayed."

"I'll take you back myself. Wait here while I talk to my trail boss."

Lucy's spirits flagged. He wasn't even going to give her a chance. He was just sending her back. Her shoulders drooped. She should have let the rustler steal those stupid longhorns. At least she could have avoided detection until they were farther away.

Nate came back. "We'll leave in the morning. You'd better get some rest."

There was a strange gleam to his eyes Lucy didn't understand, but right now she was too angry to care. She stormed off. She was too mad to even tell him about the land they owned. He didn't deserve to hear that news.

Before she'd gone ten steps, Nate grabbed her arm and hauled her against his chest. "Where do you think you're going?"

"To bed!" she spat. "You don't even care about why I came. You just want to pack me off home like a child."

Nate gave a heavy sigh. "Lucy, this just isn't the time or place for an argument. We have a camp full of observers."

Lucy glanced around and heat crept up her neck. At least ten men were watching them with great interest. "Fine," she snapped. "We'll talk tomorrow. I'll go back to my bed."

"You're staying here. I'll send Jed for your bedroll and horse."

Lucy clenched her fists. "I've been doing just fine on my own."

He shook his head. "While I trust my own men to be respectful of my wife, there are some here who signed on just for the drive. I'll not have you vulnerable."

She stalked over to a tree and flung herself down. If he thought he was holding her hand tonight, he could think again.

When Jed brought her bedroll, she kicked it open and clambered into it. But it was a long time before she slept.

THIRTY

 ⚜

He had to tell Lucy. Jed lay in wait for his sister behind a tree near where she slept. The whole camp had been full of the news that she'd come on the drive dressed as a boy. Though he could talk to her in front of Nate, this was private stuff and he wanted only his sister.

Nate finally rose and moved off in the dark. Jed crept closer until he could touch her arm. "Lucy," he whispered urgently. He shook her, and her lids fluttered then opened.

She sat up. Confusion raced across her face. "Is something wrong?"

He crouched beside her as the memories exploded in his head. "I know what happened that night. The night Dad died. I remember!" He shuddered. "It's horrible, Lucy. More horrible than you know."

"Oh, Jed." She grabbed his hand. "Are you all right?"

His chest tightened at the compassion in her voice. "I didn't want to remember." She was going to be upset when he told her, but she had to know. "It was my mom."

"What do you mean?"

He could still see his mother's twisted mouth and threatening stare. "She came to the shop with Albert. She told Dad she wanted the coins. That she was going to disappear but she had to have money. That he owed her for putting up with the kind of life they'd lived."

"Where were you when they were arguing?"

"Putting stuff in the storeroom."

"She didn't see you?"

He shook his head, still feeling sick as the memories poured in. Lucy gave his hand a squeeze. "He'd told her about the coins?"

"The day before." Jed could still see the greed in his mother's eyes. He'd blocked it out.

"What did Dad say?"

"He told her no. That if she wanted to leave him, she could leave like the pauper she was when she came. Sh-She picked up a heavy statuette thing and hit him with it." Jed swallowed hard. "I was peeking around the door. Then Albert and another guy I'd never seen put Dad's body in the buggy. It was parked in the back. I hid when they came through the storeroom." He couldn't help the tears that started down his cheeks. "I should have made them stop."

"They were grown men, Jed. There was nothing you could do."

"She saw me when she followed them and made me get into the driver's seat. I took off in the buggy before they could get in. I was trying to get Dad to the doctor, but the rain was coming down so hard." He gulped and wished he didn't have to tell her it was his fault.

"Oh, Jed." Lucy's eyes were moist. "She's pure evil."

He had to tell her all of it. "The horses went faster and faster. The next thing I knew, the buggy was tipping over. Then I woke up at home with you beside me. If I hadn't been driving so fast, maybe I could have gotten him help."

"It wasn't your fault, honey. She killed him."

"I wish she weren't my mother." Jed swiped the moisture from his face with his sleeve. "I hate her."

Lucy buried her face in her hands. "We have to forgive her somehow."

"I can never forgive her," Jed said fiercely. He jumped to his feet and ran back the way he'd come.

NATE THOUGHT HE saw Jed with Lucy, but by the time he got back to camp, she was sleeping. He couldn't get over her courage as he watched her sleep in the flickering glow of the fire. And the danger she'd put herself into. What if someone else had discovered she was a woman and taken advantage of her? A chill shuddered up his spine.

Bo moved into the gleam of the light. "Here's her pack, Boss." He tossed it at Nate's feet.

Nate thanked him, and when the man melted back into the shadows, Nate picked up the pack and hauled it over by his. It would be easier to combine them all in one. He began to pull items from the roll and grinned when he recognized some of his old clothing from his adolescent years. A warm sensation lodged under his rib cage at the thought of her wearing his clothing. It seemed so intimate.

"Stanton?"

He turned at the sound of the man's voice. O'Brien stood in the shadows. The other rancher usually had his herd ahead of the Stanton cattle. "Slumming tonight?" Nate asked with a grin.

"Not exactly." O'Brien moved closer to the fire and held out his hands to warm them. "I always knew you were nobody's fool, son, but I didn't realize just how crafty you are."

"What are you talking about?"

O'Brien nodded at Lucy lying curled in her blanket. "Marrying that little gal was a smart move. I wondered why it all happened so undercover, especially when me and your pa had it all planned out. How we were going to merge our land and eventually acquire the Thompson acreage."

"I have no idea what you're talking about."

"Did you think I wouldn't find out? Now you and your pa have more land than the rest of us put together. No wonder you had no need of Margaret."

Nate pointed to a rock near the fire. "Have a seat and tell me what you're talking about. The last land Pa bought was the Larson spread. We're still far behind you in land ownership."

O'Brien stared at him. "I'm beginning to think you really don't know."

"I'm getting tired of this game, O'Brien. Say your piece so I can get some shut-eye."

"Ten thousand acres of land is what I'm talking about. And your little gal owns it. So that means *you* own it."

Nate had heard O'Brien wanted to buy up the big spread on the Stars Above's back side. It was mostly Indian territory right now, roamed only by deer and rabbits. Pa had eyed it as well, but the cost would have been astronomical, even if the owner was around to be found.

"You're sure?" he asked finally.

O'Brien's nod was jerky. "I've spent a pocketful trying to track down the owner, and here it's your own little wife."

"Lucy owns the old Thompson spread," Nate repeated, still unable to wrap his mind around what the rancher was saying. "How is that possible?"

"Her ma's maternal grandmother was a Thompson. She had tied the land up in a trust so it always passed to the eldest daughter. She wanted the women in her family to be able to be independent. The land passed to Lucy's mother, who is dead. Lucy is the oldest, so it belongs to her. You really didn't know?"

"I don't think *she* knows." Nate couldn't believe Lucy would keep something like that from him. But then, she hadn't told him about the coins either. If Jed hadn't spilled it, he might not know even now.

O'Brien snorted. "Bet your Pa did." He shook his head. "If you want to sell, let me know." His voice held no hope of that happening though. He turned and stalked away.

Lucy was sitting up and rubbing her eyes. Her golden hair spilled over her shoulders and caught the light, but Nate hardened his heart at the beautiful sight. Could she have deceived him? Maybe his father had told her not to tell him the marriage was a business arrangement, though Nate had no clue why Pa might hide it.

"I heard voices," she said, her voice soft.

"O'Brien was here. He wanted to buy your land." He hoped she would at least appear confused, but she looked away. "Why didn't you tell me?" he demanded.

"I just found out." She reached for her pack and dug into it, extracting a creased paper. "It was in the bottom of my mother's chest. I found it when I was packing to come on this trip. I'm sure Dad assumed it was worthless, if he even remembered Mama owned it. I wanted to make sure it was real, so I checked with the county clerk before coming to find you. I wanted to surprise you."

Longing to believe her, he took the heavy, yellowed paper gingerly in his fingers and held it up to read in the fire's glow. It was a deed to ten thousand acres of land.

Her gaze stayed on him until he looked up. "We weren't destitute after all." She bit her lip and looked down at her hands. "I-Is it worth a lot of money?"

"Yes. I wonder if Pa knew about it."

"How could he?" Her head came up quickly and she frowned. "Wait a minute," she said slowly. "He mentioned that Mama had inherited some land but that she wanted to live in the city so they packed up and moved away. So he knew she owned it at one time. He even said he would have bought it if it hadn't been left to my mother."

"Pa is no fool. I reckon he went looking for you so he could get control of this." Nate held up the deed. "He knew your pa had died when he arrived, right?"

She nodded. "He said Catherine wrote to ask for help."

"I bet he'd hoped to buy it from her, but it was passing from your mother, not your father. So he figured he'd get it through marriage."

"I—I thought he truly cared about me and the children. That he had come out of love for my parents."

He heard the waver in her voice and wanted to take her in his arms. To reassure her that he loved her, but since he'd never told her his feelings in the first place, this wasn't the time. Not when she seemed to regret having married him. "We need to talk to Pa about this."

Her slim shoulders squared and she stood. "To what purpose,

Nate? With his heart condition, can we risk upsetting him? He may have known nothing about it."

"Oh, he knew. I'm sure of it." As anger washed over him, he wanted to jump on his horse and ride back home to confront his father. But Lucy was right. His father's health might not take the stress of an altercation. "We can't ignore it. I have to know the truth."

"If we approach him calmly to discuss it, perhaps he won't become upset."

Nate nodded. "I can try." He studied her face and wished he could see what she was thinking. "What would you have done if you had known?" he asked softly, already knowing the answer.

Her small teeth gleamed in the light as she bit her lower lip. "I wouldn't have had need of your father's offer."

The knowledge caused an ache under his breastbone. When had he begun to love Lucy? It felt as though this feeling had always been part of him. His life would be so empty without her.

"So what do you think about our marriage now?" he asked.

"Nothing has changed. If God had wanted me to know about the land, I would have found it before I married you."

Her words calmed his heart. "You're my blessing," he said, brushing her lips with his. "Get some sleep. We'll deal with Pa tomorrow."

BY THE TIME Nate came leading the horses the next morning, Lucy was sitting on a tree stump sipping a cup of vile coffee. She'd coaxed some sugar from one of the hands. She longed for milk though. Then the coffee might be drinkable.

When she saw Nate, she poured out the rest of the bitter brew and rose. "I'm ready."

"I'd pour it out, too, if it had sugar in it," he said with a teasing grin.

She examined his expression. "I should have brought some tea."

He walked her to Wanda. "Those britches never looked that good on me." He helped her mount.

What had gotten into him today? He seemed almost happy to be leaving the cattle drive.

They rode in silence to the south, back toward the ranch. At only twenty miles from home, they should reach the main house by early afternoon. The cattle were only able to make fifteen miles a day, but the horses could do forty.

Nate finally broke the silence. He began showing her wildflowers along the way and told her their names. He pointed out the hawks flying overhead and the eagles atop the bluff they passed. Wasn't he going to bring up the land? Maybe he didn't want to talk about it so he kept his anger with his father in check. The landmarks began to be familiar to Lucy. They would be home soon.

At the crest of the hill above the ranch, Nate reined in his horse. He cleared his throat. "Was Pa in on this all along? About you coming on the cattle drive?"

She shook her head. "He had no idea until I showed up with Eileen. I had planned to take her with me, but she was sleepy and cranky, and I realized it wouldn't work."

"At least you showed some sense." He turned in the saddle and stared at her. "Why do you feel this need to prove yourself, Lucy? You have many talents. They just aren't with the cattle. I'm not saying you didn't do a good job as a cowboy. Bo said you were better than most of the tenderfoots he's worked with. But you hate it."

"It's part of your life, and I want to share your life, Nate. I don't want to be an appendage who has no relevance to your real life. Your passion is the cattle empire you're building. You said when we first met that you needed a wife who would work alongside you with the cattle." She still smarted from those words.

Nate sighed. "I was wrong, Lucy. I've told you I was wrong. I didn't know what I needed, but God did. I needed you."

Tears stung her eyes, but she sniffed and wiped her nose on her sleeve. Was he just saying that? She thought back to the words she'd overheard last night when he was talking to Margaret. She'd tried to earn love all her life by controlling things and being what people needed her to be. Was she even capable of stopping that?

He reached over and laid his hand on hers. "You don't have to earn anyone's respect, Lucy. You have it already."

Respect. For a moment she'd hoped he would tell her he harbored stronger feelings than respect. She longed to hear words of love from him. She managed a smile. "We'd better get going."

They started down the hill, and Lucy saw the ranch in the distance. Her backside hurt, and she craved a soak in a hot tub. And the softness of a real bed. The horse must have sensed her eagerness because the mare's pace picked up. Nate kicked his gelding into a canter as well, and they rode the final distance home. The horses plodded to a stop in front of the barn, and Lucy slid to the ground. Her stomach was in knots at the thought of the coming conversation.

Nate handed the reins to a hand who came to help him. Taking her elbow, he led her to the house. The aroma of chicken cooking wafted to her nose. They found Henry in the parlor reading a story to Eileen, who was sleeping with her head leaning against his knee. He had a blanket over his knees, although the day was far from chilly. Lucy thought the thermometer must read close to ninety. She listened to his deep voice as he read about Alice and her adventures through the looking glass.

Henry glanced up. His bushy eyebrows rose. "He wouldn't let you stay, eh, Lucy? I suspected as much." He closed the book and laid it aside. "Eileen was missing you."

Lucy took the chair farthest from her father-in-law. "I missed her." Aware that her jaw ached from clenching it, she forced herself to relax as Nate dropped onto the sofa near his father. She hoped there was a logical explanation.

Henry stared at his son. "You seem tense, Nate. Don't be too hard on Lucy. She did it for you."

"I'm not upset with Lucy. I know she has a big heart and wanted to please me." Nate slowly reached into his pocket and withdrew the deed. "This is what threw me." He opened the document and smoothed it out on his knee.

Henry craned his head to look. "Looks like a deed." His voice was eager.

"It is. For the ten thousand acres on our back side."

Henry's eyes widened, and he snatched up the document. Holding it under his nose to read it, he began to smile. "You found it."

Not even a pretense of ignorance. The satisfaction in his voice made her ill, and Lucy pressed her hand against her stomach. "You knew," she whispered. "You didn't come to see me out of concern for me and the children."

Henry's smile faded. "It wasn't quite like that, Lucy. Of course

I wanted to help you. And Nate here was never going to take a wife without a push. It seemed the logical solution."

"You get the land you wanted, and you manage to get me married," Nate said. "Then everything is right with your world."

Though his voice was deceptively calm, Lucy saw his jaw harden, and she prayed for Nate to stay calm even as her own temper rose. *Just sit quietly and let your husband handle it.* But it was hard to bite her tongue.

"We'll put the land to good use. It was being ignored and wasn't helping anyone."

"And you feared O'Brien would get it first," Nate said.

"I didn't want to be boxed in."

Nate glanced at Lucy. "It's your land, Lucy, not mine. You can do whatever you want with it."

The way he took his hands off of the property touched her. "I'd like to give some of it to my uncle."

Henry leaped to his feet. "That's ridiculous, Lucy."

"Which would you rather have? All of my land or my uncle's spread?"

"I own your uncle's spread now," Nate said.

They locked glances, and she couldn't read his expression. Was he disappointed that she would want to do this? Did he feel she was choosing her uncle over him?

"Are you trying to force my hand, Lucy? I thought you wanted our differences put aside, not compounded."

Lucy laced her fingers together. "I don't want my family to have nothing. Uncle Drew's spread is small. Only a thousand acres. If I compensate him with the same amount of land, that's a tiny portion of the land I own." Nate stared at her and she held her breath to see his reaction.

"Please, Nate. Let go of any hard feelings. I heard you talking to Margaret, you know. What you said about being loved for ourselves. I love my family because they are part of me. Can't you do the same?"

His face was impassive until he finally gave a slow nod. "Then let's give him back his land plus another thousand I own that borders it. We'll keep yours intact for our daughter someday."

Her heart swelled to bursting, but before she could tell him how she felt, his father leaped to his feet and raised his fist in the air.

"You can't do that!" Henry shook his fist again. "Larson's land is mine."

Nate ran his hand through his hair. "It's not, Pa. You signed it over to me last spring."

Henry sank back onto the sofa. "You're no son of mine."

THIRTY-ONE

⚜

The dismissive tone in his father's voice made Nate draw in a quick breath. His dad would come around. "You don't mean that, Pa."

His father snorted, then his gaze went past Nate. "Watson. What are you doing here?"

The detective stepped into the parlor. "Reporting on what I discovered, Mr. Stanton. Am I interrupting?"

"Another time might be better."

"This concerns my wife, so we're interested in what you have to say." Though Nate didn't trust the man, he hoped to put an end to the danger that had been swirling around Lucy.

Why was his father scowling? Nate couldn't put his finger on the mood in the room as Watson dropped into a chair by the fireplace.

The man opened his briefcase and extracted a paper. "I tracked down the owner of the coins. They were reported stolen six months ago. The owner is a well-known collector in Boston, a Mr. Ralph Johnson. The police are still investigating the theft, and so far have no leads to the thugs who took them."

"Thugs?" Lucy was cradling Eileen on her lap.

Watson nodded. "A guard was killed during the theft. From the evidence, it appears there were three men involved."

"I'll give them back, then," Lucy said. "I want nothing to do with them if they were stolen."

"I'll take care of it for you," Watson said.

"I'd rather do it myself," Nate said. "Do you have the man's address?"

Watson's gaze darted from Nate to his father and back. "I have it back at my room. Not with me."

"I'll stop by and get it."

His father waved a hand in the air. "Oh, Nate, don't be ridiculous! Hand over the coins to Watson and let him take care of it. You can't be spared from the ranch to go gallivanting off to Boston."

Watson was shifty and wouldn't look Nate in the eye, and he didn't like his father's insistence that he needed to hand over the coins. Pa was greedy. Nate recognized the sin for what it was now.

Nate glanced at Lucy. "I think I'll ride back to town with Watson and get that address. Want to come along?"

She nodded and Eileen squealed. "I want to see Aunt Sally!"

"May we?" Lucy asked.

He nodded. "We'll have dinner in town."

"There's no need to rush off," his pa said. "Percy has chicken cooking. Stay and eat."

Hadn't his father just told him he was no son of his? Why was he suddenly so genial? Or was it that he was trying to prevent them from going to town? Nate didn't like the way every part of his body was on alert. He hated that he was filled with distrust toward his own pa. It didn't seem right, but he was unable to shake the feeling.

He rose and held out his hand to Lucy. "I'll talk to you later, Pa."

Watson pressed his lips together. "I wasn't planning on going to my room just yet."

"You're staying at the boardinghouse. I know Mrs. Hopkins. If you tell me where to find it, I can get it myself."

"I don't want anyone rifling through my things."

Nate folded his arms across his chest. "You don't have it at all, do you? This is a scam to get possession of the coins." He glanced at his father. "You're in on it too, aren't you, Pa? This was your plan all along, to get those coins for yourself."

His color going gray, his father shook his head. "It's not like that, Nate. Everything I've done, I did for you and Roger. Not that your brother appreciates it. Neither of you ever had to be hungry like I was. You never had classmates whisper about your drunken father like I did. I want the Stanton name to mean something in the legacy of this state. My wealth has wiped away every stigma from our name."

The strength went out of Nate's legs, and he sank back onto the sofa. Even though he'd accused his father, he'd held on to a hope that there was another explanation.

Lucy rose. "You knew about the coins before you talked me into marrying Nate too, didn't you?" Her voice trembled. "You hired someone to break in and try to find them. If you'd found them, would you have left me in Indiana to starve?"

"Of course not, honey," his father said. "I just wanted the coins to be safe."

"Catherine mentioned them, didn't she?" Lucy's voice rose

and she waved her hands as she spoke. "You thought you could swoop in and take everything for you and your sons?" She drew out a harsh sob. "Did you hire someone to force me to give up the coins? To follow me?"

Henry massaged his left arm. "Of course not! I'm hurt you would think I would do such a thing. I care about you, Lucy. And Eileen and Jed too. I've made sure you and your family were well taken care of."

Nate couldn't speak, couldn't formulate the full horror he felt as his father stood and took a step toward Lucy. She backed away when he held out his hand.

"Did you know anything about this at all, Nate? Anything?"

Still mute, he shook his head, but he could see the doubt in her eyes. The betrayal in her voice hit him hard. And he didn't blame her. The revelation of his father's despicable deeds left him feeling frozen and bereft as if the ground under his feet had suddenly given way.

She shuddered and clasped her arms around her. "Is everything a lie? *Everything?*" She stared at his father. "Did you care anything about me at all? And Eileen? You acted as though you really loved her."

"I do!" His father tugged on the collar of his shirt. He stretched out his hand and stepped toward her.

"Don't touch me." Her voice was low and impassioned. "You used me to get what you wanted." She grabbed up Eileen, then rushed out the door.

"Lucy!" Nate started toward her, but his father groaned. Glancing back, he saw his father topple toward the floor. "Pa!" He leaped to try to catch him but wasn't in time, and his father fell facedown on the carpet.

Nate rolled him over and stared into his pa's lifeless eyes. He was gone.

"WHERE WE GOING, Lucy?" Eileen's voice was plaintive.

Lucy swiped at her eyes. "To find Jed." She stuffed their clothes back into the trunk. When everything was packed, she dragged it to the door of the cabin. How was she going to get it loaded in the wagon? Her vision blurred again, and she took another swipe at her wet eyes.

She didn't want to believe Nate had anything to do with this, but had it all been a good performance? After all, he hadn't come after her when she left. Didn't that indicate guilt? And he'd wanted to know where the coins were. In a sudden panic, she realized she hadn't retrieved them yet.

She rushed out the back door, hurried down the steps to the cellar, and opened the pickle barrel. Cool, pungent vinegar encased her arm as she plunged her hand into the pickles. She only dared breathe when her fingers touched the oilcloth. Carrying the dripping bundle outside, she paused when Bridget came to nose at her leg.

She would miss the dog. Tears fell faster now. Her pain wasn't just for the dog but for her home here. For Nate and the life she'd thought to build. She patted the collie on the head, then took the coins inside where she washed them off and tucked them back into the dress where she'd found them. It took only a few minutes to whipstitch the hem back in place and cover them. No one but Jed knew where she'd found them, so they should be safe there.

Now to get the chest into the wagon. And how was she going

to get to Jed? He was on the trail. She couldn't take the buggy on a trail. Maybe they could take the stage to Kansas City and meet him there. It was getting dark, though. Was it safe to take the buggy alone to town? The darkening sky put her aback. She sat on the chest and buried her face in her hands.

"What am I going to do, God?" she whispered. "I don't think Nate loves me. I've been a fool."

"Nate loves you," Eileen said. "He told me so."

Lucy's pulse stuttered, and she raised her head. "He told you?"

Her little sister nodded. "When we were playing with the kittens." Her eyes grew round. "I wasn't s'posed to tell you."

The frantic pounding in Lucy's chest eased a little. "What did he say?"

Eileen clapped her hand across her mouth. "I promised," she mumbled past her palm. She lowered her hand. "Don't tell him, okay?"

Lucy didn't want to insist Eileen break a promise, but knowing what Nate said might help her know what to do. Was it possible he harbored fond feelings for her? She shook her head and got up from the chest. Eileen's words made her want to stay, at least tonight. Just in case there was hope that Nate might come after her.

She took Eileen's hand. "Time for bed, honey." Once her sister was tucked into bed, she took her Bible outside to the porch rocker and settled in. The light would be gone soon. A crocheted cross marked the spot where she'd left off reading. It was Matthew 19. She read the first verses, then came to verse 5.

"And said, For this cause shall a man leave father and mother, and shall cleave to his wife: and they twain shall be one flesh? Wherefore they are no more twain, but one flesh. What therefore God hath joined together, let not man put asunder."

Though their marriage had not been consummated, the Bible said they were one flesh. If she wanted to follow God, didn't she have the burden of at least talking to Nate before she left? Of asking for an explanation? Her thoughts flashed back to the moment when she'd realized what Henry had done. Nate stood there without a word to say. Shouldn't he have vehemently protested his innocence?

She sighed and rubbed her head, which was beginning to throb. Sometimes it was hard to do what was right. And she knew it was wrong to leave. Closing her eyes, she prayed for the strength to wait and see what God could make of this mess. All the control in the world couldn't solve this. As she prayed, she felt the load lift. It was freeing to turn her burden over to God, to admit she was powerless to fix this.

As she rocked, she became aware of the rattle of tack on a horse. She rose with her hand to her throat as Nate came riding toward the cabin. From the tenseness of his shoulders and the straight line of his mouth, she could tell something was very wrong. She said nothing as he dismounted and stood staring at her in the twilight.

"Lucy," he said, his voice hoarse. "Pa's gone."

"Gone?" She struggled to understand what he meant. "With Watson?"

Nate stepped nearer and shook his head. "He's dead."

She gasped and moved to embrace him. "Oh, Nate!" He picked her up and carried her to the chair, where he collapsed and buried his face in her neck. She wanted to cry, but after seeing Henry's true nature, she found it hard to summon more than sympathy for Nate and regret for a life wasted in chasing power. His breathing was harsh and ragged in her ear. She held him as tightly as she could, willing him to take her strength and love.

When he raised his head, his eyes were wet. "I still can't believe he did all this."

She clearly saw that Nate had nothing to do with his father's schemes. His pain was too raw. "I'm so sorry, Nate. I should have believed you immediately. I know the kind of man you are."

He pulled away and stared into her face. "What would it take for you to believe I love you, Lucy? Just like you are."

Lucy gulped the tears in her throat. "You do? Truly? I overheard you talking to Margaret about love that is earned is no love at all. I realized that's what I've been doing my whole life. With everyone, not just with you. I've always felt I had to earn love. I think it started with my father. I was the oldest, and I was supposed to do more, to give more. I always felt like a failure. But I want so badly to be loved for myself, for who I am."

Nate's gray eyes grew solemn. "I love everything about you, Lucy. Everything that makes you who you are. Your fire and spirit, your determination to right any wrongs, your love for people, your compassion. I love you even if you hate tending cattle."

"I realized I try to control too much and don't let God do it."

He grinned. "'A man's heart deviseth his way: but the LORD directeth his steps.' You just didn't realize God loved you so much that all the time you were trying to make sure you had the love you craved, he was directing you right here to me."

Lucy buried her face in his neck. He pressed his lips against her hair. "I'm so blessed God brought us together," she whispered. "You're what gives meaning to everything I do."

His fingers lifted her chin, and he gazed into her eyes. "I love you, Lucy Stanton. I only hope our children are just like you."

His lips found hers, and she was lost in his kiss. It promised all the things she'd longed for all her life. A home, acceptance, and approval. She rubbed her hands across the rough stubble on his face, relishing his maleness and strength.

"I love you, Nate. I've loved you for a long time, but I was so afraid you would never accept me. I'm never going to be like Margaret."

"I reckon I had plenty of opportunity to marry Margaret. I always knew something was missing. You're more important than anything, Lucy. More important than the ranch even. What would you say if I told you I wasn't going back to the cattle drive?"

"You have to go back!"

Nate shook his head. "No, I don't. I have a good foreman and good cowboys. My foreman will watch out for Jed. There's no reason to go back and a very good reason to stay." He cupped her face in his hands. "You are that reason, Lucy. It's been hard trying to woo you with Jed and Eileen in the house. We have that time now. Let's take it and get to know one another better. I wish I were a poet so I'd be able to tell you how much I love you."

With an inarticulate cry, Lucy burrowed into his arms. "I wanted to be a blessing to you, just like the Bible says."

"You already are. My life was empty without you. I can't imagine living without you. If you couldn't adapt to ranch life, I'd leave it all behind and find a job in the city. You're all I want, Lucy. You and Jed and Eileen. And our own kids, of course." He smiled crookedly.

"I love the ranch. As long as I don't have to share it with Zeke."

Nate grinned. "Zeke's gone, but you're here and I'm here. Can we have a honeymoon here, or would you like to travel somewhere? I have money tucked away, if that's what you want."

"Keep your money, Nate Stanton. All I want is you. This cabin with you is where I want to be. I won't have to share you with anyone here."

Nate's eyes grew bright, and his lips came down to claim hers again. Lucy reveled in his love and in who she was in his sight. She lifted her face to the moon beginning to rise. "It's not the blue moon yet, but I can't wait. I want our marriage to be real."

EPILOGUE

Carriages rattled by the Wabash hotel that Nate had chosen for their belated honeymoon. Lucy stood in the window and stared down at the people hurrying by on the street below. She checked the watch pinned to her bodice. "She's late."

"Patience, love. It's only ten after." Nate's gaze went to the tiny swell of her belly. "You'll get young Stanton riled, and she'll be demanding more pickles."

She put her hand on the small bump and felt the baby kick. "He's already kicking me."

"She," he corrected.

It was a familiar argument. Nate swore he wanted a girl, and she wanted a boy. But they would be happy with whatever they had. She stepped into his arms and nestled her head against his chest. "I just want this meeting to be over."

"Soon."

She listened to the beat of his heart against her ear. He was a good man, and she was so blessed. Every time she thought about her uncle's reaction when Nate had freely given him the land, her eyes welled. The stoic man had broken down and actually sobbed.

He'd asked Nate to forgive him for trying to burn down his barn and wanted to go to the sheriff and confess, but Nate had told him it was all in the past—that together they would move forward and be a family.

The last few months had been sheer bliss. Family was everywhere Lucy looked, and she had never felt so loved.

The knock they'd been waiting on came. Nate left her and opened the door. Resplendent in a blue satin dress, Catherine stood in the hall. "Come in."

Her gaze sharpened when she looked past Nate and saw Lucy. "I didn't expect to see you too." She entered the room and glanced around. "Rather posh surroundings for you, Lucy. Where are my children?"

"Home," Nate said.

Catherine smiled. "Then you've agreed to my terms. You brought the coins?"

"I have them," Lucy said, struggling to keep disdain from her voice. "Did you bring the document agreeing to turn over full custody to us?"

"I have it here." Catherine touched her beaded bag. "Let me see the coins."

Lucy wanted to scream at the woman, but she forced herself to get the bag containing the coins and hand it to Catherine. The woman loosened the drawstring top and stared greedily at the shimmering silver dollars inside.

"The agreement." Lucy held out her hand.

"I didn't want the brats anyway." Catherine withdrew the paper from her bag and signed it with a flourish, then handed it to Lucy. "Good riddance."

She turned to go to the door, but before she'd taken two steps, the door behind them opened. A man with a big nose held another man by the arm. Yet another man was in cuffs and was guarded by an officer. Lucy immediately recognized the prisoner with the big nose as the man who had broken into the house. The man with the strong hair tonic.

Lucy held her breath as the policeman pointed at Catherine. "That the woman who hired you?"

Both prisoners nodded. "That's her," the man who had broken into the house said.

Catherine's face paled. "What's this all about?" Her gaze darted to the door, but Nate stepped in front of it.

The officer approached her. "Mrs. Marsh, you're under arrest for the murder of your husband."

Catherine held her hands up. "No! You have no proof."

"Jed remembered what happened," Lucy said.

Catherine whirled to run for the door, but Nate grabbed her as she approached. The detective wrestled the bag of coins from her hand. She made a grab for them. "Those are mine!"

"They belong to Mordecai Mitchell in Detroit," the detective said. "He's in the lobby to receive his property back."

Catherine sobbed as they took her away, but Lucy felt no pity. Only a deep sadness that a woman who had sworn to love her father had killed him instead. When the door closed, Lucy buried her face in Nate's chest. Tears finally came, but they were mostly for Jed who would never forget what his mother had done.

"Shh, it's over," Nate whispered in her hair. "We can put this behind us."

She lifted her head and looked into his gray eyes. "So much pain. And all for money."

He cupped her face in his hands. "You brought sanity to all of us, Lucy. Your heart, your spirit, your generosity. We're free from the taint of greed now. It died with Pa."

It hurt her to see the pain in his eyes when he mentioned his father. But she would do her best to make him forget the past and look only to the future.

He turned her gently toward the door. "Let's go feed you. I hear the café down the street has the best pickles in town."

ACKNOWLEDGMENTS

I'm celebrating ten years with my Thomas Nelson team this year—truly my dream team! Publisher Allen Arnold (I call him Superman) changed everything when he came on board. Everyone in the industry loves him—including me! Senior acquisitions editor Ami McConnell (my dear friend and cheerleader) has an eye for character and theme like no one I know. I crave her analytical eye and love her heart. She's truly like a daughter to me. Marketing manager Eric Mullett and publicist Katie Bond are always willing to listen to my harebrained ideas. Fabulous cover guru Kristen Vasgaard (you so rock!) works hard to create the perfect cover—and does. And of course I can't forget my other friends who are all part of my amazing fiction family: Natalie Hanemann, Amanda Bostic, Becky Monds, Ashley Schneider, Jodi Hughes, Ruthie Dean, Heather McCoullough, Dean Arvidson, and Kathy Carabajal. I wish I could name all the great folks at Thomas Nelson who work on selling my books through different venues. Hearing "well done" from you all is my motivation every day.

I've heard legendary things about Julee Schwarzburg, and this was my first opportunity to work with her. She is indeed the master editor I've heard so much about! Thanks so much for all the ways you improved this book, Julee.

My agent, Karen Solem, has helped shape my career in many ways, and that includes kicking an idea to the curb when necessary. Thanks, Karen—you're the best!

Writing can be a lonely business, but God has blessed me with great writing friends and critique partners. Hannah Alexander (Cheryl Hodde), Kristin Billerbeck, Diann Hunt, and Denise Hunter make up the Girls Write Out squad (www.GirlsWriteOut .blogspot.com). I couldn't make it through a day without my peeps! Thanks to all of you for the work you do on my behalf and for your friendship. I had great brainstorming help for this book in Robin Caroll and Cara Putman. Thank you, friends!

I'm so grateful for my husband, Dave, who carts me around from city to city, washes towels, and chases down dinner without complaint. As I type this, today is the first day of his retirement. Now he will have more time for those things—and more. Thanks, honey! I couldn't do anything without you. My kids, Dave and Kara (and now Donna and Mark), and my grandsons, James and Jorden Packer, love and support me in every way possible. Love you guys! Donna and Dave brought me the delight of my life— our little granddaughter, Alexa! This year at Christmas she was interested in watching her Mimi sign copies for her daddy to give away. When I told her that Mimi wrote the books, I'm sure I saw shock in her face. Okay, maybe I'm reading too much into her little two-year-old mind, but she will soon understand what her Mimi does for a living.

Most important, I give my thanks to God, who has opened such amazing doors for me and makes the journey a golden one.

READING GROUP GUIDE

1. One of the first things we try to do as Christians is to examine the idea of self-sacrifice. It goes against our nature as humans to put someone else above ourselves. Why do you think Lucy was good at this? Is it something innate, or was it something she learned?

2. Did you identify with Lucy's insecurity? Why or why not?

3. What are ways we try to prove our self-worth to ourselves and to others? Where is our true self-worth found?

4. All families face strife from time to time, just as Nate and Roger did. What are some ways to handle strife in a biblical way?

5. Nate was hurt when he realized Lucy didn't trust him enough to bring her worries to him. Is deceit ever warranted?

6. The Bible talks quite a lot about money and how an unhealthy attachment to it can affect our lives. Greed can be more than just the desire for money. What other things can we humans be greedy for?

7. Did you identify with Lucy's desire to be a blessing to her husband? Why or why not?

8. Lucy's compulsion for control was an illustration of what I've been going through myself. How about you? Are you able to turn things over to God, or do you continually try to fix things?

After *Blue Moon Promise* comes . . .

THE RED RIVER BRIDE

More romance and intrigue await in
the next Under Texas Stars novel.

AVAILABLE JANUARY 2013

THOMAS NELSON
Since 1798

Libby arrives at the Tidewater Inn hoping to discover clues about her friend's disappearance. There she finds an unexpected inheritance and a love beyond her wildest dreams.

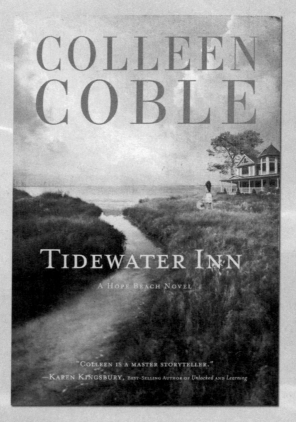

The first novel in the Hope Beach Series

AVAILABLE JULY 2012

THOMAS NELSON
Since 1798

"*The Lightkeeper's Bride* is a wonderful story filled with mystery, intrigue, and romance. I loved every minute of it."

— CINDY WOODSMALL —

New York Times best-selling author of *The Hope of Refuge*

THE BEST-SELLING MERCY FALLS SERIES.

ALSO AVAILABLE IN E-BOOK FORMAT

THOMAS NELSON

Since 1798

ESCAPE TO BLUEBIRD RANCH

ALSO AVAILABLE IN E-BOOK FORMAT

THE ROCK HARBOR MYSTERY SERIES

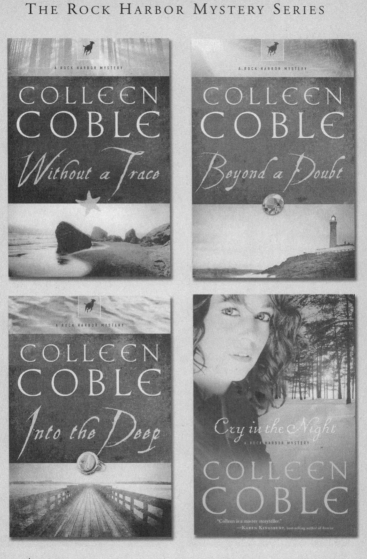

ALSO AVAILABLE IN E-BOOK FORMAT

*F*our friends devise a plan to turn Smitten, Vermont, into the country's premier romantic getaway—and each finds her own true love along the way.

Colleen Coble,
Kristin Billerbeck,
Diann Hunt
& Denise Hunter

Smitten

Love is on the way

THOMAS NELSON
Since 1798

ABOUT THE AUTHOR

Author photo by Joe Saxton

Best-selling author Colleen Coble's novels have won or finaled in awards ranging from the Best Books of Indiana, ACFW Book of the Year, RWA's RITA, the Holt Medallion, the Daphne du Maurier, National Readers' Choice, and the Booksellers Best. She has nearly two million books in print and writes romantic mysteries because she loves to see justice prevail. Colleen is CEO of American Christian Fiction Writers and is a member of Romance Writers of America. She lives with her husband, Dave, in Indiana. Visit her website at www.colleencoble.com. Twitter: @colleencoble